A CROWN FORGED IN BLOOD

THE FORGED QUEENDOM BOOK ONE
POPPY L. ROBERTS

CONTENTS

Content Note

This book is intended for adults and may contain graphic or distressing content including violence, death, and explicit sexual content.

A detailed list of content notes can be found at **au thorpoppyroberts.com** if you believe something is missing from the website list please email me.

For everyone who wanted to be a fairy but became a bitch instead.

THE QUEENDOM OF SUVIEL
THE CELESTIAL COURT
THE TIDAL COURT
ARACHIN
THE HEARTH COURT
THE ARCANE COURT

Lexicon

Aduna /ah-DOO-nah/

The Goddess of Life. Aduna created all of Suviel including the fae and all magic comes directly from her. The elemental magics were directly gifted from her own magic during creation.

Amphipter /AM-fih-teer/

A form of legless dragon classified as a winged serpent. The females of the species are large with muted black and grey coloring while the males have brightly colored feathers and scales.

Hema /HEM-ah/

A species of giant spider. They nest mainly in the mountains and are highly venomous. Most concerning however is the airborne hallucinogenic toxin they excrete that causes extreme rage.

Lachis /LAH-khiss/

Souls that are trapped on the mortal plane. They are also referred to as shades or ghosts.

Mab

The first High Queen of Suviel and the first to wield all four elements.

Nassella /nah-SEL-ah/

The offspring of a voxis and fae mating pair. They have powerful glamour magic and when their blood is used to fertilize the felbore plant it creates a powerful drug that subdues the nassella's victims.

Necsite /NEK-sit/

Water demons, may take the shape of a horse or their natural demonic form, they most often live in deep waters and do not pose much threat to fae unless they enter their territory. The Tidal Fae are well-versed in this boundary.

Prime

The ruler of an individual court. There are four Primes in Suviel, one for each court and all four are under the governance of the High Queen.

Thahaos /THA-ohs/

The God of Discord who was cast out of Suviel to become The God of Death.

The Beneath

The underworld, where the souls of the dead reside in an accord with Thahaos to maintain balance.

Voxis /VOks-is/

Wild fae who possess much of the same simple magic as the fae but are also powerful shapeshifters. The voxis are not a part of the court system but are bound by the treaty with Mab to maintain balance and self-govern.

"In a realm where shadows dance, the whispers weave an unseen path. Those who dare to walk it must wield hope like a sword, for only in the pits of darkness will they find the light that leads to salvation. Though take with you this word of caution: in the land of blackened dreams, the line between friend and foe is as thin a thread as spider silk."

High Priestess First Order of Aduna
Temple of the Unseen

PROLOGUE

With every step, life sprouted beneath Aduna's feet. Trees grew full and strong with deep red and brown bark and vibrant green leaves. Flowers bloomed in every shade, creating a tapestry of color, and earthy green and gold lichen spread across the rock, softening its rough surface. Water poured into the impressions of her heels, creating vast lakes. All the while, the dragging of her cloak connected the bodies of water as they formed with a rush of water, carving rivers into the landscape.

In her hands, she molded the small creatures of the world, dropping them in their homes and watching them take on a life of their own. Tiny animals burrowed into their dens, and birds nested in each tree. Creatures both large and small took to the water. Some formed from the water itself. She continued, hoping to form a world to nurture. She turned to admire her creation and saw that in her wake all the land was cloaked in thick darkness.

She sat in a large clearing of tall grasses, each blade stretching towards her light. As she sat, mountains pushed up to cradle her back, and then, closing her eyes, she began to weave. Fire poured from her fingers in the thinnest threads. As she wove, an orb of delicate gold fire began to take shape. Where the orb lay, the land dried out, and the plants shriveled, but still, she continued to weave. Once the orb was strong, flickering and dancing with flames, she stood and hung it in the heavens.

She placed it in the skies, higher than the tallest peak, so its light and warmth would reach into all the valleys, around the mountains, and banish the darkness. With a tap of her finger, she set it into motion, making it glide across the skies to give life to all her creations in turn.

She carried on her journey, stopping only to dig for more clay to form the inhabitants of this place. As she dug deep, she admired the life stirring around her and began to weep at its beauty. As she wept, her salt-filled tears started to fill the cavernous hole at her feet, dividing the land and forming the sea. The sea was vast, and she paused to create new creatures to live in the unknown depths. As she dropped the largest creation into those waters, it began a perpetual shift, causing salty waves to lap at the shores in an endless push and pull.

As the fiery orb made its passage overhead, she saw that in its wake there was a cool, still darkness. From the sea, she gathered water in her hands and pulled the frost from the mountaintops to freeze it into a glass orb to match her orb of fire. She imbued into the glass her own light, cool and blue. She hung this in the sky much closer to her creation and admired its splendor, but the orb was too heavy for the skies. So it fell, shattering into infinite shards. The shards each glistened and whorled. They were a beautiful kaleidoscope of flickering colour and magic, so she swept them into her palm and blew them deep into the heavens, creating a tapestry of light in the skies.

Admiring these small lights, she ran her fingers through them, swirling them and painting the heavens with their glow. She created artful whirls and dips; she positioned the brightest into constellations, telling the stories of her past. While they were a splendor to behold, she knew she needed something more. She found the largest shard, polished it into a much smaller orb than the first, and rehung it in the skies.

At last, Aduna made her way around her creation and found she was back to the place where she began. Again, she sat, new mountains rising around her like a throne. She ran her fingers through the grasslands, and new creatures appeared, some with magic and some without. She touched the treetops and creatures of flight burst forth, singing an ethereal song. Stirring the seas, she found that life there was just as diverse, creatures slipping in and out of the waves. Though her creation was grand and beautiful, she felt something was missing.

She began to form in her hand creatures shaped to be like her. Strong bodies, delicately pointed ears. She formed many, each a little different, and she placed in each of them the smallest kernel of her own magic. It would help them grow and sustain their lives, as well as the lives of all her creations. Each kernel of magic took root in a different part of these creatures. In some, it burrowed into their feet, grounding them to the land. In others, it was held in their core, giving them the equilibrium to balance the water. Sometimes, it settled like a crown, drawing them into the skies, so she gave them wings to help them find their way back. In the last, it slipped, burying itself in their hearts, stoking the embers of passion into a raging inferno.

Once she had created an abundance of these creatures, she distributed them across the lands and seas. In the forests, she hid those with the ability to manipulate the land and help it thrive. To the sea, she gifted guardians of its tides and keepers of its secrets. Those with flight and mastery over the heavens, she guided to the tallest mountain range. Finally, at the base of the fiery mountain that housed the amphipteres, she placed the last, fire and shadows dripping from their hands.

These creatures were magnificent, compassionate, and intelligent. They worked tirelessly to help her creations flourish. They took time naming each of her creations from birds soaring through the skies and necsites stirring the seas, to the sun, moon, and stars. Aduna knew they would honor her creations, and she had grown weary from the loss of so much magic. So, she rose from her place and left to watch her new creation from afar. As she left, one of her creatures flew into her path.

"My Goddess, wait!" he implored her. "Before you leave us, would you name us? We have named all the others of your creation, but we are left with no name. Would you please honor us one last time?"

The goddess smiled down at him and continued on her path. Just as she took the last step, she said, "My dear child, you are fae."

An eon passed after Aduna stepped from this world to the next. Other gods and goddesses visited, leaving their own fingerprints on the landscape before moving on. Thahaos, the God of Discord, saw in the land an opportunity to create something of his own. He carved through it and created a new realm, The Beneath, guarded by wraiths and monsters, a place of vicious beauty.

Slowly he lured fae into his realm, but quickly they learned that once they entered they couldn't leave again. Thahaos, stirred the souls of the dead, collecting them to fill his realm, but found that the life span of the fae meant that there weren't enough. He needed more. In his greed, he sewed the seeds of discord throughout the land Aduna created and watched them grow.

In the midst of the chaos and fighting, a weary general sat at the base of the first tree Aduna pulled from the soil. Battle-worn and gravely wounded, she lay in its roots, her blood dampening the moss. The tree cradled the fae in its roots, sending its own magic to heal her wounds. At last, she pulled in deep lungfuls of air and whispered her thanks into its bark as she sank into a still sleep.

In this stillness, she saw visions of the goddess, of all of creation. She was given whispered words from the goddess herself. With this knowledge of the past came magic, wild magic that she would use to end the bloody conflict. She would rise from those roots and walk onto the battlefield and pull the magic from the very air around her, from the fae and the land itself. It would nearly kill her.

They would leave that war with a treaty and a new world forged from new magic. A queendom formed of four elemental courts and the wild fae ruled collectively by one queen.

The Queendom of Suviel.

LITHIA

"Why, in the goddess's tits, did you only call in a fraction of the legion?"

The deep voice vibrated through her bones. Lithia looked up sharply as Calcas slammed back the flaps to her command tent. She would castrate whoever was on guard duty for letting him pass. Her gaze locked on a mismatched pair of eyes–one iris a depthless black, the other stormy blue, both rimmed faintly in gold–that churned with shadows.

Calcas stalked towards her, a muscle in his jaw ticking, fighting back his explosive anger. She straightened her back, crossing her arms over her chest. The creak of her leathers was the only sound besides his heavy footfalls. He pulled to a stop a breath away from her, the toes of his boots nearly touching hers. She leaned her head back only enough to look into his eyes; he would not make her cower. She stood there in silence, refusing to be the one to break.

"Well?"

She narrowed her eyes before turning back to the map spread out before her.

"It is unbecoming to question your commanding officer, Calcas. I am your general whether you like it at the moment or not. You should be with your men."

"Don't fuck with me right now, Lithia. You have signed all our death warrants."

"That is a bit dramatic, even for you. Our plan is working, and if there were too many troops in place it would do more harm than good. Are you so incapable of trusting me?"

He huffed, falling into a nearby chair and swiping her ale from the table.

"It has nothing to do with trust and everything to do with common sense. We are cornering nearly 20,000 voxis and their ilk in the Valley of Atropin with only around 12,000 of the legion. Why not call in more to camp outside the valley as a precaution?"

His mistrust set her teeth on edge. They had spent centuries trusting each other, and now, at a crucial moment, he was needling at her plans. Was she not Legion High General? Did she not have the gift of battle strategy from the goddess herself?

"Cal, the plan will work best with a smaller force; we don't need to play a numbers game. The voxis will be cornered into the valley. The sentinels I have recalled are our best fighting units, along with the more highly skilled teams, like yours. The voxis are unorganized and undertrained—with their backs to the mountains we'll bottleneck them into the valley and they will fall."

Cal sat straight in his chair, his shoulders stiff, the muscles in his jaw flexing as he watched her. Something other than simple mistrust was bubbling under the surface, but Lia wasn't sure there was time to pick at that thread with battle looming. He leaned forward, lacing his fingers together, elbows on his knees.

"Have you not been watching? They are not the same disorganized resistance they used to be. They have a leader somewhere who has them working as cohesive units. This is a mistake. We can not go at them expecting a sure win."

"From what our intelligence says, they don't have a leader, just a slightly common goal."

"You are underestimating them, Lia," he growled.

"And you are underestimating me."

"Calcas, leave her alone."

They both whipped their heads towards the newcomer. Seren entered the tent, pulling her helm from her head, her hair matted with sweat from her ride. She grinned at them both, ignoring the tension that always seemed to crackle between them.

The captain was stunning. Her rich brown hair shot through with gold, and her warm bronze skin made her honey-bright eyes sparkle. She stood and finger-combed the knots from her braid, a lopsided grin on her face.

"You too love each other too much to fight so often." She chuckled. She sauntered over and swiped the mug of ale from beside Cal and sat in an unoccupied chair, throwing her feet up onto the table and winking at him. "What are you two hens clucking about?"

Cal huffed but softened, as he always did around Seren.

"We were politely discussing how Cal thinks I'm going to get everyone killed."

"Aw! Cal, don't worry, I'm indestructible, didn't you know?"

He stood abruptly and Seren's face fell.

"This is not a game."

"Cal, love, I'm sorry. I was just—"

He shook his head, and glossy black strands of hair loose from his bun bounced against his cheek. Lithia thought in this moment he seemed to fill the space more than he had in the previous breath, still the same muscled warrior, the same scarred olive skin, but more. A breath shuddered out of him and he left the tent.

Lithia leaned on the table in front of Seren's chair, crossing her arms. She looked down, and the scent of lemon and thyme floated under the salty scent of sweat and dust. She let the familiarity of Seren's smell calm her racing thoughts before she spoke.

"Are they gathering?"

"Yes. Wil and I tracked a group of voxis through the lower peaks and they were gathering just inside the valley. They aren't organized, so they are hard to count, but there are fewer than we anticipated, closer to 16,000 than 20,000. They have some fae with them, but not many. It's possible the few fae they have are how they are so organized."

"Good, and Wil?"

"Talking to a bird somewhere."

Lithia shook her head at the grin settling back onto Seren's face.

"She's checking for messages before she comes to see you, probably to give you the more formal version of the information I just gave you."

"Then why are you here, Captain, if she is the one giving me the report?"

Seren stood from her chair, bringing her nose to nose with Lithia. Without wasting another breath, she pulled Lithia to her, tangling her hand into copper curls at her nape, and crashed their lips together. Lithia stepped lightly into her and tipped her head back to deepen the kiss, her tongue flicking out to explore the sweet warmth of Seren's mouth.

After a moment Seren pulled back and began planting hot kisses down the length of Lithia's throat. She nipped the soft flesh beneath her ear, causing Lithia let out a short moan.

"Alright, Little Siren, that's enough. I have a battle to plan, I'll find you later."

"If that's an order, General."

Lithia laughed and watched the way the light bounced through Seren's eyes, admiring her ability to remind her that she wasn't alone.

"Alright, Lia, I'm going to find Cal and calm him down." She winked theatrically, drawing another chuckle from Lithia before she sobered. "He only worries because he loves us. You know that, right?"

"I know."

Lithia forced a smile and Seren pecked her on the cheek before bouncing out of the tent, and Lia watched while the thread in her heart pulled taut.

The clouds crept thick and grey through the sky, mixing with smoke from near the edge of the lake. A distant echo of thunder rolled around the clashing of steel and the groans of the injured. The ground beneath Lithia's feet was a mire of mud and gore, her footsteps clinging to the ground with each step. Moving through the chaos, she searched for Seren.

Lithia caught sight of her, sword locked with a mangled voxis, still clinging to battle. Seren's sword slashed with vicious grace as it sliced through the last of her opponent's remaining strength. She looked like an avenging angel as she kicked out, sending the voxis to join its ilk in the mud. She looked around, looking every inch the warrior.

As she turned, they locked eyes. Lithia moved across the spongy ground towards Seren, eliminating the distance between them. With no regard for the gore covering them, Lithia grabbed the back of her head and pulled her into a kiss, pouring emotion into her, before throwing a wink and turning back to the battle raging around them. For a moment of ever-fleeting hope, she thought she would see Seren at the end of all of this, that the people she loved would come out of this unscathed.

Battle is the enemy of hope.

A scream split the air, desperate and raw. She looked over her shoulder in time to see the spear leave the small voxis's hand a breath before it plunged into Seren's back. Lithia looked down to find the bloodied point emerging from Seren's chest as time seemed to freeze around them. Seren met Lithia's eyes for a fraction of a second, her honey-gold eyes wide in terror before her knees buckled and she crumpled to the mud.

"SEREN!"

Lithia could hear nothing but her own voice. She moved her hands frantically around Seren, panic clouding her logic.

"SEREN, LOOK AT ME!"

The pounding of her own heartbeat filled her ears. Blood was bubbling from Seren's mouth as she stared up at the sky, the battle moving in silence around them.

"SOMEONE FIND A HEALER!"

All she could think was how unfair it was for her heart to beat so loud as Seren's ceased beating at all.

Someone ran up, dropping his sword in the mud and shouting that he could heal her. Lithia nodded absently, staring into Seren's eyes and watching as they slid in and out of focus. She sat in the mud, the realization that no healer was going to fix this settling in as a dark-skinned fae with small tattooed constellations on his ear ran glowing hands over Seren's abdomen.

She carefully lifted Seren's head and laid it on her lap, motioning for the healer to stop. With shaking hands, she smoothed her hair away from her face.

"Seren, please," Lithia whispered, leaning down and placing her forehead on Seren's, the sob thick in her throat. "Please, I need you. I love you. Please, stay."

Seren's eyes focused on Lithia's above her. Hot tears fell from Lithia, mixing with the blood and tears on Seren's cheeks. As Seren breathed, small droplets of blood peppered Lia's lips that hovered a breath away. Lithia could see the light leaving her eyes. She knew Seren's soul would not leave this battlefield, and she knew hers would be trapped here with it.

"I love—" Seren hacked another cough and pulled in a ragged half-breath. "I love you." Her breath rattled ominously in her chest. "In this life and the next."

"Please don't go, Little Siren."

CALCAS

T he hot air clung to his skin, sweat and blood rolling in rivulets down his neck. Calcas stood in the middle of the valley, chest heaving, as he stared up at the mountains, trying and failing to blot this from his memory. The mountains loomed at the end of the valley, their snowcapped peaks casting a shadow across the land. His eyes slowly tracked down from the mountains, taking in the carnage all around him.

The valley floor was littered with bodies. Patches of fire were being doused by several Tidal Fae, limping between bodies and doing what they could to stifle the flames. He watched as his fellow sentinels carried their dead off the field toward a battered-looking fae with a roll of parchment taking down the names of the fallen to be honored. His heart ached in his chest, heavier than the armor clinging to his skin.

There were several fae bound in iron-laced ropes waiting to be executed. He scanned their ranks, taking note of the fae among the voxis being held, wondering what had brought them to the point of turning on their kin. It pained him to see his brethren turn on their own for no discernible reason but power.

His eyes raked over the wreckage, his body slowly beginning to feel the toll the battle had taken. His limbs were heavy, and he could feel at least one broken rib aching as he tried to catch his breath. He should be heading to the healer, but he needed to find her first, to lay eyes on her, to know she was okay. The tug in his chest needed to see her.

Slowly moving across the field, Cal scanned the face of each survivor, hoping it was any of the faces he was desperate to see. Coming towards the rim of the valley, he leaned his sword with its onyx and emerald hilt and his morning star against the base of a nearby tree, their weight too much for his battered body.

He caught sight of the copper braid he was looking for. She was seated with her back to him, her elbows resting on her knees, her head hung low. He watched her for a moment, reassuring himself that she was alive. He took in her features before he approached, lithe arms and powerful legs wrapped in blood-soaked leathers set off her fiery waist length copper braid caked in mud. In opposition to her powerful figure, her facial features were soft and delicate, although they too were caked in blood and dirt. As his frustration began to settle like a pit in his stomach, he moved towards her still form.

Cal circled to stand in front of her, casting a long shadow over her hunched form. He saw the moment she registered his presence: her body stiffened, head slowly raising to meet his gaze. Tear tracks carved through the soot and blood below the deep voids of her black eyes, and seeing her grieving when every death was her fault stirred the rage in his gut.

"You did this. You did all of this."

Her jaw slackened and fell open as she stared up at him. She looked far more helpless than he had ever seen. Something about the depth of the grief on her face didn't fit the self-assured general he met with just a day ago.

"You should have listened—we needed more sentinels. An unnecessary number of fae died at your hand today because you refused to listen to anyone but yourself. Your selfishness killed countless fae today and, you're just sitting out here in your own little world thinking your grief is more important. Have you seen how many are still out there?"

Lithia continued to stare up at him slack-jawed, tears streaming in tracks down her cheeks as he berated her, his frustration fizzling out in the face of her grief. Cal shook his head, wincing in pain at the movement.

"Fine. I'm going to the healer's tents to find Wil and Seren."

He took two steps toward the tree where his weapons waited, his muscles protesting each movement before a quiet voice stopped him in his tracks.

"Seren's not there."

Cal's chest heaved with exertion. Sweat rolled down his chest, mixing with the blood splattered across his abdomen. He wasn't entirely sure if it was his blood at this point. The fae in front of him had gotten in a few good swipes with the bone-tipped gloves he wore acting like talons. He circled out towards the boundary of the worn wooden ring, watching as the smaller fae shook the last blow from his vision. His pupils had blown wide. One more hit to the temple, and he would go down.

He noticed the limp setting into his opponent's left leg; the adrenaline beginning to fade. He lunged, sending his shadows out and into the fae's injured leg, and brought his fist down on his temple as he fell. His opponent hit the boards and didn't move, a trickle of blood coming from his ear. There was a breath of silence before the crowd erupted into cheers and money swiftly changed hands.

He might have killed him. It didn't matter; he wouldn't be the first, nor would he be the last. It had only been four months since he deserted the legion. From what he'd heard, Lia had covered it by discharging him in his absence to save face. Not his face, of course, but hers. He couldn't possibly care less about what anyone thought of him at the moment. The fae he loved was dead, his goddess-damned mate was responsible for it, so why the fuck should he care about any of it.

He turned towards the now open gate on the side of the ring and stalked out. Jofin, the sleazy fae who owned the fighting rings, stood with a sack of gold by the door but Cal ignored him. He ignored the males jeering at him as he made his way to the stairs. He ignored the catcalls and invitations to private rooms from the females who had gathered. He ignored all of it.

Finally, in the silence of the stairwell, he heaved a breath. He could never seem to burn off the aggression entirely. Entering the tavern that hid the ring, he nodded to the older female behind the bar and made his way over, scooping up the ale she poured for him and downing it in one go. He turned, finding a beautiful pair of honeyed eyes upon him. Everything else was wrong, it wasn't her. Her hair was too blonde, her chest too large, and her lips nowhere near as pouty, but the eyes. They drew him in, and he leaned towards her on the bar.

"Would you mind helping me stitch up these cuts?"

She bit down on her soft lower lip and ducked her head. He smiled a wolfish smile, reaching up and gently tugging her lip from between her teeth with the pad of his thumb. Her pupils dilated, and she hopped off her stool, grabbing him by the hand and dragging him towards the stairs.

He followed her, latching the door behind them. They undressed each other quickly, peppering kisses as they went. She pushed him to sit and lifted the rag and washbasin, Slowly, she washed the blood and sweat from his skin. As the last of the filth was wiped away, she kissed and nipped a hot line behind the rag, marking the clean skin. Cal's patience snapped, and he snatched the rag from her hand, tossing it to some far corner of the small room. He grabbed her around the waist, turning and tossing her onto her back as she giggled.

She was sweet, warm, and dripping wet when his cock finally sank into her. The pace was quick and frantic, Cal having no intention of her staying past this encounter. His breathing turned ragged as his climax approached and she arched into him, her eyes closed. Why were her eyes closed? He needed to see her eyes.

"Look at me," he growled.

Her eyes popped open, and she made the most beautiful sound as her pussy convulsed around him as she came. Her chest heaved contented sighs, eyes fogged with lust. Cal came a breath later, looking into the honey eyes—Seren's eyes—before he remembered. As his climax waned, his shadows crawled up her body, filling her eyes and nose, ripping the air from her lungs. Her hooded eyes grew wide in terror as her breath was ripped from her body.

His shadows retreated, and he stared down in horror at the lifeless golden eyes staring up at him.

L ITHIA

L ithia stood outside the walls of the citadel and faced out over the Cliffs of Lorelei. A sheer cliff face dropped into the roiling sea below her. The sea spread out before the rise like a blanket of whirling blues and greens. Close to the craggy rocks at the base, the smaller of the sea serpents were playing in the waves as vessels pulled towards port for the evening. Far out, just under the horizon, the Twin Harbors framed the moon, the round swell of silver perfectly filling the gap like it was rising from the sea. She loved this view—the expanse of water between the ports like a pathway beckoning her to search for distant shores.

She scanned the shoreline as it curved around the bay, disappearing from her line of sight behind the high walls of Arachin. The capital of Suviel was situated in the center of a circular bay nearly a mile from any shore, like the bullseye on a target, the mainland forming a crescent around it. The island held the entirety of the capital, a great walled city accessible only by a bridge formed an eon ago by the first High Queen.

She turned back to the moon, wishing more than anything she could catch hold of its tail and escape on its flight. She shook the thoughts from her head and turned back to her companions: her personal guard, Tadhg, who always followed her in the capital, and her second-in-command, Neda. Despite being the second highest-ranked officer in the legion, Neda, a Hearth Fae and earth elemental, seemed to be pestering Tadhg by softening the stone under him, making it nearly impossible for him to stand.

"Neda, didn't you track me down out here, disrupting my peace and quiet, to update me on the voxis?"

Neda smiled broadly at Lithia. "I did. I got several updates in. It looks as though there are small groups of them gathering but nothing like the attacks has happened again. They have also not done anything to breach the treaty again. Their numbers don't seem to have rebounded in the eight years since the battle which is unexpected. The spies we have tracking them seem to think the ones forming groups are doing so for protection, not rebellion this time."

Lia nodded silently. The voxis had broken the ancient treaty that formed Suviel eight years ago when they began to rebel against the courts, and Lithia still couldn't understand what spurred it. Their magic was wild, but it was strong. Neda cleared her throat and Lithia blinked hard, coming back to the present.

"Sorry, thank you. Was there anything else?"

Neda chewed her lip. "I had a crow from Wil. She said she's on her way to Arachin to meet with you."

"Alright, have you already briefed the High Queen on the voxis?"

Neda smirked. "Yes, your mother caught me in the hall while I was searching for you."

A great crashing noise followed by a blood-curdling shriek tore through the night, ripping Lithia from her sleep. The sheer curtains of her rooms danced in the breeze off the bay, the moon casting cold light across the bed. Her heart beat wildly in her chest as she tried to catch her breath. Was the scream her? Had she woken herself from a nightmare? The thundering of guards running past her room told her the truth. A sense of foreboding hung in the air as she leaped from her bed and ran into the hall.

Several guards ran past, headed towards the stairs at the end of the hall leading to the High Queen's chambers. She followed behind them at a run. The tension held her heart in a vise.

Not again.

She barreled up the stairs and through the ornate doors, blinking rapidly, trying to make sense of the scene in front of her.

Gerania, the High Queen of Suviel, her mother, was lying on the ornate rug by the fire in her nightdress. Her throat was slashed from ear to ear, a pool of blood like a halo around her body, her once vibrant green eyes staring lifelessly into the fire. Lithia's breath caught in her throat.

"Don't touch her."

Her voice came out stronger than it felt, decades of life commanding armies taking over.

"Call for the priestesses. The queen is dead."

Five guards turned and ran for the door to follow her orders. She turned to the others.

"Do you know what happened?"

"No, General. We heard her attendant scream and entered to find this only seconds ahead of you."

She walked over to her mother, kneeling by her head, paying no mind to the blood soaking through her nightclothes. Hundreds of years of memories flew past her eyelids. Her mother, once warm and full of light, would no longer be the hand guiding them through the darkness. A once-great ruler, now an empty shell, cut down by a coward. Anguish and rage burned through Lithia as she whispered a vow to her mother. She would deal the same fatal blow to her assassin and watch the light leave their eyes.

Reaching down with a trembling hand, she closed her mother's eyes gently. She ran a tender hand down her mother's face, soaking in her soft features.

Leaning down, she placed a soft kiss on her mother's forehead and squeezed her eyes shut on the last image of her mother.

"Rest where no shadows fall," she whispered.

The words echoed through the room as they were repeated, the sound of scraping armor as the collected guards kneeled. The commotion in the hall grew louder. Lithia turned to the nearest guard and wordlessly motioned to the door. No one but the priestesses needed to be let in here. He barred the doorway with his frame, and the footsteps scraped to a halt, replaced with hushed whispers.

Four priestesses slipped into the room, their faces covered as always even at this late and unexpected hour. Lithia wondered absently if they slept with their faces covered, or if they slept at all, for that matter. Then her wandering thoughts crashed back to her mother's cold hand in hers.

One of the faceless women placed a heavy hand on Lithia's shoulder.

"Come, let us cover her."

Lithia stood on slightly trembling legs and shifted to the side of the room, the priestess never letting go of her. She watched as they covered her mother's body with a clean sheet, the same pale green as the ones on her mother's bed. The priestess beside her spoke to the guard nearest to her in a tone too low for Lithia to catch, and soon everyone was being ushered from the room.

"General, we will remove the queen's body to the temple to have it prepared for her pyre, the room should be looked at before it's cleaned."

Lithia nodded. "Wil is on her way to the city. Seal the room until she arrives."

"Yes, General. There is also the matter of starting the marking. We shouldn't wait long."

Lithia took a deep breath through her nose, the thi patchouli and vanilla smell of her mother's room soured by the iron of blood.

"Let's do it now."

The priestesses paused a moment.

"Why don't you go get cleaned up first?"

Lithia looked down, the bottom of her soft white nightshirt was soaked in blood, it was streaked up her bare legs and smudged on her feet. Her hands looked like she had dipped them in the tacky substance. She felt the burn of tears and clenched her jaw. The moment she was alone, she knew she would break.

"No. Now."

LITHIA

Two of the priestesses accompanied by twelve of the Queen's Guard would be taking her mother's body through the guard tunnels to the temple on the other side of the island. The bells would not announce her mother's death to the queendom until her body was secure and the transfer of power had begun.

The two remaining priestesses led the way out of the queen's chamber, Lithia pausing in the doorway and breathing in the last breath of their mother before they sealed the door. Turning, she found the small landing surprisingly empty save for Tadhg and began making her way down the stairs. Before they reached the doors at the bottom, one of the priestesses placed that weighted hand on her shoulder again, stopping her and gesturing to Tadhg.

"I was able to clear this hall but I wouldn't be surprised if you have to face a few of them on the other side of this door," he said, shifting uncomfortably.

Lithia squared her shoulders, taking the last few steps and pushing through the doors. It wasn't a few. The eleven remaining Queen's Guard, Neda, and the dozen other advisors and high-ranking legionaries were standing in the hall watching her with grief-stricken faces. The priestess to her right took a small step forward.

"Gerania Caileanach, Decendent of Mab, High Queen of Suviel is dead."

The silence in the room thickened until Neda stepped forward and took a knee in front of Lithia, bowing her head in deference. Like a wave, the others followed the priestesses, turning to do the same. It took a moment for Lithia to realize they were going to stay like that until she told them otherwise.

"Please." Her voice cracked. "Please, stand. I am honored to have you all at this moment, but this is a very sensitive matter. Please return to your rooms and posts and do not spread the news until the bells announce it."

A ripple moved through the gathered crowd as they bowed and began to leave. One of the priestesses held up a hand towards Neda before speaking.

"Commander, would you mind coming with us?"

Neda bowed her head in assent and joined their small group. The priestesses began walking again, leading the way down the hall. Lithia widened her stride just enough to bring herself level with Neda. When they were walking in stride, she reached over and grabbed Neda's hand in a vise grip, intertwining their fingers, needing desperately something to tether her to the ground again.

They moved through the residential wing in silence, the bustle of the castle nonexistent at this hour. As they passed through doorways, guards bowed lower than normal and she caught the sheen of tears on several cheeks. They moved quickly through the small courtyard that separated the residences from the public areas of the citadel and down the wide hall that housed the major meeting chambers and led directly to the wide doors of the throne room.

They stopped outside the closed doors and she nodded to the guards stationed there, who looked at each other with concern at her current state. She paused a moment to allow Tadhg to fill the two sentinels in and admired the ornate opal inlays of the door. She loved them any time of the day, but especially the late evening when they glinted orange and red and truly looked like the flames they represented. Now in the low light, they were their natural pearly sheen.

They quickly pushed the doors open to allow them entry before dropping into low bows. She bowed her head before they stood, closing the doors behind their small party. Tadhg quickly checked the one other entry point into the room, alerting the guards posted there of their presence before taking up a post by the main doors as the others made their way toward the throne.

Every time she walked through this room during the day it stretched endlessly. Everyone would stop their conversations as she passed, turn, and watch her walk by like she was some sort of exhibit. It made her skin crawl. Every pair of eyes was another ant creeping along her body. The deep black stone of the floor and walls made even the silence seem to echo, and it was a crushing weight. She locked her eyes on the throne, shutting out every whisper and judgmental pair of eyes.

The Ember Throne was a marvel of amphiptere magic. Seated on a dais, the throne was crafted from perfectly clear glass, filled with swirling smoke and floating cinders. The amphiptere, a race of legless dragons, had forged the throne in the first age of Suviel, when Mab formed the queendom as it exists today. As a youngling, Lithia would inspect every inch, needing to know how the fire still glowed, and what made the smoke move. Even after her two centuries of life, she still thought the throne was a wonder.

The throne was the only adornment in the room, save for the gold braziers along the walls. Behind the throne was a wall of windows overlooking the Cliffs of Lorelei. Apart from the fae it was always full of, this room was her favorite place in the citadel. Now, however, it was cold and lifeless.

Lithia was startled by the raspy voice of the priestess who had been silent so far.

"General, if you wouldn't mind sitting on the throne."

Lithia didn't move. Her heart raced as the realization that she was effectively about to become queen sunk in. Neda squeezed her hand tightly.

"Before I allow you to perform unknown-to-me magic on my general and the heir apparent to the throne, would you mind if I ask what exactly is about to happen?"

Lithia let out a small breath at the delay, silently thanking Neda for understanding she needed a moment.

"Of course, Commander, I understand your hesitation. There is no need to worry, however. Lithia has been preparing for this throughout her life, but we should have had more time."

They all paused a moment, the realization that her mother had been alive only a couple of hours ago making Lithia's stomach turn. The quiet priestess had moved onto the dais where she was drawing small runes around the base of the throne with what looked like oil from a small vial at her belt. A small sniff came from the direction of the priestess before she continued speaking.

"When Mab first joined the courts under the Ember Throne, she was blessed with a mark of magic from each of the four courts after returning the magic to Suviel. This act established her as the first High Queen."

She shifted on her feet and began indicating some of the runes as she spoke.

"Water from the Tidal Court, earth from the Hearth, air from the Celestial, and fire and shadow from the Arcane. These blessing marks were imbued with the power of the courts, granting Mab control of the magics tied to each court. So, once the rite was completed, she became the only being to walk this plane with all the elements of magic. This, of course, is something all fae know."

Neda nodded along, a furrow forming between her brows as the priestess spoke. Few understood how the royal magic was passed down, and given their long lives, many had not been around the last time a queen was crowned.

"In its simplest form, Mab created a new court that day: the High Court, though we don't often name it as such." The priestess continued, "It is why those born of Mab's line, all women, do not hold any elemental magic until they are crowned. We believe that instead they were gifted with well-honed wild magic rather than belonging to a single court. Lithia's grandmother, for instance, was a powerful seer while her mother had potent mind magic."

She paused for a moment and turned that blank face to Lithia. "Your magic is unique too. Where your grandmother's sight was broad, your sight has made you a master of strategy, of knowing your opponent's moves, reading their intentions."

"Back to my point. What we are doing tonight is the beginning of the marking. We will begin the marks to signify that Lithia is Mab's heir and the heir of Suviel. The first part of the marking syphons all traces of magic from Lithia's body. The purpose is to humble her in the first full year as queen, to show her the importance of power, and to cleanse her body, effectively making her a pure vessel for the magic of the marking."

Lithia felt Neda tense beside her. She knew what she was in for, but Neda didn't. She took a deep breath, knowing if she didn't speak now, she never would. She ran her thumb over Neda's hand before letting go of it slowly and moving toward the throne.

"In one year, the Primes of all four courts and their heirs will meet here and complete the marking, and my magic along with the magic of my line will be returned. This is my duty and I am not afraid."

It was a lie. She was terrified, but Neda didn't have to know that. She turned when she made it to the throne and gave Neda's concerned face a small smile. As her bare thighs met the warm stone of the throne, she sat and closed her eyes.

The priestesses hummed and slowly drew the same runes in ink and oil on her skin, beginning on the insides of her wrists. As they reached her inner elbow, she opened her eyes and focused on Neda, the only other figure in the room.

Neda was tall and muscular, albeit far more intimidating in leathers and armor than she was in her nightclothes. Ashy blonde hair cropped just above her shoulders was still tousled from sleep. Lithia's body went rigid as the burning started in her fingertips but she continued to focus on Neda, determined to fight the discomfort as they continued up her arms towards her shoulders.

Her commander had soft features with pouty lips and high cheekbones, but the most distracting thing about her was the startling green of her eyes, like the bright green of a peridot. Around her right eye was a black tattoo mimicking the scar that her twin, Narcos, had running through his eye.

Her study of the commander was cut short when the priestesses made their final marks on either side of her throat near her collarbone. The pain in her body multiplied, fire clawing its way through her limbs, trying to find a way out. No one had told her it was going to hurt. The room shook slightly and the fires in the braziers went out.

Everything was pain, but she was nothing.

CALCAS

Calcas leaned back in his chair, staring over the rim of his mug at the mess in front of him. His hair was still damp and his skin was still raw from the hour he spent trying to scrub his sins from his skin in the shower. He supposed calling the poor dead fae on his bed a mess was a bit dismissive, but at a certain point he stopped really knowing what to think. Over eight years this was number eleven, or was she twelve?

Goddess damn it, what was wrong with him? The building rage he had been running from all those years ago had done nothing but get fought out in the ring just to reform in his chest by morning. He had quickly become Jofin's prize fighter, the Shadow of the South. He made the slimy fae a lot of money and in return Jofin kept him hidden and moving.

He had likely been to every shady inn and tavern in Suviel, and had most certainly graced every illegal fighting ring. This inn was one of his favorites, near enough to home to catch news, but not so close that his mother would catch wind of him. He stared at the girl on the bed for another moment before plopping a rather large sack of gold on the dingy table and gathering his bag.

He would find another place to stay after his fight tonight; he didn't have time to clean up his mess. Even more concerning, he didn't have time to figure out why they kept fucking dying. He had never been so out of control of his magic as he had in those moments. His shadows had never not listened to him before.

He moved quickly through the pub downstairs, sidestepping a pair of men coming to blows over a game of cards and slipping through the small door near the kitchens. The sounds from the pub cut off as the door closed, and he was left alone in the dim hall. Just before he pushed open the next heavy wood door, he thought he caught a familiar scent, but it left him too quickly.

He pushed into the ring and the sound hit him like a battering ram, the fight before his just starting. Calcas muscled his way through the spectators as he made his way over to Jofin, who looked mildly like someone who had a fish hook constantly tugging at their lip. The large man ran a hand through his oily, deep blue hair as he listened to the mousy man in front of him explain why he couldn't pay. In Calcas's experience, that never went over well.

"You know how long you have to get the money. Come in here during a fight and waste my time again and you won't leave."

Calcas averted his eyes as the man left, ashamed at how many times he had done this exact song and dance. Jofin brought a meaty hand down on Cal's shoulder, steering him to the small room to the side of the ring. Cal tossed his bag onto the small bench and pulled his shirt off, tying his hair into a knot on top of his head. Jofin watched him with his head tilted to the side.

"Those tattoos finally finished?"

Cal shrugged. Through the years, between fights, Cal had found himself under the tattoo magic of a fae in the Tidal Court. Swirling black tattoos curled around his chest and shoulders, a warrior's mantle made of shadow. He was no longer a sentinel, but he still carried the burden. He pulled on his leather leggings and strapped the two small daggers to his thigh before lifting his morning star and saluting Jofin.

They stepped out toward the ring. Two young fae were just finishing sweeping the sandy floor when Jofin stepped out into its center.

"GENTLEMEN," Jofin started before looking up and locking eyes with someone Calcas had no interest in discerning. "And ladies, of course," he finished with a wink. "I have a special fight for you this evening." He gave a dramatic pause for the cheering to die down. "We have a crowd favorite in the ring tonight, the Shadow of the South."

A beat of silence followed his announcement before an eruption of noise. Screaming cheers and the clank of hastily made bets. The crowd pulsed towards the platform as Cal stepped into the ring.

"His opponent for the evening is a brand-new challenger. Nerisei, the Sapphire Dragon!"

A slender woman slipped into the ring, circular knives gleaming in her hands. She cast a feral grin toward Cal as she mirrored his movements around the sandy edge of the ring. He had never heard of her before, but the way she moved was feline and predatory. She wasn't an amateur set up to win the ring money. He cut a look towards Jofin, who locked eyes with him and shrugged, then gestured to a rather large trunk being moved toward his office.

Lovely. So not only was someone here to kill him, but they wanted to make a show of it.

"The rules are simple. To the death"—another of his infuriating pauses—"and no magic."

Calcas could practically feel his molars cracking with the pressure of clenching his jaw. Like hell would he die in this ring to line Jofin's pockets.

The roar of the crowd echoed through the underground arena as Calcas tracked Nerisei's steps. The spiked head of his morning star glittered in the flickering light as he spun it. Across the ring and pacing closer, Nerisei held curved blades poised for attack, her lithe form and sharp eyes reminding him of a mountain cat.

Nerisei wasn't quite what he expected from an underground fighter. She was too clean, too sharp, and her movements too focused. She was small and lean, with long golden hair in a single braid that fell nearly to her hips. Her eyes were a deep blue and gold and upturned at the corners, playing into that feline look. She wore sleek black leathers and was barefoot, much like Cal. Jofin seemed to want to make sure his fighters weren't given any protective advantages.

At some internal signal, Nerisei lunged forward, her movements a blur as she closed the distance between them in a breath. Cal swung in a wide arc to halt her approach, but the smaller female ducked under his massive weapon, rolling to the side and slashing out at Cal's leg. Her blades glanced off his leathers, missing his flesh just barely.

Cal's morning star slammed into the sand a hair's breadth from her moving limbs sending sand flying. Cal's chest heaved as they circled each other again. Nerisei's knees bent a fraction just before she lunged a second time. Cal was ready for her, aiming the morning star at her chest in a vicious backswing, sending her sprawling into the sand and choking on an inhale. One of her blades embedded itself in Cal's left arm as it flew from her hand on impact.

Pain seared through his arm, hot and wet, sending little spits dancing in his vision. He pulled the blade from his flesh, sending another searing lick of pain up his arm. Just as he tossed it to the side, Nerisei swiped out at him after regaining her feet, slicing shallowly into his cheek. He caught her arm on the backswing, yanking her towards him, feeling a pop of bone as he kicked her feet out from under her, sending her sprawling into the sand once again.

Desperation flashed in Nerisei's eyes as she swiped out looking for her dropped blade, blood pouring from her mouth with each breath. The fight came too easy, over too quickly. Even if he walked away now, the blow from the morning star had likely already killed her, but it would be slow.

In his moment of hesitation, Nerisei called up the dredges of her strength and pulled a small blade from the front of her vest. Cal turned as it left her fingers, burying itself in his ribs just under his heart. A roar of pained fury tore itself from Cal's throat and his grip faltered for a moment, his morning star slipping lower in his hand.

Before the flush of victory could settle on her face, Cal's morning star was finding its home in the center of her head, blood and viscera splattering the sand. His stomach roiled, and he quickly turned his back on her and faced Jofin, who was opening the ring door, a malicious grin consuming his gnarled face as Cal stumbled bleeding from the ring.

As soon as he stepped into the night, a hand shot out, pulling him bodily into the alley beside the tavern.

"You would think a prize fighter wouldn't be so easily kidnapped."

Cal turned, looking into the glittering white eyes waiting behind him, and smiled for the first time in longer than he could remember.

"There has been a crow on my windowsill for three days, Wil. I knew you were coming."

Willow stepped out of the inky pool of shadows against the wall and Cal took her in for the first time in nearly five years. She looked every inch the royal spymaster with her lithe frame and rich ebony skin clad in black leathers, her thick amethyst braids coiled in a large bun on the top of her head. Her opalescent eyes scanned the alley once more before jerking her head in the direction of the street.

"Come on, I have a room."

No part of him particularly wanted to go with her, as it meant someone sent her looking for him. He followed her in silence into the nicer part of this small village. He tended to stay in the seedier places this close to the Arcane Court to avoid the eye of his mother. Astris Lavar, the Prime of the Arcane Court, was Calcas's mother and her position over the court made it particularly difficult for him to hide within its borders. If she wasn't already aware of his presence, she was about to be.

Calcas plopped down at the table in Willow's room, swiping the decanter of wine and filling both their glasses before downing his quickly.

"Did my mother send you or did our illustrious general?"

"The queen."

Calcas froze halfway to filling his glass a second time.

"Why would she need me?"

"Unfortunately for you, Cal, I travel much faster than news makes it to the underbelly you exist in these days."

Cal shifted in his seat, straightening as Wil continued.

"Gerania was murdered a fortnight ago. Lithia is queen."

The thoughts running through his head were a chaos he was struggling to decipher. Of all the things he expected Wil to say, this wasn't one of them. He had been running from Lithia for so long that he avoided any news of her, but all he wanted to know was if she was okay. Was she hurt? Was she hurting? Who was with her?

Instead, what fell from his mouth was, "What happened?"

Wil swirled the wine in her glass a moment, watching him before she answered.

"An assassin slit her throat in the night. I found the assassin's body in the courtyard the next morning. It seems like she drank something rather than risk being caught alive."

"That ... that's actually a bit anticlimactic."

Wil raised her chin. "She did a coward's job and died a coward's death. She will be a footnote for it."

"So you came here to what? Let me know?"

Wil narrowed her eyes at his dismissal. "No, I came here because even though I tried to talk her out of it, Lithia wants you to lead her Queen's Guard."

Cal downed the rest of his wine because he would rather dance naked in The Beneath than be a member of the Queen's Guard.

"Even if your answer is no, and it should be, you are still going to have to get over yourself because the court heirs are required to be a part of the marking and you, Calcas, are an heir."

LITHIA

Lithia stood staring into the mirror, taking in the facade she had created. Her hair was loose and wavy, with the top braided around her onyx crown, making it seem a part of her. Her eyes had been lined with black kohl and her pouty lips stained a red so deep it was near black. She had been dressed in supple black leather armor over her leggings. The bodice was a sculpted corset, intricately crafted with gold inlay that mimicked the grooves of her metal battle armor.

Slung over her shoulder was her soft green leather baldric with its row of gold-handled throwing knives, her great sword hanging on her hip. There were also two small knives in her boot and an ornate jeweled dagger on the front of her hip. The overall look was an elegant reminder that before she was queen, she was a warrior. She looked intimidating, and she desperately needed to feel intimidating. The lack of sleeves and arm guards showcased the runes that marked her as the High Queen, adding to the aura of power.

The runes. They started at the knuckle of each middle finger, running in a straight line up her arms to her collarbone where they formed a collar around her throat. Near the hollow of her throat was a gap where it looked like a few were missing. They wouldn't be missing for long. As she looked into the voids of her deep black eyes, she realized she was afraid. She hadn't dealt with fear like this since Seren, but she swallowed it down and turned to the fire.

"Ugh, I can't believe you're going to marry my brother."

Neda sighed dramatically from where she lay on the chaise in Lithia's room, dressed in her own formal leathers. After stalling for nearly four months, she had finally moved into the queen's chambers a week ago but had forced Neda to stay with her every night because she couldn't bring herself to sleep alone with her mother's ghost. Lithia laughed lightly as she ran her fingers through her unpinned hair.

"Well, you have had nearly five years to get used to the idea, Neda, no need to sound so grossed out. We won't get married until after the marking anyway, so don't worry."

"Oh goddess, I've just realized you'll have to have his babies."

Neda made a fake gagging sound as Lithia moved, plucking a glass of wine off the sideboard to stand at the end of the chaise. She laughed lightly at Neda before responding.

"You'll be more disgusted to learn we've already practiced."

Neda threw her arm theatrically over her face. "Oh unholy goddess, I'll never recover from such knowledge."

"I promise to be disgustingly affectionate when we greet Narcos."

Lithia chuckled, staring off into the flames, sipping slowly, and letting the lighthearted conversation fade. She watched Neda shift on the chaise to pull on her boots, allowing Lithia a moment of silence.

"Do you miss her when you're with Narcos?"

The wine in Lithia's throat dropped like molten steel into her stomach, burning her from the inside. The smell of lemon and thyme filled her senses and honey-colored eyes looked back at her from the fire. The ghost of a thread in her soul panged with the loss of a love that would stay just out of reach. She swallowed down the remainder of her wine and set her glass down.

"It doesn't matter."

The look of pity in Neda's eyes made her want to vomit, or maybe it was the wine, or something else entirely. Whatever it was, the room was getting smaller, and they had places to be.

"Come on, General, your brother should be here soon. Let's go do our jobs."

Lithia winked at Neda, who rolled her eyes and smiled.

"It's only been a few weeks, but it's strange not calling you general."

"Fret not, I'm still in charge."

Lithia tapped her crown, and Neda made those fake gagging noises again and the steel weight in Lithia's stomach lightened the slightest bit.

The sun was blazing down on the entry courtyard as Lithia, Neda, and a few courtiers watched as the small group of Hearth Fae crossed the bridge into Arachin. The Infernum Bridge was created an eon ago by Mab, the first High Queen. It stretched from a small fort on the mainland to the island across the water, ending in the citadel's main courtyard.

It was truly a beautiful bridge. Ornate stone was carved with intricate images depicting the elements of all four courts, a picture of balance. Its walls were low so as not to obstruct the view and wards were weaved in intricate patterns on its surface, both holding the bridge up and preventing anyone from falling from its sides.

Lithia squinted into the sunlight at the approaching group of fae. At the front was a glinting suit of armor that could only be her new Captain of the Queen's Guard, Cian. Her heart still ached at the memory of reading Cal's rejection in Wil's neat script. A deep part of her had been prepared for it but another part of her had hoped that in her pain her friend would return to her. It seemed that wound would remain raw and bleeding for longer.

As they reached the entry, her face split into a grin as Neda's mirror image stepped out from behind Cian. The planes of his face were sharper, with a narrow nose and high cheekbones. Ashy blond hair was pulled into a high knot, and wisps escaped in the breeze coming off the bridge, prominently displaying his ears—one with a point, the other blunted. Her gaze tracked from his ear's mangled tip to the scar that ran across his temple, through his right eye, and down the length of his face, ending at the soft corner of his mouth, stretched wide in an answering grin.

There was a blur of motion in Lithia's periphery before Neda pounced on her brother, who nearly crumpled at the contact. They embraced, laughing in a way that made Lia's heart warm, the steel in her gut lightening again at their joy. She smiled as Cian made his way to her, bowing before stepping behind her and clapping Tadhg, ever her shadow, on the shoulder.

The remaining few members of the small crossing party bowed to Lithia before dispersing toward their respective destinations and their waiting friends before the still-smiling twins made their way over to her. Narcos bowed low, his joyful grin for his sister turning wolfish as it landed on Lithia.

"My Queen," he said, reaching for her hand.

A scoff from Neda sounded at the formality.

"You didn't address me by my title!"

Narcos rolled his eyes playfully as Lithia stifled a laugh.

"Why don't we go inside where there are far less ... spectators," Lithia suggested.

She glanced around at the usually bustling courtyard and found a large number of people pretending to look busy. The small groups of advisors and social climbers scattered throughout the courtyard, listening for any gossip to pass along. Lithia caught one of the ladies tilting her head in their direction in the hopes of catching something to use to make herself look more important to whatever group of twittering girls she was a part of. It was the worst part of being who she was. No part of her life had ever been private, and it was even worse now.

They moved through the courtyard towards the large stone doors that served as the entrance to the citadel and down the wide hall that housed the public meeting chambers. They stopped at a small stairwell flanked by two of the Queen's Guard. Cian bowed and took his leave of their small group before they made their way up to the private offices. Each of the Primes, as well as the two highest-ranking legion officials, general and spymaster, had studies on this floor along the western-facing side of the hall. The eastern side of the hall housed only studies for the queen and her consort, as well as the council chamber.

Tadhg took up his post outside the door to the queen's study as the three of them entered. As soon as they entered Lithia's sitting room, Narcos scooped her into his chest. With one finger under her chin, he tipped her head up to look into her depthless black eyes.

"I've missed you, Lia."

He kissed her lightly on the tip of her nose and she smiled, leaning up and pressing a kiss to his lips.

"Disgusting."

Lithia looked over at Neda, who despite her words had a rather sweet smile on her face. The guilt at her own happiness made her stomach turn, but she shrugged it off, kissing Narcos again, before letting go and moving towards the plush chairs.

"How was your journey? I'm sorry I can't stay long, I have a meeting with Cian about the security for the marking." Neda said, perching on the arm of Lithia's chair.

"It was fine, a bit boring. We did have a bit of excitement when I was leaving the Hearth capital though. Four of the citizens of Fernholme have gone missing in the last few weeks and they can't seem to find any reason as to why or where."

"Is your brother looking into it?" Lithia asked. concern thickening in her voice.

Narcos nodded. "Nylian is doing everything he can. He was writing to Willow when I left to see if there was anything similar happening elsewhere."

A furrow had formed between Neda's brows. "I am supposed to be meeting with several unit leaders and captains later this week who are stationed throughout Hearth. I'll ask them if they have seen anything too."

"When Wil was here, she said they had a missing girl in Arcane," Lia added, chewing on her lip. "I hope they are isolated and just poor timing. It would be a shit time to have to hunt down flesh traders."

"I'll send notes to Primes Cassara and Osharus and see if Celestial and Tidal have had any issues too," Narcos added, laying a comforting hand on Lithia's knee that had begun bouncing. "At least all the Primes and heirs will be here for the marking in a few months, so hopefully if it is a widespread situation we can find a solution then."

Her knee abruptly stopped bouncing. Shit. Shit. Shit. Heirs. She was fine dealing with his rejection and distance as long as it was, well, distant, but Cal was an heir.

A small knock sounded at the door and broke her spiraling thoughts as Narcos squeezed her knee in understanding before he hopped up to answer. He returned with a small stack of papers.

"Cian dropped off some things for you to sign Lia and he said to tell Neda your meeting started 10 minutes ago and he'll be in your study."

"Thahaos's balls!" Neda huffed, hopping up from her seat and kissing Narcos on the cheek on her way out the door.

Lithia stood, grabbing the papers from Narcos and moving towards her desk.

Dropping the papers onto the desk, she plopped in an entirely queenly manner into her plush high-backed chair. She kicked her boots up onto the polished granite of the desk and narrowed her eyes at Narcos. He looked so ... smug.

He was standing straight, with his feet shoulder-width apart, hands clasped in front of him in his usual stance, showcasing his broad chest and strong arms. He caught her appraising look and the small grin turned into a dazzling smile, a small dimple appearing on the unscarred side of his face.

"See something you like, My Queen?" he practically purred at her, heat singing through her body.

"You only ever use my formal title when you want something from me. What did you do?"

His smile turned feral, and he began walking towards her desk, a faint click telling her that he had just used magic to lock the door. As he rounded the desk, she moved her feet from the desktop to the floor, her spine locking straight and eyes tracking every one of his movements. The predatory look in his eyes sent a hot bolt of desire through her body. When he finally stopped directly in front of her, he leaned back on the desk and looked down at her.

Reaching out, he tucked a few of her wild curls back into her braid. Then, running his thumb across her bottom lip, staring into the fathomless voids of her eyes, he leaned down, placing a soft kiss on her lips. Well, it started as a soft kiss. Her built-up tension and the sudden wave of desire quickly had her fisting her hands in the soft cotton of his tunic and dragging him closer, deepening the kiss. Narcos wound his fingers into her hair near the of her neck and tilted her head as he pulled back, breaking the kiss to look into her eyes again.

"Lia, you are queen. Don't let one man's presence make you forget that you are powerful. You are the moon. Do not bow to the stars."

Calcas

C al strode up to his large mount, a blue-black warhorse called
Redmaw, and ran his hand down his neck, scooping his
reins before slipping a boot into his stirrup and hoisting himself
into the saddle. He motioned up to his mother's carriage and indicated that they could continue before looking over to a grinning
Wil riding beside him.

"I hope Lord Fancy Pants had a lovely ride in his cozy little
carriage," Willow said with a teasing lilt.

He huffed, "I don't think being stuck in a carriage with my
mother and being lectured is exactly cozy. Have you had any updates?"

"So grumpy. Not really, more of the same, but it's getting
worse, of course. Four more have disappeared, eight more have lost
their magic entirely, and a grove near the western shore has stopped

blooming as the void creeps closer. They can't seem to find a link between any of the missing or magicless fae in any court. They have taken to calling it The Voiding in the updates. It's never fun when they give it a name."

Cal bit down hard on the inside of his cheek. Whatever this was, name or not, it wasn't good, and it happening at the same moment Lithia became queen was concerning. It was almost stressful enough to distract him from the pit in his stomach every time he remembered he was about to see her for the first time in nine years, but not quite. He had made it this far without her realizing she was his mate and he didn't want proximity to fuck that up. Wil's voice clanged into his thoughts.

"All the Primes should have arrived in Arachin in recent days for the marking this evening, we are the last to arrive. Lithia has already set a meeting for after the marking to come up with a plan since there won't be any time before. You do plan on not acting like the giant ass you are, correct?"

"I plan on doing exactly what is required of me and nothing more, Wil. I can't ... I can't do anything else."

"I know you believe that and don't want to hear it, but we need her."

Something in his chest cracked open, and boiling rage spilled out. "Last time someone needed her they fucking died. I don't need her."

Several hours later near late afternoon, the bridge fort came into view. It was a squat square building, its sole purpose to allow passage to the bridge. It was not heavily manned, but he could see the archers tracking their progress from the parapet as they rode. All were likely Celestial, so their power over the air would mean those arrows never missed a mark.

As their party grew closer, he saw that stables and paddocks had been expanded to accommodate the influx of horses and carriages coming to the capital for the marking. Since there was no need for them on the island, most wouldn't even fit on the bridge. There was no quick escape in the form of a horse from Arachin, much to his dismay.

Their group approached the heavy iron gate, and Calcas dismounted and led Redmaw off to a stable hand who was waiting, hand outstretched. He passed the slight boy the reins and turned back toward the gate with a firm pat to the horse's blue-black shoulder. He took in the sentinels milling around the fort's entrance.

A tall guard moved through open gates toward Cal with purpose. His black breastplate bore the seal of the Ember Throne, a sword piercing a flaming crown, marking him as one of the Queen's Guard. As he drew closer to them, Cal recognized the emerald cloak that established him to be the captain of the guard. Cal shifted uncomfortably, turning to the carriage to offer his hand to his mother as she exited.

"Arcane Prime." The tall male bowed his head as his mother straightened her skirts. "Welcome to Arachin. I am here to escort you and your heir"—he nodded to Cal—"across the bridge. The High Queen is awaiting your arrival on the other side."

"We shouldn't keep her waiting."

His first time crossing the bridge as a youngling, he was convinced any breeze would knock him from the side. Now he very much wished he could pitch himself off rather than get any closer to the flaming copper head he could see growing closer in the distance. The moment he stepped off the bridge onto Arachin, he looked up and all the air vanished from his lungs at the sight of her.

Wil threw an "I'm begging you to behave look" over her shoulder, clearly hearing his reaction to the nearly unrecognizable queen in front of him. She was formidably beautiful. Tall and lethally graceful, she was wearing a nearly sheer black gown that swept the tiles of the courtyard, the fabric catching the light like a sea of gleaming stars. The sheer skirt split up each leg to her hip, cinching in at her waist then gathering at her shoulders with emerald brooches. Under the sheer fabric of the bodice, it looked like an armor-plated corset with a deep vee. As his eyes finished the torturously slow path from her feet to her face, he met her eyes. Eyes that were locked onto his, smugness hidden in their depths.

With a shake of his head, she turned to look at the others and found Narcos was looking at him with such venom it was clear he would have killed Cal on the spot if there weren't witnesses. Turning, he thought it may be safer to avoid that particular confrontation for now. He stayed at his mother's right hand as they approached Lithia, bowing deeply.

"Lia, my love, you cut a fierce figure as High Queen."

Astris opted to swoop Lia into a hard hug after her more formal curtsy and she melted into the maternal embrace as Cal averted his gaze from the tender moment. The realization that his own vitriol hadn't tainted their relationship knocked him off balance. The Prime pulled back, still holding onto Lithia's arms.

"Prime Astris, I am so honored to have you here. I have missed your council."

Their polite conversation faded to a hum in his ears. As Lithia and his mother spoke, he finally took in the splendor of the crown she wore. It was towering spikes of obsidian, woven into her hair as if it grew from her skin, like it was a part of her. A single emerald dripped onto her forehead.

The pair laughed at something he missed and Lia placed a kiss on each of Astris's cheeks. "I do hope I have more time to speak with you. I have missed you Astris. I am sorry that dinner has to wait, but the marking needs to begin at sunset. I did have some food sent up to your rooms, so you can have a bite while you change."

"It's no problem, dear, we will wash up and be down quickly."

His mother moved past Lithia and through the citadel doors. Lithia looked up at him expectantly, her mouth opening, black eyes glittering. He could see words building on her tongue, but before they left her mouth he bowed deeply. His heart began to race, the thread in his chest started to hum, his shadows churned around his arms. He needed to breathe, but when he inhaled all he smelled was her. Violets and cedar. He had to run. Again.

"My Queen," he said with a bow and continued through the doors behind his mother.

The four Primes and their heirs stood in the chamber outside the throne room just over an hour later. The urge to flee was making Cal sweat, but here he was sulking in a corner instead. A small door opened and Narcos stepped into the atrium, his tailored black tunic a perfect match to the dress Lia had been wearing earlier.

Narcos stood with his hands behind his back, chest out. "Thank you all so much for coming so far. This evening is a monumental moment that hopefully we won't see again for a long time. We will begin the marking immediately and dinner will be served in your chambers after."

Cal sneered at the future king consort. What a pompous ass. Narcos turned, and the guards opened the massive doors to the throne room. Cal shifted, offering his arm to his mother as they fell into step behind the others.

The processional formed behind Prime Nylian and Neda, his sister and acting heir until Nylian has an heir of his own, from Hearth. They were followed by Prime Cassara and Halos of Celestial, Prime Osharus and Aegaea, of the Tidal Court, and finally Prime Astris and Cal. Only the Primes, their heirs, the consort, and the High Priestess were party to the marking. Its magic was a highly guarded secret. The incantations would be wiped from the minds of the Primes and heirs upon completion held only in the minds of the current High Queen and High Priestess.

When they entered the throne room, Lithia was already seated on the Ember Throne, the High Priestess to her right and Narcos to her left. The broaches on Lithia's shoulders had been undone, revealing the entire expanse of her arms and throat, the sheer fabric falling to become a part of her skirt. The runes tattooed from her hand to her shoulders were left exposed.

The priestess began when they were all standing in a crescent in front of the dais.

"The marking is the oldest form of magic, given to Mab by the goddess when Suviel needed a beacon in the darkness. The magic of all courts is given to the ruling queen so she may maintain the balance. Each Prime and their heir will come forward to mark the rune of their court onto Lithia's collarbone, completing the path of runes and entrusting her with your court's power. The marking is more than a bestowing of power; it is a contract of loyalty. Not just of your court to Lithia, but it is the promise that she will always act in service to all courts and that the courts will remain in service to the Queendom of Suviel."

Lithia's knuckles were white on the arms of the throne. The tension in the room was palpable.

"After the inking of the final rune, Lithia will enter a stillness until the magic has taken hold. After she wakes, she will be fully crowned High Queen of Suviel. Before we begin, are there any objections to Lithia's right to the throne?"

Astris tensed as if she expected Cal to object, but he held his head high, meeting Lithia's eyes. His pain surrounding her was personal, and he would not use it against her now.

"Very well, let us begin."

The High Priestess began to chant.

"In halls of power, four courts unfold,
Magic's dance, a tale retold.
Beneath an emerald canopy, they convene,
Mystic realm with strength unseen."

"Celestial Court, please come and place your palms on Lithia's chest."

Cassara and Halos fluttered a mere inch from the stones as they laid hands on Lithia.

"Court of Skies where whispers weave,
Mystic currents winds conceive.
Sovereignty in skies untold,
Breath of power pure and bold."

A blast of wind swept through the throne room.

"If the Hearth Court would please come and place your palms on Lithia's chest."

Nylian and Neda stepped up the dais with looks of pride and each placed a hand across Lia's collarbone.

"Court of Earth strong and wise,

Rooted power where empires rise.

Stone and soil, a foundation strong,

Whispering trees where wisdoms belong."

The ground shook beneath their feet.

"Tidal Court, if you please, come place your hands."

"Court of Water currents deep,

Where emotions softly sweep.

River of influence emotions guide,

In strength, their waves abide."

A wave broke against the window outside, despite the distance to the water.

"Finally, Arcane Court, place your hands to seal the final runes."

Cal held his out arm to lead his mother up the steps. He looked into the inky pools of Lia's eyes. He saw the barely concealed pain. This was hurting her, but she hadn't flinched once. He placed his hand directly over her heart and measured its frantic pace. His eyes would be the last ones she saw before she went into stillness. The thread in his heart thrummed in a frantic need to reach her. His breathing quickened.

"Court of shadow sight unseen,
Mysteries dance in veils between.
Locked in darkness, powers conspire,
Magic elusive a moonlit choir."

Shadow burst from the point where Cal's hand met her skin, blackening the room. Lithia went limp on her throne. The only indication she was alive was the subtle rise and fall of her chest. As the shadows receded, the priestess waved a hand and the throne turned into an altar, Lia's body arranged on it reverently.

"Please step down," the High Priestess said as she stepped forward, placing her hand in the center of Lia's chest.

Cal stumbled back slightly, his mother reaching for his arm as she led him back to their places around the dais.

"Through ancient rite courts entwine,
Eternal realm power's design.
Fourfold dance, harmonious play,
A queen to hold their powerful sway."

A blinding golden glow overtook the room before it plunged into darkness.

LITHIA

She was floating. No, not floating—she didn't think she was really anything. There was nothing but blackness all around her. She couldn't feel her body, like she was suspended in a pool of tepid water. She could hear a voice calling to her. It could have been her mother, but it was richer, layered like several women were trying to talk to her, to pull her to them, but some hazy void blocked them.

As their voices faded, a more melodic voice took its place, this one clear and crisp like it was brand new but ancient too.

"I'm sorry, sweet one."

A searing pain ripped through her core, and everything went silent once more.

Slowly, her senses started returning. She could smell the faintest trace of burnt herbs and feel the soft pressure of a blanket. How long had it been? It seemed like moments and years all at once. She fell back into the blissful void.

The next time her senses returned, it started much the same. The smell of something bittersweet, like tea and the touch of soft-spun bedding. However, there was also the feeling of someone seated next to her and the low murmur of voices. She strained her senses to feel more of what was happening around her, still unable to move or open her eyes.

There was a soft brush on her arm before a sweet-smelling cloth was pressed to her cheek, the herb smell lulling her. After a few moments, there was a soft huff before the bed shifted, the cloth continuing to dab at her cheeks.

"What is it?" asked a raspy older voice Lithia didn't recognize.

"I can feel her magic getting stronger, but her connection to Aduna and the land seems frayed? Or weak? I'm not sure. And I'm not picking up any of the elements in her core like I should be. It's been nearly six days."

Ah, priestesses.

"I will call for the High Priestess. She has started stirring already and will likely wake in a day or so anyway. Maybe she can sense something you are missing."

"I don't know. When I reach into her magical core, it seems off, like it's clawing at me."

The priestesses' worried conversation faded to black as she drifted back into stillness.

That layered voice, like her mother's but not, called for her again, as if from the other side of fogged glass, and she couldn't seem to find the door as everything faded to blackness.

She slowly peeled her eyes open as soft early morning sunlight made its way through the stained glass windows of her chambers. Her mouth tasted like it was filled with sand and her head was nearly too heavy to move.

A soft snore made its way to her ears, and she turned her head in search of the source. In a chair beside her slept Neda, feet propped up on the edge of the bed, head slung back and a line of drool making its way across her cheek. Lithia slowly sat up and looked around the room, finding Narcos asleep on the chaise and the High Priestess seated in the wingback chair to his right, her faceless mask directed at Lia.

"Good morning, dear. Your friends will be relieved to see you awake."

Lia smiled a devious smile. "Oh, in that case, I think we should wake them."

With one push she knocked Neda's legs from the bed, slamming them to the floor. Several things happened at once. Neda startled awake, jumping and grabbing for her sword, looking frantically around the room. The commotion woke Narcos, who jumped up, eyes blazing, daggers in hand. Both of their panicked gazes landed on Lithia at the same moment.

"You're a real bitch, Lia," snorted Neda, immediately plopping onto the bed beside her.

"I'm so glad you're finally awake, Lia. We have been worried; it's been nearly seven days."

Lia's head snapped to the head priestess who stood from her chair.

"My dears, now that you have seen that the High Queen is safely awake, I must ask you to leave so I can speak with her alone. It would also be a good time to inform the council and Primes that she has awoken."

Neda planted a sloppy kiss on Lia's cheek before climbing off the bed and moving towards the door. Narcos, however, hesitated, looking to Lia for guidance.

"I'll be fine, Nars. I'll call for you as soon as I can."

He leaned down, placing a chaste kiss on her lips before following his sister through the door. They sat in silence for a few moments until the sound of both sets of footsteps retreated. The priestess waved her hand and one of her acolytes appeared with a tray of food and tea for Lia, who gave the youngling a quick smile.

"Seven days? How could it be that long? That's nearly as long as Mab, isn't it?"

The older female drifted over and settled herself in the chair Neda had just vacated.

"Yes. The magic manifests differently in everyone, and therefore, the periods of stillness last for differing times. Generally, it is believed the longer the stillness, the more potent the power. The longest we have on record was Mab herself, who took eight days to awaken. Typically, five to six days is normal."

Lia took small bites of food as she listened, worried that her stomach was going to turn.

"From what we know of the queens' power, the magic is what we would call a syphon. You are aware of the history correct? Of Mab wiping out all the magic on the battlefield? "

Lia leaned in, her attention completely ensnared.

"Well, from what we have discerned, that may be an exaggeration, as most histories are, given they are told by the victor. But we do know that the way that your wild magic works is by consuming."

The High Priestess shifted in her seat uncomfortably, casting a wary glance at the door.

"High Priestess, is something wrong?"

Lithia balled her sheets in her fists, blanching her knuckles. The High Priestess breathed deeply before she continued.

"We aren't sure. You have magic, we can feel it, it's extremely powerful magic but–"

The priestess fidgeted again, which was the third time making it three more times than Lithia had ever seen the other fae fidget in her life. Lithia bit down hard on the inside of her cheek, the metallic taste of blood pouring over her tongue. She could feel the failure settling around her before the priestess said anything, but how in the goddess had she failed at this?

Clearing her throat, the priestess continued, "But we can't seem to find your connections to the goddess and the elements. Your magical core won't let our magic near it without trying to feed off it. It seems as though something in your connection to your ancestors or Aduna frayed, and the magic didn't cling to your core properly."

Lithia laid back down, staring up at the slats of her ceiling. She closed her eyes and dug for anything to make it make sense. As she lay there, something clicked.

"In the stillness there were voices. They called my name, but they couldn't reach me. All I remember was thinking it was my mother." Lithia took a shuddering breath, the tears hot as they slipped past her lashes. "It was her, wasn't it?"

The priestess laid a papery hand on Lia's. "If I remember correctly, your mother told me she spoke to several generations of your line in her stillness as well as the goddess Aduna. Your family line has the only direct connection left to Aduna, as she no longer walks this plane."

"I have failed."

The priestess shifted to sit on the side of Lithia's bed and clutched both her hands.

"You have not failed. You survived, Lithia, and that is more than any other fae would do in your position. Your strength is not determined by the power you wield, but by the courage you display in the face of opposition. We will figure this out, and you are not powerless, Lithia. Now, rest until they send a bunch of people up here to dress you for the coronation."

The priestess squeezed Lithia's hands before pulling the blankets back up to cover her. Lithia rolled over, staring at the same morning sunlight filtering through the stained glass, and cried until sleep pulled her back under.

The dress was splendid, a green so deep it was almost black, the top layer a fine mesh that sparkled in the firelight. The sleeves draped off her shoulders, leaving them bare before a split exposing her arms collected at her wrist with a gold bangle shaped like a snake. The bodice flowed into a tasteful plunging neckline, accentuating her full breasts and nipping in at her waist before spilling loosely to the floor. The high split up her right leg gave her access to her thigh sheath and exposed the muscular expanse of her legs and the dagger-sharp heels.

Her hair was unbraided, soft, and perfumed before it rolled down her back in waves. She stared at this version of herself; she looked powerful. It didn't match the anxiety roiling in her stomach.

She rubbed at her chest as if that would work the tangles out of her emotions. She heard sure footsteps coming through her sitting room. As they passed the threshold, however, they faltered. Looking over her shoulder, she saw Narcos in the doorway, frozen mid-step. He was raking his gaze up her body, causing a flush to color her chest. His tongue darted out to wet his lips as he finally met her gaze.

"Lia, you look stunning." His voice had taken on a low rasp. "Do we have to go?"

She chuckled lightly. "To my coronation? Yes."

He kissed her tenderly, leading her out of the small waiting room to the inlay doors of the throne room.

"Ready?"

"Nope. Let's go."

The doors opened on a silent wind and the throne room, more full than usual, welcomed her into its depths. She had walked this path thousands of times, but this time seemed like a lie. She shouldn't be here. Suviel itself had rejected her. The priestess bowed to her as she approached the throne, turning to face the crowd.

She found herself entirely incapable of looking down at a single face. She was terrified to find disdain, disgust, or pity written there, so she stared out over their heads. Cold and distant. Thankfully, this was more a presentation than a ceremony and would be over quickly. The priestess stepped forward on the dias.

"With the completion of the marking, I give to you The High Queen of the Fae, Prime of Suviel, and Daughter of Mab, Lithia Caileanach."

Lithia sat on the Ember Throne and the priestess lifted Lia's crown from its ebony box and placed it on her head, a little sleight of hand magic fixing it in place.

"My Queen," she said quietly as she finished, then louder and in the old tongue, "*Mo Bhanrighit.*" She knelt. "Long may she reign."

The phrase echoed throughout the room as, for the second time, the crowd fell to its knees in a wave before her. Finally, looking down, her eyes landed on a mismatched pair of eyes looking up at her, and a pang shot through her heart.

CALCAS

He sat down on the chair by the door and pulled off his boots. He hated formal events; they were too rigid and choreographed. While the evening was rather simple and was really more of a presentation of Lithia to the court, he still ached like he was the one who had just woken from an ancient magical nap, not her, although she didn't look anymore rested than he did.

He had checked on her every day. He couldn't stand the uncertainty, it was eating him alive. One of the flower twins seemed to always be around, which made it exceedingly difficult to sneak in to see her, so he started tagging along with Wil. He was a fucking idiot, to be honest, he needed to be getting away from her, but all he wanted was to be near her. He had to get off this goddess-forsaken island.

He paced across the room and dropped onto the plush mattress, knowing he wouldn't sleep. A maid had left a cup of tea and a few cardamom cookies on his side table. The tea smelled of snake root and valerian with a hint of honey. He sipped it, grateful for the rest it promised.

He had no idea how long he had been asleep when he was woken by a soft rapping on his door. Judging by how dark the sky outside his window was, it was still the middle of the night. The knocking got louder and more urgent. Groaning, he rolled out of bed and dragged his heavy limbs to the door. He expected it to be Wil or even his mother. What he was not expecting was an exhausted-looking High Queen.

Lia stood outside his door twirling the end of her copper braid, a nervous habit he teased her for in their youth. Her expression, however, was a careful mask of neutrality. He stood there wordlessly staring at her, not sure whether to let her in or tell her to bother someone who cared. Unfortunately for both of them, he was someone who cared, despite his determination not to be.

"Are you going to let me in before someone starts a scandal about me visiting your room in the middle of the night?"

He let out a huff, but moved to the side to let her in.

"You know your *lovely* fiancé's door is on the other side of the hall, right?"

"Your humor is astounding, but given this has been your door for a century now, I assure you I knocked on the correct one. To be honest, I was sure you would leave me outside."

Cal crossed his arms. "If you were so sure I would turn you away, why even come?"

She plucked a bottle of wine and glasses off his sideboard before she settled into a chair in front of the fire. She filled both glasses and sat back in her chair, watching him.

"I think it's time we talked because I need your help and it won't work if you still hate me."

With a sigh, he sat down and drained the glass she poured for him, the familiar sweet bubbles dancing along his tongue and frothing his memories.

"I could never hate you, at least not fully. But Lia, I just—" he paused to refill his glass. "I just don't know how to be around you without that old feeling of betrayal coloring every little interaction. I look at you and I am so awed by you, but I don't feel the same feelings of comfort or confidence in you that I used to. You really fucked up, and it's been almost ten fucking years and this is the first time you've even tried to talk to me."

"Talk to you? How would I have spoken to you, Cal? Tell me, because you walked away from me on that battlefield and never came back. We both lost her. I know I made mistakes, but you left me to battle them alone. You. Left. *Me*."

"MISTAKES? YOU KILLED HER BECAUSE YOU WERE TOO PROUD TO LISTEN TO THE PEOPLE AROUND YOU! You might as well have wielded that blade yourself."

Lia reeled back as if he had dealt a physical blow. He deflated immediately, wilting into his chair as the emotions of that day came rushing back. His emotions still so raw. He had trusted Lia so fully, and when he began to doubt her plans, Seren had assured him between breathy moans that Lithia loved them too much to put them in danger. Then, in a breath, he was looking at lifeless honey-colored eyes. Who was he supposed to trust?

Lia shifted uncomfortably and stared into the fire, her eyes rimmed in silver. "If you think I haven't had all those same thoughts about myself, you're wrong. I would do anything to be able to redo those choices, but I can't. I can't keep going without you, though. You are the only person I have left. Narcos is incredible but he just—he isn't you. I need my best friend back. I can't ... I can't get Seren back, but I can't keep existing as if I lost both of you, Cal, I can't."

His heart cracked open, molten pain seeping out. He hardened it again. Not again.

She drained her glass and stood. "I'm sorry, I shouldn't have come. I'll see you at the meeting tomorrow, Calcas. I apologize for waking you."

Cal drained his glass and stood from his chair. "You said you needed me. What for?"

"Really, Cal, I don't know if it's okay to burden you with this when we have so many open wounds between us already."

He sighed, running his hands through his hair. "You are still my queen and I will still do whatever I can to help you, Lithia, please tell me what you need."

She perched back on the lip of the chair she had just vacated.

"My magic is … I think, well, the priestesses think it's broken."

"I'm sorry, but you are going to have to explain so much more."

"That's what I need help with, to be honest. I can explain all I know, but it's not a lot. The priestesses said they couldn't find my connection to any of the elements, nothing. In essence, the only magic I have access to is Mab's syphon magic. but I'm not sure how that's useful. I'm afraid I'm already failing, Calcas."

He swirled the dregs in his glass.

"Have you tried to call on any of the elements?"

"Not really, I've been asleep most of the day." Her smile was weak and half-hearted.

"Well, come on, let's give it a try."

Lithia gave him an unenthused look but stood, placing her glass on the table next to her. She squeezed her eyes closed, concentrating. Several minutes passed and nothing changed except the deepening furrow between her brows.

"I'm assuming it's not working?"

Her eyes popped open, and she glared at him.

"Obviously."

"What element were you trying?"

She flexed her hands by her side several times before speaking. "Air, it seemed to be most readily available."

"Ah, maybe go for fire or shadow. That way I can stop it if it gets out of hand."

"Cal, this is ridiculous. There is nothing there; the priestesses could sense nothing."

"Did *you* feel nothing, though? Just stop being stubborn and try."

She closed her eyes again, the furrow reforming between her brows. Just as he was about to tell her to stop, a searing pain pulled at his magical core and the flames in the Hearth shot into the air.

She gasped, "I did it!"

Another searing tug at his core and the flames bounced higher.

"Lia, stop," he groaned, doubling over.

Her concentration broke, and the flames danced back to their normal size, the pain ebbing. He panted for a moment, trying to puzzle out what the fuck just happened.

"What happened? Are you okay?"

"I ... I don't know what happened."

He stared into the fire for a moment, the pieces floating into place.

"Lia, do that again."

"Do what?"

"The fire, do the magic again."

She gave him an odd look, but shrugging, focused on the fire. Braced for it, the pain still seared but didn't catch him off guard.

"Stop. Stop."

She did, looking back to him with worry etched around her eyes.

"I think you are using my magic."

She looked back and forth between him and the fire for a moment, connecting the threads in her head. He saw the moment the calculation turned to panic.

"Shit, did it hurt? Cal, I'm so sorry."

"No, I just wasn't expecting it."

He wasn't sure why he stopped short of telling her how painful it was to share that power. Well, he knew, but he had lied to himself for so long, why stop now?

"So definitely syphon magic, not elemental magic. Do you ... do you want to try the shadows?"

"If you're sure it isn't hurting you."

"Go for it."

He braced himself, but this time the pain wasn't bad. He wouldn't call it pleasant, but his magic seemed more inclined to share with her this time around now that it knew her.

She took a few deep breaths, and he watched as tendrils of shadow swirled around her, dancing. She got a look in her eye before they drifted, forming a pair of smoking wings. They reminded him of an amphiptere but in a deep iridescent black. As he watched, the edges seemed to pulse in time with his heart.

"That's enough," he said in a low rumble.

She let go of his magic and he took a steadying breath as it coiled back in his body. The thread in his heart reached out, wanting to twine with her. He hardened his heart again.

"You need to go, Lithia."

She looked up at him, a mix of confusion and abandonment playing out across her features. He couldn't let her in again. He could feel the thread in his heart reaching for hers and he needed her to leave. He moved her towards the door, closing it quickly behind her as she left.

LITHIA

L ithia closed the door to her room behind her as quietly as she could. She slid off her slippers and padded towards her bedroom. She hung her robe on the hook beside her door and made her way to her washroom to run some water over her wrists to cool the frustrated flush that had settled over her skin.

"You know, I came to make sure you were resting before the meetings tomorrow, but you were—"

She whipped around at lightning speed, releasing a throwing knife towards the intruder's voice. Narcos, however, was fully prepared for her reflexes and smoothly dodged the blade. He stood smirking in his soft linen sleeping pants, his broad chest and lean muscle on display. He fell back into bed, pushing the blanket back and indicating that she should join him. With a roll of her eyes, she climbed into the bed beside him, allowing him to gently unbraid her hair. When he finished, she rested back in the crook of his arm and twined her legs with his, letting the warmth of his body chase the chill from her toes.

"You went to see Cal."

It wasn't a question. His fingers ran through the ends of her loose hair as she let out a deep sigh.

"He feels like the only family I have left, Nars. I wasn't expecting some kind of apology or sweeping forgiveness, but I just wished he would talk to me. He's this massive piece of my life that has been missing. He's my best friend. Was."

He nodded stiffly and pulled her more firmly against his chest. "I would never begrudge you his friendship. I just wish you wanted to be friends with someone less—"

"Grumpy?"

"Well, I was going to say less of an ass, but grumpy works, too."

Lia laughed. "I'll work on finding more agreeable friends."

Narcos nuzzled into her hair, and she heard the deep inhale as he breathed in her scent.

"I find myself a very agreeable friend."

"Friend?"

Lithia arched her body into Narcos, his hard length pushing against her. He brought his hand down on her hip, pulling her into him, his thumb drawing small circles down her thigh. Stretching, she ground back into him eliciting a low groan as he nipped lightly at her ear. He slid his hand down her leg and slowly hitched her nightgown up her leg, exposing her and sliding his fingers down to meet her pussy. He buried his face in the crook of her neck, letting out a harsh breath at the wetness he found between her legs.

"Mo Lunath," he growled in her ear, his breath fanning down her neck.

She shivered at the endearment: my moon.

She reached back to twist her fingers in his long silken hair while he pressed hot, open-mouthed kisses to her throat, tracing her runes with his tongue. She arched into him, his fingers tracing firm patterns on her clit and pausing just when she was near the edge.

"We should really sleep. We have meetings in the morning," she murmured through the fog of lust.

He began slowing his movements and she chuckled. "I didn't mean stop. I meant if you won't make me come then move so I can do it myself."

He pulled his hand back and freed himself from his pants, palming his cock. With his other hand, he ripped her nightdress in one quick movement before hauling her back flush against his chest. He watched the rapid rise and fall of her breasts before slowly rolling a peaked nipple between his fingers.

"I intend to have you filled with my cock, Lia. But don't rush me."

She was starting to squirm, certain she would combust if he didn't fuck her soon. Just as she had that thought, he reached down and hooked her leg up over his arm and sank fully into her.

A shudder wracked her body and stars danced behind her eyelids. Narcos's head fell and his rumbling praises filled her ear. He stayed perfectly still, seated entirely inside her until she was writhing and whimpering, begging him for friction.

He bit down on the tender flesh of her collarbone before he began to pound into her, the room filling with Lia's whimpering moans. She reached down and stroked her clit, throwing her head back to rest on his chest. He leaned down, taking her mouth in a plundering kiss and swallowing her moans, keeping them for himself. Her pussy contracted around his cock, and she cried his name, toppling over the edge of oblivion. At the sound, his cock pulsed, and he came deep inside her, moaning and whispering incoherent nothings into her hair. She stilled and their labored breathing fell into a rhythm.

She leaned up, giving him a soft kiss and smiling at his flushed cheeks. He slowly pulled out of her, peppering her shoulder with kisses before rolling onto his back. Lia slid out of bed to relieve herself and rinse the salty sweat from her skin before slipping back into the bed. She curled into Narcos, resting her arm on his chest and nestled her cheek in the hollow of his throat, inhaling his earthy sage scent.

She stared out at the watery moonlight, Narcos's breathing slowly becoming deep and even with sleep. She could feel how much he cared for her. She could feel the growing pit in her stomach each time she realized she may never return those feelings. As she drifted off into sleep, her dreams smelled like lemon and thyme.

The things Lithia had missed the most without her magic weren't the flashy magics she used in combat or even the powers she had with persuasion and battle strategy; it was the little magic. She had missed being able to summon her own shower and change its temperature, or being able to glamour her own appearance, and the healing. The blessed prickles of her fae healing had been sorely missed, quite literally.

She stepped under the spray of the water, adjusting the heat to soothe her pleasure-tight muscles. She only had a few minutes to get ready; she wanted to meet with the priestess and invite her to the meetings today early this morning before the day got moving too quickly. She stepped out, drying herself quickly and banishing the water from her hair before placing a smaller, less formal crown made of intertwining branches of silver set with emeralds on her head and glamouring her hair into a woven circlet around it.

Stepping into her closet, she pulled on a soft pair of leather leggings and a gold inlaid corset over a flowing linen top. She let out a small sigh as the baldric of throwing knives settled across her chest, a comforting weight, before quickly strapping on the sword belt and thigh sheath and slipping the small knives in various places across her person.

She let out a shaky breath as she turned to head out of her chambers towards the temple. On her way past the bed, she let out a soft chuckle at where Narcos had fallen back to sleep, snoring softly. Her smile faded as she chewed her bottom lip. Narcos was wonderful, kind, and fair. He would make a good king. That was, after all, what her mother had insisted when she set the match just a few short years ago. Lia had hated him on principle, of course; her heart had died in the shadow of the mountain, on a smoke-hazed battlefield. Slowly, Narcos had become a confidant, then a lover. He loved her, she knew that, but her heart was still on that battlefield. Turning her back to him, eyes shining, she headed for the door.

Lithia trudged up the steps to the temple, the sun just rising on between the Twin Harbors. She stopped at the top of the steps, taking in the sight of Arachin just waking up below her. The temple was poised directly opposite the citadel. The highest point of the island city, the temple boasted 150 steps to the doors, penance before you reached Aduna, The Mother.

The steps, like the rest of the temple structure, were a glistening rose quartz, a stark contrast to the black volcanic stone of the citadel. Looking down into the capital sprawling between the two, she could see the market square just beginning to stretch and yawn in the bluish-gold light of dawn, the first of the merchants cleaning up their stalls before opening.

She loved this city. She knew the majority of its inhabitants because of the relationship the city had with the crown. The city was inhabited by advisors, foreign emissaries, the citadel staff, sentinels, and their families. It was a beautiful grid of stepped streets and limestone buildings. Taking a lungful of the salty air, Lithia turned to the daunting carved ebony doors of the temple. As she reached for the knocker, the door swung inward revealing the blank mask of the High Priestess.

"Good morning, Mo Bhanrighit," she bowed her head, moving to the side and inviting Lithia into the temple.

"Good morning, High Priestess. I apologize for interrupting your morning."

"You aren't interrupting anything, dear; come."

She followed the older fae through the doors into a sanctuary with ornate floor-to-ceiling windows overlooking the bay. The floor was swirls of soft colored stones with a shallow bowl of hammered gold taking up the majority of the room. Seated along the edge, various priestesses and acolytes sat praying, or counseling the locals who had made the trek up the stairs.

The High Priestess led her to a small alcove with floor cushions in a crescent shape around a low table, set with a steaming tea service and small biscuits that smelled like fragrant cardamom.

She sat down across from the priestess as the other female poured their tea. They sat quietly, listening to the gentle sound of string music floating in from somewhere deeper in the temple. The silence slowly became oppressive as they finished their tea.

"Now, what is it we can do for you?"

"Well, it's a couple of things, really. First, last night I found out that while I don't have any connection to the elements, as you thought, I can apparently channel them through others. Though, I'm not sure how that process affects them so I don't want to do it again until we can research it further."

The priestess tilted her head slightly. Not being able to read her facial expression was infuriating at the best of times, but Lithia pushed on.

"I would also like to request your presence at the meetings today with the Primes. There have been concerning reports throughout Suviel that I don't want to detail in public, and I think your knowledge and your connection with Aduna would be a valuable resource."

The priestess nodded slowly.

"Of course. I am honored that you seek my counsel, Mo Bhanrighit. About your magic, it sounds like the syphon magic at work. I have an idea, but give me some time to pull it together and we'll give it a try this evening, if that works for you."

"Of course, thank you."

Lithia rose to leave the temple, chewing on her lip in thought. A papery hand caught hers as she turned, and she paused turning back to the High Priestess.

"Do not walk into that room looking like you failed, Lithia, or they will use your weaknesses against you. Be a queen."

CALCAS

Cal hadn't been able to go back to sleep after Lithia left his room so he found himself in the training pits used by the Queen's Guard hours before sunrise trying to fight out his aggression with any inanimate object and training sentinel that crossed his path. He nearly lost track of time and rushed to his room to shower as the sun rose.

He pulled a soft grey tunic with black detailing over his head before looking at himself in the mirror. The tunic left his arms on display, which his mother would hate, but to him it was more like he was entering battle unarmed, so he needed some level of comfort. His mother hated his tattoos because they reminded her that he spent his time around arena fighters more than doing his duty. But that was nothing compared to how she loathed his piercings.

The sleek black hoop in his bottom lip was from a Tidal Fae who had taken him diving with the sharks off the coast of Nightstone, the prison island. It was originally a fish hook as a trophy, but now it was thin black stone from Darke Mountain. His nose piercing was from Wil. She said it was a marker of a battle fought; she had a similar piercing but through her septum. His nose ring tonight connected to one of his various ear piercings with a delicate gold chain.

He wrapped his long black hair into a neat topknot, exposing the shaved sides and securing it out of his face. His face looked different than it had over the last few years. His skin no longer looked flat and sallow, but golden and healthy. His mismatched eyes, one black and one blue, both ringed in gold, still looked tired but no longer lifeless. The gold glittered again. He gripped the counter, his knuckles bleaching. He knew being near her was what he needed, but it was the furthest thing from what he wanted. Fate was a bitch, and she could keep her mate. He stalked away from the mirror, snatching his pants from the counter as he turned.

After sliding on the leather leggings and hard boots, he made his way towards the weapons he had haphazardly thrown on the bed in his haste to shower. It would be uncouth to enter a meeting of Primes fully armed, so he situated only his onyx sword on his back and his thigh sheath. With a deep sigh, he made his way towards the large council chamber.

Wil fell into step with him as he stepped into the public corridors, shooting him a sidelong glance as he raised his chin and pushed open the doors. Several of the Primes and their heirs were already present, seated in their respective seats around the large table. The nearly circular table was a perfect topographical map of Suviel. It was crafted an eon ago from a black stone set with colored gemstones and imbued with magic that mirrored the land perfectly. If a cliff were to topple into the sea, so too would the cliff on the map.

The last time he was here, there had been figures placed strategically throughout, showing the locations of the battle lines at the time. Today, though, it was cleared of all wartime chaos, gleaming in the morning sun. He leaned down, greeting his mother with a kiss on her cheek before pulling out a seat for Wil and taking the seat between them. Wil chuckled as she sat down and adjusted her long braids over her shoulders.

"So formal today."

Astris chuffed a laugh, poking his exposed arm. "Not quite, his tunic seems to be missing some pieces."

Wil leaned in, still chuckling. "My crows have brought me more of the same, but no new insights. They say more land has turned barren."

At that moment, the last of their numbers entered, followed by Lia, who was dressed in a more formal and less practical version of the uniform she would have worn as general, reminding everyone in the room that she was a general long before she was queen. Cal stifled a smile at the gesture. To his surprise, Lia was speaking quietly to the High Priestess, whom she led to a seat at the table opposite hers before moving around to take her own.

Wil leaned over and whispered something to Neda in greeting as she took the seat to her left, at Lia's right hand. Neda gave him a tense nod as her gaze swept the room. Lia's stride toward her place was assured and measured, even as her fingers had a white-knuckled grip on her sword's hilt.

As everyone settled into their seats, Lia stood. "Thank you all for coming to this meeting. There have been some disturbing reports recently and I think it's important that we come together as quickly as possible. The stability of our queendom has always come from the united front of the courts and the magic given to Mab by the goddess Aduna. As you know, I am not one for small talk so I would like to skip ahead to ask for a rundown of the intelligence we have so far."

The formal atmosphere snapped as tension rolled through the room. Wil gave him a sidelong look and gestured to him.

He rested his elbows on the table and clearing his throat. "Wil and I have been collecting reports as much as possible. The broad problem is we have been getting reports of fae going missing or losing their powers. From what we've gathered, there are similar occurrences in all the courts." He paused for a moment, allowing for nods of assent from the gathered Primes. "We have also been informed that the land at the southernmost point of Suviel is becoming barren. The crops are withering, even the grass is dying.

From what we have been told, it's like the earth is turning to ash. The fae and animals alike are being forced out."

He gestured toward the area on the map he was referencing, and it did indeed look darker, the stones having lost their vibrancy, becoming as dull and lifeless as the land. If you weren't looking for it, it almost seemed to be covered in a layer of dust. Or ash. Lithia moved around the table, looking at the indicated point on the map, gesturing for him to continue. Instead, however, Wil took over.

"We haven't been able to locate any trace of the missing, from any court, no bodies, no trace magic, nothing. As for those losing their magic, the healers say it's almost as if their magical core never existed. We have taken to calling it The Voiding. I am not a fan of giving something a name because the name gives it power, but even I must agree it has reached that point."

Lia sat down sharply. "It sounds like the magic itself is dying. Have you located a source?"

Lithia sent a fleeting look towards the priestess sitting silently across the table.

"We haven't had time. We only learned it was widespread in recent weeks. Wil has been gathering information, but so far nothing points to a single source."

"And it is truly this widespread?" Lia asked, scanning those gathered.

Nods and murmurs of assent rolled through the room.

A soft voice rose from the far end of the table. "Heir Calcas, this news has not yet reached the High Temple. Could you explain more about what is happening to the land?"

"Of course, High Priestess. From what we have gathered, the land seems to be green and fertile one day, then ash the next. One of the farmers whose land has been affected said that it looks like a shadow moving across the land as everything dies."

"Hmm. Prime Osharus, have you noticed any change in the waters?"

"No, High Priestess. However, the waters to the south are deeper than is livable, so it is unlikely we would notice until it encroaches further."

"High Queen, it is impossible to be sure without further information, but it sounds like something is fraying the threads of magic." The priestess tilted her head before she continued, "The temple's resources are, of course, at your disposal. I have an idea of where to begin."

Lia nodded. "Thank you, High Priestess. Heirs, if you would, please update us with the numbers of missing and voided fae from your courts, as you know them to be."

Cal cleared his throat. "19 missing and 26 voided in the Arcane Court."

"8 missing, 10 voided in the seas," Came Aegaea's melodic voice.

"Hearth has 11 missing." Neda's voice cracked. "And 39 voided."

Cal heard the soft intake of breath from Narcos as his sister relayed the numbers of their court. Hearth was the most heavily populated, but that was still an incredible number.

"3 missing and 9 voided from the Celestial Court. That is, however, just what is known. We are spread wide, so the numbers are likely greater." Halos's low rumble faltered slightly as he spoke, the stones in his hair clinking as he straightened in his chair.

Lia turned her glazed eyes to Neda. "The legion?"

"40 missing, but none voided," Neda said with a sigh.

Lia sat back. "How did this escalate so quickly?"

"With the few recent voxis attacks in the mountains, we attributed the missing sentinels to deserters, until the spymaster came to me with questions," Neda explained with a nod towards Wil.

"I think we all saw it as a localized problem until we came together, Li—My Queen." Cal's tongue stuck to the roof of his mouth.

A murmur of assent rolled through the room.

"Mo Bhanrighit, I agree with the Arcane Heir. It was not until we received word from the spymaster inquiring that we realized the issue was happening in other courts as well," Nylian said.

"The seas and skies are so widespread that it is not unheard of for fae to go missing and turn up later, having ventured further than normal. So it was odd, but we didn't see the real pattern until we arrived and thought it best to wait until after your marking to burden you," Aegaea added in her lilting tone.

"It makes no difference now. What matters now is moving forward and how we go about making sure we come through this whole. Is there anything else pertinent?"

Neda straightened.

"Yes, Mo Bhanrighit. I got several reports this morning and last night of wild fae, mainly voxis, and one report of a banshee, attacking travelers through The Singing Wood over the last few weeks. More are also beginning to filter in from the mountains, though they aren't what we were expecting. They all seem to be solo attackers, most of them subdued. The more detailed reports say they seem to be sick or weak. With the current issues, I wonder if this Voiding is affecting them as well."

These caught Cal's attention. From what he remembered, the wild fae were still tied directly to Suviel's magic. If something was killing the magic, or fraying it, as the priestess said, then it makes sense that the voxis would be directly affected as well. His thoughts tumbled, kicking up all the boring books his tutors had forced him to read as a youngling.

Lost in his contemplation, Cal completely missed the meeting's dismissal and found himself one of the last in the room. Lia was standing to the side in a heated discussion with Neda and Wil, while a few others floated around by the door, waiting to get Lia's ear. He finished his scan of the room, landing in the warm gaze of his mother.

"What are you thinking? I saw that look."

"I was thinking I might be grateful for that horrendous tutor you forced on me."

"While I appreciate the century-late gratitude, Calcas, I was referring to the fact that you are about to run from the room with your High Queen in it yet again."

Cal could hear his molars crack as he clenched his jaw. She placed an always-too-warm hand on his arm.

"Calcas, dear, look at me." Taking a breath, he looked down into his mother's amber eyes. "We are allowed to love the people who hurt us. Don't give up on yourself while you heal."

LITHIA

Narcos and Neda sat sprawled in the chairs by Lithia's fireplace, eating the spiced pork that was currently perfuming the air. Lithia paced back and forth, her stomach turning. The evening meeting was starting in a few minutes and the High Priestess had sent word earlier that she had found what she thought was a promising lead. Something in her gut, however, told her that it was going to be a tangled web to unweave.

As she turned on her heel, a piece of bread came flying at her head. She caught it a breath away from her ear. She turned to find Narcos scowling at a grinning Neda.

"Time to stop pacing, your royal broody queenliness, it's time for the meeting," Neda said, slapping her thighs as she stood.

Narcos and Lithia exchanged eye rolls as they followed her unnaturally peppy walk from the room. She reached out to grab

Narcos's hand as they descended the step. Squeezing it firmly as he raised it to place a kiss on her knuckles. As they came to the bottom, he released her hand and fell into step with his twin just ahead of Lithia. Several Primes were making their way to the council chambers as well, stopping to give short bows at her presence. The formality turned her stomach.

Taking a slow breath, she entered the mostly filled room to find everyone anxiously standing around the table, with the exception of Calcas, who was reclined in his chair, his gaze heavy on her as she made her way to her seat. The High Priestess stood looking relaxed, wearing an entirely expressionless mask, as always, by Lithia's chair.

"High Priestess, if you wouldn't mind going first, please let us know what you learned."

The older fae curled into herself, a posture she had never seen from the stoic female.

"The consensus of the temple elders is that the Queendom's magical core is dying. If not dying, the magic is at the very least being frayed. The way it is drawing the magic from the land leads some of the elders to believe it is not a natural death but some external magic is attacking it. Time being a factor, we do not have knowledge of the type of magic involved or where it has come from."

No one breathed.

After three heartbeats of silence, the room erupted into a cacophony of questions.

"What do you mean, dying?"

"How are we supposed to fix it?"

"How do you not know? Who knows?"

With a gentle raise of Lithia's hand, the room fell into a thick silence.

"Unfortunately, it sounds a lot like what we feared from our earlier meeting; however, the confirmation is jarring. Did the elders have any further insight?"

"Yes and no. The queendom's magical core is a physical thing, The Heart of Suviel. The biggest problem we have is that we no longer have knowledge of its location. When Suviel was created, as part of the treaty, Thahaos the God of Discord became the God of Death, giving him access to the souls that passed to fill The Beneath."

Wil fidgeted in her seat, and Lithia cast her a look before addressing the priestess.

"What does Thahaos have to do with the heart, though? It was Aduna's magic."

The priestess tilted her head before continuing, "His final act, as he was sent to The Beneath, was to steal the heart. Since the gods no longer walk this plane, we do not know where it was hidden before he was banished."

Lithia was starting to become frustrated with this non-answer.

Halos cleared his throat, leaning forward in his seat. "This is a fine story, but how does this help solve the very real problems we have that we have laid out in front of us?"

While Lithia may have been a bit more diplomatic, she had a very similar question. Judging by the way several others leaned in, the sentiment was shared.

"We believe the only place answers would be found about its location is from the priestesses at the Temple of Thahaos, in The Tipping Peaks."

Halos scoffed, opening his mouth to speak, his mother reaching out a gentle hand to stop him. Litha watched Halos. The male was ethereal, with deep brown skin and grey-white hair braided into a mohawk before spilling small braids down his back. His ears each sported moonstone piercings and constellations were tattooed across his cheeks like gleaming silver freckles. His mother, Cassara, just as ethereal and stunning, stared down her nose at the priestess.

"That is a fool's errand. The temple is the entrance to The Beneath and is unplottable. It could take weeks or longer to find, and that is just once you are in the mountains."

"There is no one else who knows where he hid the heart." The High Priestess shifted in her seat straightening her spine.

Lithia needed to divert the conversation for now before anything escalated. She spoke over the start of Cassara's rebuttal, cutting the Prime off.

"Nylian, you found something as well?" Lia prompted, sitting forward.

"Yes, Mo Bhanrighit. We believe that magic killing the land is a form of withering curse. From the way they have described the land dying, it is presenting much the same as it would a single plant or fae. However, no one I spoke to has ever seen it on such a scale and it's never disconnected someone from their magical core."

"What is the standard treatment for such a curse?"

"Removal of the infected area, such as amputation."

"Mm, I'm not sure we could just cut off a chunk of Suviel, but that does make sense, thank you."

He sent her a weary smile.

"Does anyone else have anything to add?"

Cal cleared his throat. "I do. I did some reading and looked through the reports Neda got on the voxis attacks. From what I can tell, and Priestess, please correct me if I'm wrong, when the group of fae that decided to shun the court system joined the wild fae, they became the voxis. While they gave up their elemental power, they didn't give up their connection to the wild magic and by extension to Suviel."

The priestess nodded, so he continued.

"The reports Neda is getting make it sound like the voxis that are attacking are sick or weak for some reason. Each one that has been killed has been incoherent. Two reports have even mentioned putrid black blood. I think whatever is killing the land is killing the fae. It's killing magic and it's killing voxis as well. We are all connected to the same core and if it's dying, we all are."

Lithia sat back in her seat as a hum of conversation picked up around her. Wil's voice rose above the others.

"There is a slightly larger implication, Mo Bhanrighit. We are not the only creatures with magic that walk this plane. If the voxis are attacking, other things may start attacking as well."

A hush settled over the gathered fae, and Lia realized she needed to clear the room before the silence detonated. They had another meeting set for just after sunrise, which was only a few hours away. They all needed to sleep on whatever rash decisions they were about to throw out.

"If you would all return to your chambers and reconvene here at six bells tomorrow, as planned. I fear nothing pertinent will come from the rest of this evening. High Priestess, please stay a moment."

As the Primes and their heirs filed from the room, Lithia motioned for Narcos and Neda to stay before speaking quietly to Wil just as she rose from her chair.

"Willow, would you and Cal both remain as well?"

With a nod, she sat, yanking Cal back into his seat. After the last of the group slipped through the door, Lithia rose from her chair, motioning for the others to follow as well.

"Let's move to my study. I need a drink for this."

"Goddess, I was hoping you would say that!" Neda exclaimed as she moved towards the door.

Once there, they settled around the Hearth in Lithia's study, a maid slipping in with some fruits and leftover tarts from dinner. Lithia stared into the crackling flames, watching the embers dance in the air and absentmindedly sipping her wine, the deep spiced flavors coating her tongue. The burden settled like a woolen blanket in the peak of summer, the weight of duty like an anvil on her chest. She had made heavy decisions for a century as High General, every strategy costing lives. Narcos's low rumble pulled her from her trance.

"Lia, I can see you moving pieces on your board. Tell us your plan."

"I don't have a plan; I have a confession. My magic is fucked. The marking didn't work. Well, it did work but not properly. I don't have any elemental magic. From what we can tell, I only contain my own magic and Mab's syphon magic."

"I had a thought about that when Cal was speaking, Lithia," the High Priestess said, leaning forward in her chair. "He is correct that all magic is tied to Suviel's core. You, however, are more intricately linked—your magic comes directly from Aduna. I don't think your marking just failed. I think it failed *because* of the voiding."

Wil leaned her chin on her fist. "It would make sense. If the threads of magic are frayed, they wouldn't have been able to reach you."

Narcos was rubbing small circles on the nape of her neck, soothing the tension that was building, but it wasn't enough. Her muscles began to tremble as she spoke.

"If my magic is tied to Aduna, what happens to me if Suviel's core dies? What happens to Suviel?"

The priestess tilted her head. "I don't think it would be easy, and I think we would lose much, but we could survive without magic."

"What would happen to me?"

"I do not know, but I imagine your magical core would not survive being cut off from its source."

There were several sounds Lithia couldn't place, but Neda's voice cut through them.

"I'm sorry, are you saying if magic dies, Lia dies? Because that's just ... no."

"I don't know that; it is just a guess based on how the marking reacted to the voiding."

There was a sound like rushing water in her ears and those light circles on her neck started to feel more like claws raking down her spine. She needed to get out of there, but she was frozen.

"I need to go."

She wasn't sure if anyone responded, but she could feel the fiery tendrils of panic as they licked down her spine.

Lithia rose and left the room without making further eye contact with any of them. She stumbled as few times, making her way quickly down the stairs and through the nearly empty corridors towards her rooms. As she pushed open the door into the courtyard, she heard quick steps behind her. A glance over her shoulder told her Narcos was jogging to catch up to her.

They continued down the hall and Lia paused as she reached the stairs to her rooms. She turned, placing a trembling hand on Narcos's chest.

"Please, I need to be alone for the night."

She leaned up, placing a soft kiss on his lips before turning and continuing up the stairs, not waiting for a response. She pulled her body up the stairs, it seeming heavier with each step. The panic reached her bones, turning them to lead.

She slipped through the door and leaned her back against the smooth wood. Hot, she was so hot. The flush slowly crept up her neck, and her head began to spin. She made her way towards the bathing room on numb legs, frantically pulling off her clothes as she went.

She summoned cold water from the shower and plunged her body into the icy stream.

She crumpled to the floor, desperately rubbing feeling back into her limbs.

Her breath came in quick, jagged gasps.

Her eyes squeezed shut against the heat pricking behind them.

The cold water needling her skin became too much.

She banished the flow, curling into herself.

Knees to her chest, the hot tears began to flow in earnest down her cheeks.

Opening her eyes, she could see nothing but spots dancing in her vision.

Gasping breaths turned to panicked gulps.

Die. She was going to die.

Calcas

He had just removed his second boot when someone pounded on his door. He moved toward it with heavy steps, slinging it open to find Wil mid-knock. Her eyes bulged and she looked more harried than he had ever seen, her emotions usually locked down tight.

"Cal, something is wrong with Lia. I went to speak with her—I just—Narcos didn't answer his door. Please hurry."

She turned and ran back towards the stairs, and Cal hesitated only a moment before following. They climbed the stairs, Wil charging through Lia's quarters towards the bathing chamber without pausing. Cal had no idea was he was expecting but it wasn't to find Lithia, High Queen of the Fae, former High Legion General, curled into herself on the floor. She lay naked and shivering, with tiny rubies of blood dripping from crescent-shaped scratches on her arms, tears glistening on her cheeks.

He grabbed a large bath sheet, sending warmth into its fibers before laying it over her body. He stared at his mate, wondering when so much changed. Was it all at once or did it happen slowly as the weight of life and choices took hold? He crouched beside her, placing himself in her line of sight. Wil stood to the side wringing her hands, her bottom lip caught between her teeth.

"Lia, can you hear me?"

She turned her glazed eyes in his direction but looked right through him.

"Wil, call for Narcos and a healer. Lia, I am going to touch you, okay?"

He reached down, wrapping her in the sheet and scooping her into his arms. He stood as she turned into his chest and her body trembled, wracked with a new wave of sobs. He carried her to her bed, placing her in the middle of the mattress and sending more heat into the bedding to bring her temperature back up. He found a glass of water on her nightstand and brought it to her lips.

"Lia, can you hear me? Can you drink some for me?"

He tipped the glass up against her lips as she slowly sipped at the water. Placing the glass back on the table, he circled the bed sitting at her back and used the bath sheet to wring the water from her long curls. He braided her icy damp hair into a simple plait, pulling the tie from his own hair to secure it off her skin.

"Lia? Can you hear me?"

A subtle nod had his muscles instantly relaxing, banishing most of the tension from his shoulders. He climbed back off the bed, moving back into her line of sight. He heard hurried footsteps on the stairs as he squatted down beside her bed, putting him at her eye level.

"Lia, do you kno—"

Something slammed into Cal from the side, sending him to the floor. Before he had time to gather his thoughts, his arm was wrenched behind his back, a knee pressing into his spine.

"What did you do to her?" Narcos snarled in his ear. "I could kill you for touching her."

"I didn't-" Cal started but was cut off by an enraged Narcos.

"What. Did. You. Do."

"Narcos! Remove yourself from the heir immediately! Cal has done nothing." Neda's sharp voice cut through Narcos' anger.

With pronounced hesitation, Narcos got up, leaving Cal on the floor and moving towards Lithia, where he sat on the edge of the bed speaking to her in low tones. Cal rolled over to find Wil's hand outstretched to help him up. Once on his feet, he scanned the new faces in the room. Wil had returned with both of the Hearth twins and, to his surprise, Tadhg.

"Why are you here?" The rage had left Narcos' voice, but something still lingered under his measured tone as he stared at Cal.

"I brought him," Wil said, staring down her nose at Narcos. "I came to speak with Lia and found her on her bathroom floor. I ran to find you, but you weren't in your room and Cal's room was the closest. I've never seen her like that; I didn't know what to do." Her powerful stance crumpled inward.

Cal jumped into the lull that followed her statement. "I found her much the same, curled on her shower floor, freezing, crying, and catatonic. What is going on? Has this happened before? Tadhg, why are you here? Where is the healer?"

Tadhg looked to Neda, who waved her hand vaguely in some form of permission before he responded. "I am the healer."

Cal watched as the guard moved Narcos out of the way, running his hands over Lithia. After a few seconds, a warm golden light seeped out into the space between his hands and Lia's chest. Cal had never interacted with the fae much before, but he found himself entranced now. He had deep mahogany skin and sharp features, with delicate constellations tattooed on his ear.

He worked in silence for a few minutes before speaking.

"It was just a panic attack. She's exhausted, but she will be okay. She had a few after her mother was killed. I'll help her as much as I can tonight, but you should all go. She would rather not wake to spectators."

Cal, Wil, and Neda moved towards the door, a stern, "You too, Narcos," following them out. Wil slipped through the doors quickly before Neda plopped into the chair in front of the low fire as Narcos crossed to the window, staring out at the sea. Cal was continuing toward the door, intent on returning to his rooms, when Neda called to him.

"Thank you for coming to her. I know it's not easy for you to be around her."

"I may not be her closest ally any longer, but that doesn't mean I would let something happen to her," Cal said, not turning to face her.

"Come sit."

With a sigh, Cal turned and sat in the chair facing the new general. Neda made a cup of a woody-smelling herbal tea and passed it to Cal before making one for herself. He sipped it slowly, watching Narcos continue to stare unseeing out the window, nerves tightening the muscles of his back.

They sat in silence for a while before Cal broke the silence.

"How normal was that?" He gestured vaguely to the door of Lia's bedchamber.

"It wasn't. She was one of the most confident females I had ever met until the light left Seren's eyes. She had just come into that confidence again when Gerania passed and her power was stripped. I think it shook her seeing her mother like that. It was brutal, Cal. She wouldn't move into these rooms for months, and when she finally did, she asked me to stay with her. This only happened once or twice, though."

"And Tadhg?"

She laughed.

"That, my grumpy friend, is a much simpler answer. Each of the Queen's Guard has some sort of special magic, it is largely kept a secret for obvious reasons. Tadhg is a healer. One day when she is feeling better and you aren't running away from her you should ask her how she found him. It will break your heart."

They settled into a contemplative silence, Cal's gaze locked on the slowly dying flames.

Cal woke to the subtle tap on his shoulder, a prickling pain creeping up his neck. When he finally cracked open his eyes, he found Tadhg standing over him with an amused smile. Rubbing the pain from his neck, he sat up and looking around realized he had fallen asleep in Lia's sitting room. Neda, in a most un-general-like fashion was sprawled across the chair opposite him, lightly snoring. Narcos was nowhere to be seen as Cal's eyes finally landed back on Tadhg.

"I woke him first, so he is already in with Lia," Tadhg explained. "You, however, are going to be in pain if I leave you like that. She is doing fine."

"Should we wake our glorious High General?" Cal asked with a laugh.

With a small chuckle, Tadhg walked over to Neda and tapped her on the shoulder.

"Come now, Neda, let's move you to your bed."

Neda groaned and turned, never waking fully.

Laughing, they headed for the door. "Let her regret being a heavy sleeper in the morning."

Cal grabbed a soft throw from the back of his chair and used it to cover the general, and with a smile, followed Tadhg from the room. They made their way into the hall.

Just as Cal was about to move down the steps, Tadhg's voice stopped him.

"I never really got to talk to you after the battle in the chaos, but I wanted you to know, I did everything I could to save Seren."

Cal turned and looked into the lapis eyes rimmed in tears turning pink at the edges, and realized he would never ask Lithia how she found this healer.

LITHIA

Lithia rubbed at her temples, as if that would make the clamor of argument somehow find a peaceful conclusion. She had started the morning meeting by informing the Primes of the state of her magic, or lack thereof, and their revelations the previous evening of its ties to the voiding. As expected, it set off a rather heated conversation about how best to go about solving the issue.

More shocking, however, was that not once had any of them questioned her ability to rule without the elemental magic. She had expected at least some dissent regarding her effectiveness, but there was none. Instead, they immediately jumped into an argument about the merits of seeking out Thahaos's temple, and Halos was pushing for them to evacuate the fae towards the capital cities.

It had been hours of partial plans and no real movement, and she was exhausted from the night before. She was struggling to focus on much of anything and was nearly ready to suggest they break for lunch when Wil cleared her throat and leaned forward.

"I believe seeking out Thahaos's temple is the most direct solution."

Lithia winced lightly, looking up at Wil, the light making her head pound.

"Why do you think that?"

Wil shifted in her seat. "The only thing we seem to have established with any certainty is that all these problems have the same cause. The magic is dying at the root. The best information we have as to how to find the source says that its last known location was in his hands."

"So we risk letting more die?" Osharus, the Tidal Prime, asked.

Cal responded before Wil, "Do we have a sure solution that guarantees otherwise?"

The sun-weathered fae leaned back in his chair with a tilt of his head in surrender, the beads clacking in his hair.

"Can we not send one of your crows to Thahaos's temple?"

She shook her head once. "The temple is the entrance to The Beneath. It is an in-between, neither on this plane nor beneath—my crows would not reach it. Someone must physically go."

"And you know this how?" Cassara asked down her nose.

"Knowing things is my duty."

Wil leaned back in her chair, but something in her posture set Lithia's teeth on edge.

"Then who exactly do you suggest goes looking for a mythical temple hidden between planes?" Cassara asked, her tone laced with condescension.

"I will—"

"Me," Lithia's voice sliced through Wil's offer and all the eyes in the room turned to her.

There was a beat of silence before a chorus of "no" came from the gathered fae.

"Listen to me," she said, slamming her palm on the stone of the table and pushing to her feet. "I am your queen. I may not be the only one who has the power to fix this, but I'm the only one in this room that we think is actively dying with it. I am not going to sit on my ass while someone else decides my fate."

"This is reckless, Lia." The parental tone of Astris's voice sent a fissure through Lithia's resolve, but she shook her head.

"I will die with Suviel or I will live with Suviel, Astris, but I will not do either sitting on its throne stagnant. I will not bow to this curse."

Neda shot forward. "You can't go alone, how many sentinels do you—"

"No, no one outside this room needs to know this information, if it can be helped, it would cause a panic. Fewer is better, we will move faster."

"I will follow you, Mo Bhanrighit."

Lithia's head whipped to her right, startled. Of all the people to volunteer to go, she was sure Cal would have to be bribed. The look on his face told her he was surprised with himself as well, but she wasn't going to push it now.

"Me too, of course."

Lithia sighed, rubbing her neck. "Neda, you have a legion to command. You cannot abandon your post."

"The hell I can't—"

"You will not abandon your post."

"Then you will take Tadhg. He is a healer and has knowledge of the mountains. You are doing this, but you are still our queen and you should still be protected."

Chucking quietly, Wil volunteered. "I will go as well. My crows can relay word faster than any other means and will keep you connected to the capital."

Lithia nodded.

"Thank you both," she said looking at Wil and Calcas. "In that case, I would like to leave Narcos as regent. Are there objections?"

"Yes." Cassara's voice grated across her ears. "He cannot be left as regent until you are married. Precedent dictates it is the most senior Prime."

"That ... would be me," Astris interjected, slicing through Cassara's haughty tone.

Lithia watched Cassara's eyes dart at her miscalculation.

"That is just as well," came Narcos's deep tenor from her left, "because I have every intention of going with you."

Lia opened her mouth to object, but Narcos held up a hand. "A party of five is large enough for protection and small enough to move swiftly."

Lithia sighed. "Let's plan to leave the day after tomorrow. We can spend the rest of today planning. Narcos, if you could pop into the hall and gather Tadgh."

As he rose, Nylian spoke softly. "Mo Bhanrighit, are you sure about this?"

Lithia straightened her spine, "This is the right path. I know it is."

The High Priestess sent word for Lithia to meet her in the temple the next morning and to bring someone to practice her magic with. Given all the developments in their plans over the day, they decided the whole group of five should go. After being led through the cavernous sanctuary, the High Priestess led them down a short hallway to a winding set of stairs as Lithia filled her in on their change in plans and quickly approaching departure.

Though she had been in the temple plenty of times through-out her many years of life, it still held a multitude of secrets she would likely never cease to marvel at. As they came to the bottom of the stairs, Lithia looked around, finding herself in a large underground cavern. Turquoise water lapped at the slick stone where the sea rose to meet it. She imagined if you dove you would eventually find your way into the bay, but she had no plans to try.

The most breathtaking feature of the cave, however, along the craggy limestone walls, was the most exquisite mosaic she had ever seen. Taller than her three times over, it flowed deep into the cave, farther than anyone with sense ought to have ventured. Each piece of glass and stone was placed with delicate precision. She moved closer and reached out. The tiles warmed at her touch, and the deep thrum of magic that crept its way up her arm seemed far more ancient than her own wild magic.

Aduna stood proudly in the heart of the mosaic, life pouring from her hands, the world forming under each footstep. Etched throughout were words in the ancient language of the gods, detailing her journey across this world and the life she created. The story seemed different from the one her mother told, and it was different from the version the historians wrote in the books she had studied, though stories tended to take on a life of their own depending on who told them.

Each new detail came to life as Lithia's eyes tracked the goddess' progression. Lithia thought it looked as if whoever had created it held intimate knowledge of the complexities of the world. The images were so detailed that she thought she could easily lose herself in them and walk beside the goddess herself. She marveled at the old and unknown magic that hummed deep within the tiles.

"Magic isn't allowed inside the main temple, however, I thought this would be a good place to do this little test given we have plenty of space and no spectators," the High Priestess said, breaking Lithia's reverie.

"Aren't you worried it could damage the mosaic?"

"No, dear. I think that will outlast us all. From what we can tell, it's been here far longer than any of us. Its magic is unlikely to allow it to be damaged. I also think you are unlikely to damage anything, as I don't plan on having you do much. Really what we want to see is how your magic is affecting the one you draw from."

"Okay. What do you need me to do?"

The High Priestess motioned to the other silent priestess who had moved with their group to come forward.

"If someone will allow you to channel their magic for a few minutes, that should be all we need."

"You can use mine," Narcos said, moving forward.

Cal shifted as if to offer but paused, falling back against the wall beside Wil. Lithia chewed her lip for a moment, remembering the initial reaction Cal had when she had used his magic.

Speaking low enough only for Narcos to hear, she said, "I'm sorry if it's uncomfortable."

"Anything for you, Mo Lunath." He kissed her on the nose and moved to stand in front of the High Priestess.

She took a breath in through her nose, concentrating on her magic. She searched for the thread of her power inside her, and when she found it she picked it up, its pulsing magic melding and forming to her like a worn glove. She inhaled again and smelled the earthy moss and soil thread of Narcos's magic. With another deep breath, she picked it up and pulled.

An agonized scream filled the cavern.

CALCAS

Calcas hadn't expected Narcos's reaction to the syphon magic. He crumpled towards the floor and was caught by the High Priestess and Tadhg, crying out in pain. He heard a sharp intake of breath from Lithia as she cut off her magic and moved quickly to him. Her hands fluttered around him uselessly before her panicked eyes found Cal's.

"It's ... fine ..."

"I'm sorry. I didn't know it would hurt that badly."

"No," Narcos said, hissing air in through his teeth. "Really, I think I just wasn't ready for what it would feel like."

Cal tilted his head. "It was like that for me as well. It's a startling feeling, but it wasn't as bad the second time."

The angry look on Narcos's face told him he might just pretend there hadn't been a third time. The High Priestess made a sound in her throat, removing her hand from Narcos's chest.

"If you don't mind trying again, we can."

Narcos nodded curtly. This time, however, he stayed in his seated position on the floor. Lithia closed her eyes, taking a few deep breaths, and after a few moments, a small flower bloomed in her palm, followed by a low groan from Narcos.

The other priestess stopped Lithia before she could rush back to Narcos with a hand on her chest. They sat there for a few minutes, the only sound the rippling of the water and Narcos's heavy breathing. While it wasn't as shocking the second time, it certainly seemed as painful. Cal wondered if the mate bond lessened the effects of the syphon magic or if it was his shadows allowing her to borrow from them that lessened the pain. Either way, Narcos was definitely still in pain.

The High Priestess stood, allowing Tadhg to help Narcos to his feet as Lithia moved to comfort him.

"From what I can tell, your magic is dipping into his magical core. That's why it's painful. While I think it is a tool in extreme instances, you should avoid borrowing magic, if you were to drain someone's core completely—"

"They would die," Wil finished from her place on the wall.

"Yes, they would die." She turned to the other priestess. "Did you notice any changes with hers?"

"Only the normal changes one would have when they use magic. So, when she syphons she isn't storing it at all."

"Not particularly good or bad news. It would be nice if your core could be charged with magic, but it does mean that in theory, you shouldn't store negative magic either."

Cal pushed off from the wall. "Thank you, High Priestess. You have given us invaluable information over the last few days."

She bowed her head. "My duty is to the land Aduna created. I do wish I knew more, though. However, I do have something for you, Mo Bhanrighit, before you go."

She motioned to an acolyte who was waiting inside the stairwell, and the slight fae flitted over with a long flat package. She handed the package to Lithia before bowing and hastily retreating. The High Priestess motioned for Lithia to open the package, folding her hands demurely in front of her. A crease formed between Lithia's brows as he watched her begin to untie the simple cord. The fabric beneath looked smooth like water, rippling and glistening as it slid through her fingers.

When the silken fabric shifted, a soft gasp slid through Lithia's parted lips. Between the silken layers was the most exquisitely crafted sword he had ever seen.

"The Sword of Mab," said the High Priestess, her voice thick.

The High Priestess waved toward the sword in encouragement as they all stared aghast at the incredible sight in front of them. A great sword in a black scabbard, filigreed in gold and studded with opal. Lithia reached out, slipping the blade from its sheath, and he heard another breath shudder from her lungs. He took a step forward, taking in the blade in front of him. The sword matched The Ember Throne.

"It's dragon glass?" Lithia asked as she ran her fingers over the blade.

It was crafted from translucent black stone filled with swirling embers that moved as if the sword were alive. The edge was razor thin—he doubted even the most skilled blacksmith could hone such a weapon. The hilt was black leather inlaid with the same gold and opal as the scabbard. Etched along the blade were the same runes running along Lia's skin.

"Why now? I don't think I ever saw Gerania with this," Wil asked, leaning so close her breath fogged the blade as she spoke.

"No, you wouldn't have. No queen has wielded this blade since Mab herself."

Lithia choked on her next breath.

"No one? Why me then?"

"There simply has not been a need. Suviel has been in balance. The sword is a conduit for power. You would be able to channel the elements into the blade as you wield it under normal circumstances. That's not to say it's still not useful without that magic at your disposal. You may yet be able to channel any recently syphoned magic into the blade as you wield but I am unsure of the energy that would take."

Lithia stared at the impossible blade and he watched as the awe settled over her features. A sword made for Mab, not wielded by any other High Queen before her, was just casually in her hands. She ran her fingers up the blade gently before sheathing it.

"Thank you, High Priestess, this is an honor. I will do whatever it takes to save Suviel."

The High Priestess moved towards Lithia and laid a weathered hand on her cheek.

"My dear, please do whatever it takes to save yourself, too."

Lithia gave the High Priestess a tight smile, but he could see her decision in the set of her shoulders. He knew now, as he'd known in the moment he volunteered, that his only goal in this was bringing her back alive. He turned, locking eyes with Wil, who nodded at whatever emotion she read in his eyes as they moved towards the stairs.

When he woke the next morning, it was to find an extremely annoyed Narcos sitting at his table eating breakfast. Thankfully, the male seemed to be eating his own breakfast and not Cal's but it still wasn't the sight he wanted to wake up to. After finishing in the bathing chamber, he fell into the chair across from Narcos and greedily stuffed a few slices of bacon into his mouth.

"To what do I owe this pleasure first thing in the morning, Narcos?"

The other male looked around Cal's rooms and leaned back in his chair, teacup in hand.

"It has been decided that you and I will focus on packing the saddlebags and preparing the cart to cross the bridge. Willow and Lia are meeting with your mother for most of the day, and Tadhg is helping with Neda and the weapons."

Narcos turned back and watched his expression as Calcas swallowed the rather large bite of eggs and sipped his orange nectar.

"What could go wrong?"

Everything. Everything could go wrong.

They spent the entirety of the day chasing down supplies. The weapons weren't ready, the bread was still baking, and they were short a bedroll. They had to do each task twice or in the case of the slowest blacksmith on the island, four times. A saddlebag ripped and Narcos had to go to the other side of the citadel to find another large enough, while Cal went to find the maid with the right keys to get medical supplies from her storeroom.

They got the cart packed to cross the bridge just before sunset and all but fell into their seats at the dinner table. It was now nearing midnight and Cal found himself on the turret overlooking the citadel's gardens, watching the moon hover over Soundless

Bay. The wind was warm and balmy, carrying the salty tang of the water. A last moment of serenity before they left. Or at least a moment of serenity would have been nice, had the shadows below not begun to move.

He watched as a shadow moved from the wall below him and began down the narrow guard path toward the cliff. Had it been a darker night, he wouldn't have noticed her at all, but the full moon illuminated the sheen of copper hair. The pull between sheer curiosity and the desire to leave her to her fate lasted less than a heartbeat as he swung his legs over the turret wall. He lept from the high wall, plummeting three stories and landed in the cushion of his shadows.

He stalked closely behind her, his magic silencing his steps. Lithia turned suddenly off the path, heading towards the cliff's edge. She skirted too close to the edge. Was she about to go over? His heart raced as he lurched forward, jerking her back from the edge.

"What in the mother's name are you doing?"

Lithia stared back at him, eyes wide in shock. He realized that startling her could have ended poorly, but he'd been too consumed by panic in that moment.

"What are you doing out here? You shouldn't be here."

"And you should be? It's pitch black out here and that's a sheer drop into the bay—what are you thinking? This might be the stupidest thing I think I've ever seen you do, and that's including that time you tried to ride a bull jackal."

Lithia smiled softly at the memory. "There's no chance of you just leaving me to my own devices, is there?"

Cal raised a single eyebrow and crossed his arms across his broad chest.

With a sigh, Lithia looked out over the water.

"I just ..." She sighed before continuing, "I used to come out here with Seren and we would talk about what it would be like to be able to just sail between the Twin Harbors and keep going. I came out here to talk to her again in case I don't get another chance."

"I can't leave you out here alone, Lia."

"That's okay."

They sat in silence. The silver of the moon danced on the water, calling to them like a little siren song.

LITHIA

When they came back into the gardens from the cave they found Wil, lounging on a stone bench feeding butcher trimmings to one of her crows, a barely contained smile on her face. The source of her amusement was the future king pacing the cobbled path in front of her. Narcos was pounding back and forth, arms crossed over his chest and a deep wrinkle between his brows.

"Have a nice little trip?" Wil asked, not looking away from the crow by her side.

Her question was met with silence. Narcos halted mid-step, head whipping in their direction. When neither Lithia nor Calcas answered, Wil looked up, snapping to attention at the tension written on their features.

"What are you talking about? Why are you out here?" Lithia asked, wrapping her arms tighter around herself.

"Why are we out here? Wil's crows let her know you were on a fucking cliff, Lia. Then *oh don't worry, Cal is out there.*"

Narcos cut Cal a glare as he finished speaking, and Cal rolled his eyes.

"I saw her sneaking away and followed so she wouldn't get hurt. I'm going to bed."

Cal gave her a sidelong glance before he and Wil left, leaving her alone in the courtyard with Narcos.

"I just needed to be alone, Nars, I'm sorry."

"But you weren't alone, were you?"

He turned and walked back into the citadel, leaving her in the courtyard, finally alone.

That was how, only two days into this months-long journey, Lithia found herself subjected to Cal's brutal pace and Narcos's cold shoulder with no buffer for either. Narcos had allowed the unexpressed hurt to take root, and for the last two days, she had only received curt answers and clenched jaws. Lithia was ready to strangle both Narcos and Calcas on sight.

Cal rode out front, setting the brutal pace. Will fell back to fall into stride with Lithia, pointing to the small clearing ahead where they were stopping for the night. The Singing Wood was full of beauty and light during the day, a proper enchanted forest. Towering trees with silvered bark and glittering green and gold leaves weaved a canopy that filtered dappled sunlight onto the road. Several streams connected to The Idris, the large river that flowed through Suviel's center. The forest floor was covered with vibrant green mosses and fungi that hid the smallest inhabitants of the forest.

Its most enchanting feature, however, was the whisper of ancient song that hummed through the branches on the wind. It wasn't ever-present, but when the wind blew through the silvery trees, their configuration created the most beautiful tone.

However, when the sun set, the shadows began to stir with all manner of dark creatures. In large groups it was relatively safe. In a group this small, however, they had to be vigilant.

She veered off into the clearing, settling her mare, Daylis, up between Redmaw and Narcos's dappled stallion, Baye. sliding her packs from the saddle, she made her way to where the others were clearing a spot for their fire. As she approached, Cal and Tadhg turned off to hunt for some small game and gather wood for the fire, while Wil began to ward the clearing. The wards wouldn't create much of a protective barrier, but they would act as an alarm should anything try to enter their camp.

Narcos knelt, shifting the ground into a small fire pit to protect the flames from the wind. Lia carefully perched across the small dip in the ground and began sorting out rations for their evening meal.

"Why didn't you just tell me where you were going?" Narcos broke into the silence a few moments later.

Blinking, she placed the rations down on top of the bag and sat fully in the grass across from where he was crouched, crossing her legs under her.

"I wasn't trying to hide anything from you, Nars."

"You could have just told me then, Lia. It's my duty to protect you. Instead, you allowed a male who left you when you were broken to. You trusted him where you never trusted me."

Her back stiffened.

"I will remind you that I was High General and am now High Queen. I do not require protection and I have a right to my secrets. I did not plan to take him with me Nars, it just happened."

"Sure. I hope those secrets are worth it."

He stood, turned towards the tree line, and stalked away. Wil came back into the clearing watching Narcos's retreating form.

Standing, she followed Narcos into the trees.

She found Narcos on the bank of a small stream, hardly wider than her foot was long, the gentle flow coming from a small ridge a few paces away. As she watched, he pulled a large stone towards him, his gentle magic enveloping it. After a few moments, the thrum of magic faded and what was left was a stone basin and cup. Narcos began to scoop water from the stream into the basin, filling it quickly. Lithia stepped out of the trees, settling beside him.

Narcos set the cup down and rolled his sleeves up further, before cupping them in the water and splashing it on his dusty face.

"I'm sorry, Nars."

"I just wish you trusted people the way you used to."

Her shoulders tensed, molars grinding together.

"I have been shown in every arena that trust is easily broken. Forgive me for not giving it freely to every person who walks into my life."

She watched as his knuckles blanched white.

"So I am just someone who walked into your life? It should be thrilling to be your husband as just a passing acquaintance."

"You are deliberately distorting my meaning, and you know it."

"Then what do you mean, Lithia?" She flinched at the use of her full name. "What else could you possibly mean? I am supposed to be your husband. We are meant to rule an entire queendom as partners. That will require a not-insignificant amount of trust."

She sat quietly, a wrinkle between her brows.

"I do trust you, but you must understand, this partnership is still new; it's been less than a decade. The people I trusted most had hundreds of years of trust built up and they still broke it."

"For goddess's sake, Lia ... I love you. I love every angry, battle-worn, anxious, powerful part of you."

The softness in his eyes shattered when he met her steely gaze, shadows crept from the trees reaching for her, pooling at her feet.

"So did they."

She followed the small stream as it grew larger, the smooth flow stumbling over larger stones before slipping into a small pool. The slow stream of water hardly disturbed the surface of the pool, the motion making the surface simmer like a rippling mirror. She stood on the bank, listening to the gentle sound of the forest around her for only a moment before a wave of awareness slid across her skin, prickling the hairs on her neck.

The serenity of the forest had, with the slow descent of the sun, become a stillness that raised her hackles. The last rays of the sun were slipping past the horizon when she saw a disturbance in the smooth surface of the pond, like a stone had been plunked in its center. In the middle of the wave, a shape rose from the bottom of the small pond.

The top of a small head shifted, so its eyes rested just at the surface of the water. With shimmering scales in an iridescent green and four small horns, the Kapora watched her with gently glowing blue eyes. She tensed. The creatures were generally no danger to a full-grown fae and couldn't leave the water, but its presence was a warning. Something was coming.

She shifted slowly, not taking her eyes off the creature, slipping her dagger from its sheath, and placing her hand on her sword's hilt. The creature's lamp-like eyes shifted quickly over her left shoulder before disappearing below the surface. The only sound in the clearing was a gentle lap of water … and two heartbeats.

She took a slow, deep breath and sent her magic out to feel for the creature stalking her. The heartbeat was there, but nothing else about the creature was familiar. It was as if it was slipping from existence just as she got a sense of it. Her eyes popped open, tension slipping an icy finger down her spine. Voxis.

She drew her blade and spun just as the breath landed on her ear, the sharp edge of her blade meeting the razored edge claw of the shifter. A face eerily similar to her own, with bright yellow eyes, snake-like slits for pupils, and a foul-smelling sneer, met her gaze. In a heartbeat, the voxis's skin rippled, revealing its mottled grey flesh.

"Hello, little faerie. Are you lost?"

Lithia smirked at the revolting creature before pushing it back with the flat of her blade. The creature hissed, venom dripping from the corner of its mouth. It lunged at her, claws out, almost feral. With a spin and swipe of her leg, the creature crashed to the leaf-strewn ground. She pinned the small creature easily to the spot with her weight.

She lifted her head, whistling into the trees for the others. Never in her hundreds of years had she seen one of the shifters behaving in such a way. As if he were no more than a scavenger, looking for scraps. He was gaunt and bore several wounds from exposure. Across his chest were scars that seemed to be from another voxis, that had festered and begun weeping pus and venom.

Wil breathed as she knelt beside the struggling creature. "Did your own kind mark you in this way?"

The voxis hissed and writhed in its restraints, venom foaming from its mouth.

"KILL ME, WRAITH."

"Who hurt you?"

"KIIIIIILLLLLL MEEEEE."

He watched as the spymaster sighed and slid the blade from her thigh.

"Wait," Lia said, crouching by the writhing creature, capturing its attention. "Can you tell us who hurt you? We can find you help."

The voxis let out a maniacal cackle before spitting venom and blood towards Lithia's boots.

"YOU WILL DIE LIKE MEEEEE."

He continued his broken laughter, whipping his head from side to side, spittle flying in every direction.

Lia stood. "Finish him, we won't waste more time trying to drag information from an already broken mind."

"Rest where no shadows fall," Wil whispered before she slid the blade across the creature's throat.

Hot black blood oozed onto the ground, hissing and popping as it killed the surrounding grass. She watched in disgust as the creature's life force drained from its body. The walk back to the campsite was silent, the tension like a palpable force between them.

LITHIA

The next morning, the sense of urgency from the previous evening bit at their heels. Cal hardly waited for everyone to saddle before he set out at a grueling pace.

Later in the evening, Cal called motioned for them to stop, gesturing to the trees ahead where a small column of smoke ahead had caught his attention. He turned to Wil with a nod and she sent a crow off into the woods ahead. After just a moment, it returned, and a confused look passed over the spymaster's face.

"He says it is a small village." She turned to Tadhg. "We shouldn't reach any villages for several days, correct?"

Tadhg, looking equally confused, shrugged. "The next village should be Mt. Haven in the valley."

Cal leaned down, and slid out a map, as Wil pulled her horse alongside him.

"There are no villages on the map in this part of the forest."

Lithia cleared her throat. "Wil did it look like there was any sort of threat?"

"No, it looks like a normal village. A few houses, shops, and a pub. Likely no more than 50 fae."

"Alright," Lia said, shifting uncomfortably in her saddle. "It is coming up on dusk anyway; let's see if they have an inn. If not, we will continue past it a few miles before stopping for the night. Narcos, you and Wil ride ahead and send word back if we need to avoid for any reason."

Lia watched as the two took off quickly into the trees while she and Tadhg followed slowly behind Cal.

As she came through the trees, she could make out the warm orange glow from several windows. It was odd to come across a village not on the map but not unheard of. As they came through the trees and into the open land, they could make out Narcos and Wil leading their horses to a small stable behind the small inn.

Lithia slid off Daylis and led her toward the stable, where Narcos and Wil were speaking to an older fae. As she approached, a younger fae girl came running out to grab the reins from her. She slid her pack off Daylis's back and smiled down at the youngling as she led the mare towards the stall to be unsaddled. She stood back with Cal and Tadhg as the others paid the stable master.

Turning to the others, Narcos said, "The stable master there says there is only one pub in town, but it has rooms. They don't get many visitors, so there should be space."

They turned as one towards the Felbore Inn. Cal mumbled something about being hungry and led the way towards the door. It was nothing spectacular, a small two-story white stone building with a bright green front door and flower boxes in the windows. Lithia ran into Wil's back as the two in front of her pulled up short just inside the door.

As they moved out of the way, Lia understood their hesitation. It was a quaint little pub on the outside, but the inside was opulent. Orante rugs were scattered across rich wood floors. Low tables were covered in golden silk tablecloths and surrounded by plush pillows, each topped with low flickering fae lights and coal pipes for smoking. Jewel-toned fabrics draped the ceiling and walls, and large chandeliers casting a warm glow over the space.

The stable master must not have been exaggerating the lack of visitors because a hush fell over the gathered fae as they entered, Seated around a few of the low tables were several equally elegant fae, dressed in similar jewel tones. Each was lounging with some sort of iridescent drink or a pipe in their hand, watching as the party shuffled through the door.

Behind the mirrored bar was quite possibly the most strikingly beautiful fae Lithia had ever seen. They were statuesque, with chin-length straight black hair and feline blue eyes. They watched them enter with a serene smile and adjusted the collar of the black shirt they wore. With one wave of a long, elegant hand, they beckoned the group over.

"Hello, I'm Nomira. Welcome. I hope your travels haven't been too rough." They all stood in silence as the entrancing fae spoke to them. "I am assuming you need rooms for the evening, correct? We have four rooms available on the second floor. Will that do?"

Clearing her throat, Lithia answered, "Yes that would be lovely, thank you. Do you serve food as well?"

Nomira's face lit up. "Of course. If you'd like to head up to your rooms and put your things away, I'll get a table ready for you. Should only take a few minutes. Lily will take you to your rooms."

A small fae with shimmering lilac skin popped up by Lia's side and smiled broadly at them.

"Follow me!"

A look of bewilderment passed between each of them as they followed Lily up the small set of stairs in the back of the room. The hallway upstairs was more modest than the main area they had just come through, but the carved scrollwork on each of the doors was still extravagant. Lithia and Narcos entered the second door on the left and pulled up short yet again at the room in front of them.

A large fireplace was set into the wall directly across from the door, with a large glass claw-foot tub situated to its right. A small shelf of soaps and linens rested against the wall, a basin of water on top. To the left was an exceedingly large four-post bed with an extravagant number of pillows. Above it was a silken canopy in the most stunning shade of amethyst Lithia had ever seen. Glittering gems dotted the fabric, creating a smattering of stars over the lush bed.

Narcos dropped his things on the low chair at the foot of the bed, turning to take in the opulence of the room. A few minutes later while Lia was rinsing the dust from her face, a quick knock sounded on their door. A heartbeat later Wil poked her head in.

"Can we come in?"

"Yes, of course, but hurry before Lily comes back."

Cal and Tadhg shuffled in quietly behind Wil, who peeked out into the hall before closing the door.

"Where the fuck are we?" Tadhg blurted.

"Not quite how I was going to phrase it, but my thoughts exactly," Cal echoed, turning to Lia.

"I'm not sure, but other than someone having entirely too large a decorating budget I don't see any reason for alarm."

Tadhg's stomach chose that moment to let out a loud growl, and the tension snapped.

Wil slung and arm around his shoulders. "Alright, let's go eat then."

Lia opened the door to find a still grinning Lily on the other side.

"Oh um, hi. We were wondering if dinner was ready?"

"It sure is; follow me."

Exchanging one last baffled glance, they followed her back to the main room to a large table laden with the most delicious smelling foods and the iridescent wine the other patrons were drinking. Lia plopped down onto a large teal cushion with gold fringe and surveyed the large spread of food they'd prepared in such a short time.

A large bowl of rice dominated the the spread. Surrounding it was spiced lamb in a fragrant sauce, warm flatbreads, savory folded pastries, and fried vegetables. There were delicate glasses filled with shimmering wine at each seat. She lifted one to her nose, inhaling a sweet floral scent with a hint of warm spice.

A hand touched her wrist as she brought the cup towards her lips. Turning, she saw Narcos motion to Tadhg, who smiled before trying the wine. He took a sip, his eyes growing wide.

"That is fantastic!"

Wil chuckled and broke open one of the warm pastries and took a bite. She chewed before looking towards Lia.

"I can't sense anything wrong with the food or wine, Lia, it is safe. I don't think anyone here knows who you are, anyway. The food is excellent."

Litha portioned some of the rice and lamb in a rich red sauce onto her plate before taking a bite of one of the same pastries Wil had tried. The filling was potatoes and a spice she had never had before. She dipped a corner of the pastry into a small bowl of green herbs and moaned in delight at how flavorful it all was.

After eating in silence for a few minutes, she looked up at Tadhg, who seemed to be facing no ill effects from the wine. She picked the glass up to her lips, breathing in that intoxicating smell, before taking a long sip. The sweet drink danced across her tongue, warmth spreading to all her limbs. Every muscle in her body relaxed. She continued to eat and drink, everything seeming to taste better after the wine.

Once they had eaten their fill and the table had been cleared, Nomira appeared by their group, a golden tray of small cakes in her hand. Each of the little cakes was adorned with a tiny white Felbore, like the one on the sign outside. Lithia took the cake; her only thought was, if it tasted anything like the rest of the food they had that night, it was bound to be delicious.

She ate the small cake in two bites, as did the rest of her party. Absently, she thought it tasted almost exactly like the wine but far stronger. At some point someone refilled their drinks and placed one of the pipes on the table, a coal burning at the top. Cal and Wil sat across from her, looking laid-back as they blew smoke into the air, adding to the haze. Narcos was sprawled out beside her, his warm hand on her thigh as they laughed loudly with Tadhg.

Lithia scanned the room, a smile on her face, watching as the other patrons drank and laughed. A few had even slid into others' laps, creating a carnal scene in the room around her. A tall yellow-haired female was sitting on the lap of a broad chested male, his hand hidden in the folds of her skirt, her head thrown back as he nipped up her neck.

As she watched, lost in the building energy of the room, a warm figure slid into her lap. She looked up into the bright blue eyes of Nomira. The fae's black top was unlaced, showing an ample amount of cleavage and shimmering pale skin. The stunning fae's long fingers traced up Lithia's arms, a single nail running the length of her collarbone. Lia's eyes fluttered closed as Nomira began to untie the laces of her leathers. Leaning in, they kissed and nipped up the column of Lia's neck, the warmth of their breath ghosting over her ear.

Lia leaned into their lips as they whispered, "Hello, Mo Bhanrighit."

CALCAS

His senses swirled as the smoky haze of the lush room created fascinating patterns as it danced through the low light. The vibrant colors of the room pulsed with a low thrum of music that had started somewhere behind him. He could hear the low laughter and chatter of the other patrons, along with soft moans of pleasure. He found himself laughing at something Wil said before he took another long gulp of the iridescent drink.

The colors of the room swirled around him.

The music thudded through his veins.

Wil was cackling out a story to one of the pretty females who had gathered near them, her voice muffled like it was pushing through water before it met his ears. He sat there in an addled daze, looking at his companions. This was so relaxing, a much-needed rest before ... well, before something, though he couldn't quite remember what. As he reclined, he saw that fae, Nomira, slip into Lithia's lap. The sight brought a lustful glow to his already fogged brain.

He watched as the entrancing fae began slowly touching Litha, leaning in to whisper something in her ear. Whatever they said must not have been important, because Lia looked up at them with ravenous eyes. One of the females beside him slid closer, molding her body to his side. She ran a single nail up his leather-clad thigh before gripping the growing budge in his pants. He sank back into his cushion, pulling the slight fae up, until she was straddling his lap.

A light pulsed in his vision.

The room spun for a moment before settling.

Looking around, Tadhg and a couple of the pretty fae were stumbling up the stairs, and Wil had disappeared. Odd, she was just there seconds ago. Had it been longer? The fae on his lap ground down on his cock, eliciting a small moan and snapping his attention back to her. She has glistening golden skin and long black hair that fell in a curtain down her back.

He slid his hands up her warm thighs, moving the small black skirt higher, baring her to him. He slipped his hand between them, finding her already bare and drenched. Pouty red lips parted on a gasp as he slid his fingers through the gathering wetness. She rolled her hips, inviting his fingers inside as she reached down, frantically unlacing his pants.

He closed his eyes for just a moment, leaning into pulsing heat around him.

A snicker caught his attention.

His eyes roamed over her shoulder finding Nomira had gone, and Lithia sat back, Narcos knelt between her legs. A warm hand grasped his aching cock, freeing him from his pants. He watched as the female on his lap—he should really ask her name—wrapped her small hand around his shaft and slid down his legs. She settled on the cushion between his parted knees, locking eyes with him and running her warm pink tongue along the underside of his cock. She grinned, flicking over the piercing on the underside of the head, before taking the tip into her mouth.

He leaned his head back.

The room pulsed around them.

Letting out a long groan, Cal laced his fingers into her onyx hair, pushing further into her mouth and forcing her to swallow to take more of his considerable length. She choked slightly, tears forming in her eyes as he slipped down her throat. He looked up to find Lia's leg thrown over Narcos's shoulder, her chest heaving with her frantic breaths. The sight sent a bolt of lust down his spine. He pulled up on the female's hair before grabbing her hips and setting her back onto his lap.

She grinned down at him, wickedly nipping at his lower lip before fisting his cock and lining it up with her entrance. Slipping the tip through her wetness, she sank down onto him, taking all of him in one motion. They moaned in tandem at the feeling. She began to move, only for his lap to be empty in the next breath, the girl flying across the room.

The room rocked on its axis.

He blinked hard a few times, looking around to find the others doing the same, except for Wil, who was standing over him splattered in blood, wrath rolling off her in waves. The bright white of her eyes pulsed with magic as she stared down at him. He couldn't imagine what could have made her angry; everyone had been so nice.

"Willow?" called Lithia from across the low table.

Lithia sat up straighter on her cushion, fully dressed, and paused with a spoonful of rice nearly to her lips. Narcos and Tadhg looked around eyes wide and pupils blown.

"Put the food down, Mo Bhanrighit, it's not safe."

Not safe? What was not safe? The food was spectacular ... and where had that pretty fae gone? Cal looked down, startled, expecting to find himself exposed to the table, but his leathers were laced and in place like always.

The room tilted.

What was happening?

Was he blacking out?

Where are they?

Why are they even together?

Something is wrong.

Everything crashed into place.

"Wil. What's happened?"

"Nothing has happened. Why are you being so rude to our hosts, Willow?" Lithia's voice had taken on a formal tone, clearly attempting to cover her embarrassment at Wil's outburst.

"Wil," Calcas growled.

Wil's shoulders relaxed only marginally as she looked into his mismatched eyes.

"It's the nassella."

She shoved a small plant into his hand. Dark purple leaves with shimmering gold spots, like a galaxy unfurling in his hand.

"Eat this. Now."

He placed the shimmering leaves into his mouth as Wil gave them to the other members of their group. As he chewed, the haze in the room seemed to lift. The food on the table shifted. What was once a fragrant dinner turned rotten. Mold clung to the rice and a black film had gathered on the sauces. The plush cushions and jewel toned tapestries became dull and moth-eaten.

Most alarmingly, the lovely fae who surrounded them shifted. They became gangly, their faces thinned, their eyes seeming to bulge from their sockets. Teeth went from pearl white and straight to vicious, yellowed fangs. Their clothing hung in tatters across their frail bodies. Their eyes all took on the same feline slit as Nomira's. Calcas saw the faces of his queen and their companions become masks of horror, the same mirrored on his own. The only thing in the room that remained unchanged was the shimmering wine and the small cakes; they looked as enticing as ever.

The stillness in the room held for only a moment before a sharp cackle sounded from the now dusty, termite-damaged bar.

"I should have known the magic wouldn't hold you long, wraith."

Willow turned to the grotesque fae, flexing her grip on her sword.

"How long?"

"Oh? Whatever do you mean, little one?"

"How. Long?"

"Only three days. A pity, too, we hadn't had any fun at all yet, and we do like to play with our food."

A low growl came from Wil as Cal struggled to catch up, hardly understanding what happened. In his periphery, he saw the gaunt creatures begin to shift towards their group. Eternally grateful now for the centuries of training they had together, he looked toward Lithia, who was subtly glancing over her shoulder. She gave an imperceptible nod and shifted her weight.

Tadhg stiffened in his place, and Cal could see the same wheels turning in his head. Most of their weapons were upstairs. That should have been the first thing that set Cal's alarm bells off. He never would have left his weapons in his room in an unfamiliar place. He was going to need Wil to explain what the fuck just happened ... right after they survived.

"It will be so sad to kill you all so soon, I really was excited to try out the big one over there," Nomira purred, winking at

Cal with a horrifying grin, which may have been seductive in her glamoured form, but made his stomach churn.

"Cal," Willow hissed, never taking her eyes off the nassella.

Cal's muscles tensed a breath before all hell broke loose.

LITHIA

Lithia's heart pounded in her ears louder than any war drum. The lingering effects of the drug made her magic feel sluggish and far away. Why in the goddess's name had they left their weapons in their rooms? How had they been so thoroughly entranced? She could hear Nomira taunting Wil while Cal caught her eye, throwing a quick look over her shoulder. She nodded subtly, shifting her weight onto her feet, bracing to spring from her seated position.

She felt the shift in her companions as they came to the same realization: they were going to have to fight their way out. At that moment, she heard Wil hiss Cal's name. She sprung from her seat, swiping a rather dull knife from the table as she spun, plunging it into the eyes socket of the small fae who had shown them to their rooms earlier.

Lily's angelic face had morphed into a scaled mask of malice. That sweet smile melted into a mouth full of yellowed, razor-sharp teeth. The knife sank into her eye, a burst of slimy black blood splattering onto Lithia's face. The small fae shrieked as she fell to the floor, writhing in pain. Lithia fell onto her, landing sharply on her chest as she wrestled the jeweled dagger from her talon-like fingers.

She plunged the dagger into the flailing fae's shoulder, drawing another wretched shriek from her before sliding the sharp blade across her throat, cutting off the horrid sound. Thick black blood pooled around the small fae, eliciting a snarl of disgust from Lia.

She stood, turning to the chaos behind her. There seemed to be fewer nassella than she expected. Only about seven remained, including Nomira, four lying dead already on the floor. Tadhg moved with practiced precision, his skill apparent in the ease of his movements. He had disarmed his opponent with half of a broken spear in his hand. The male he was fighting kept dancing just out of reach of the weapon between jabs. She could see the focus as Tadhg calculated the larger fae's footsteps.

Cal and Narcos each took on their attackers with fierce determination, Cal with cutlery from the table and Narcos with a simple dagger recovered from one of the slain fae. They weaved around their opponents, makeshift weapons flashing as they aimed for vulnerable flesh.

An injured fae came wildly towards Lia, black blood already spilling from a slash to their abdomen. With no weapon, it lunged toward her, claws out. Lithia's instincts had her spinning as she kicked out to the side, taking the oncoming fae's feet out from under them and sending them crashing to the ground. A groan of agony slipped to a whisper as she jammed her blade into their spine, severing their spinal column in one swift motion.

She turned and watched as Wil's sword swept through the air, the two fae attacking her bobbing and weaving under her blows. They closed in around her in a deadly dance. Lithia watched forever in awe of the artful way Wil fought, silent and lethal. One of the fae lunged, eyes glittering with vitriol. A slash of Wil's blade cut a deep groove in the fae's leg, sending her stumbling back, a moment of reprieve while the onslaught from the other attacker continued.

Beyond the haze of battle in front of her, Lithia saw Nomira behind the bar, a look of utter wrath on their face as they watched their minions fail to take down the previously drugged group. A dark-grey flush of rage crept up their throat. Lithia's muscles screamed at her as she moved toward the fray, the drugs leaving a deep ache of exertion in their wake. She skirted around the fight, aiming for Nomira. Coming up behind Wil's attackers as one of them fell backwards toward her, she shoved them back toward Wil, impaling them on the spymaster's sword.

Nomira caught her movement and turned, a sneer contorting their face.

"You couldn't just die like a good little fae could you?"

Lithia let out a low chuckle. "No, but you can."

Lithia sidestepped a body on the floor before she darted forward, dagger slicing through the air, narrowly missing the once lovely fae's chest. Nomira danced fluidly away from Lithia's blade, twisting and slashing out, catching Lia's chest with taloned fingers. A blinding, white-hot pain blurred Lia's senses momentarily. The other fae took this moment of reprieve to turn and kick her in the stomach, her breath catching in her throat. Lia's reflexes took hold, and she grabbed the retreating ankle and twisted, the sound of bones grinding as they snapped. Nomira yelped as they crashed to the floor, blood pouring from their nose.

Lithia kept twisting, a satisfying pop sounding as the force popped the vile fae's knee from its socket. Nomira rolled, writhing, and sunk their talons in the Lia's calf, pulling Lia to the ground as well. As she fell, she caught a glimpse of Tadhg unloading his brute force on the fae in front of him. He dipped low and rammed his shoulder into their gut, slamming them into the wall before burying the broken spear into the fae's head directly between their eyes.

Twisting as her knee hit the gnarled wood of the floor, she ripped it from Nomira's grasp, Lithia threw her other leg over the fae, straddling their chest and bringing her other knee down hard on their upper arm. Nomira's free hand scratched at the leather on Lia's abdomen, trying to reach the exposed and bleeding flesh of her chest. They only succeeded in knocking the dagger from Lia's hand, sending it skittering across the floor.

Nomira's face split into a grin as they watched it slide out of reach. Turning back to Lia, that grin faltered.

"Well, Nomira, it looks like we get to finish this the fun way," Litha said, a snarl slipping into her words.

Nomira thrashed, grabbed hold of Lithia's arm, and clawed at the exposed flesh. Lithia hissed, twisting, trying to free the hand, but only succeeding in digging the sharp nails further into her flesh. Then the magic called out. The writhing lull of shadows surfaced. Cal's magic rolled in and filled her like the first crisp breath of autumn after a long summer. She silently thanked Cal as his shadows began slipping up her arms, Nomira's eyes dilating, their breathing becoming panicked pants.

"Why?"

"Why what?" Nomira hissed, eyes teaching the shadows.

"Why did you trap us? Knowing who we are?"

An uneasy chuckle left the nassella's throat.

"You fae always act so much better than us. We've lived under our agreement with Mab for too long. We were tired of only being able to trap the beasts. Our magic is ebbing because we aren't allowed to use it. We've taken several lone travelers in recent years, then your delicious party came along. Well, the chance to change our luck was too tempting to pass up."

Lithia stared at the other fae in horror. The nassella may be a thing of myth but they would still be held to the treaty, would they not?

"You won't win this one. You may be blessed by the goddess, but she is not the only one."

"What do you mean?"

Nomira started to laugh. A soft, surprised laugh that rolled into a full manic cackle.

"Tell me!"

They continued to laugh, digging their talons further into Lia's flesh. Lia hissed at the pain, her face contorting to a look of disgust and confusion. In her moment of distraction, Nomira twisted, wrenching Lia's elbow out of place. The shadows reacted to some unknown instinct, spearing through the fae below her. Nomira sucked in a gasp of pain, and their eyes went wide as the life left their body a breath before the shadows came pouring out of their mouth. The shadows rolled across the floor to Cal, the magic leaving Lithia.

Lia sat stunned for a moment before registering the utter silence behind her. She pried the talons from her arm and stood. Adrenaline beginning to ebb, breaths coming in ragged gasps, she turned to face the room. She looked around at her companions, their faces streaked with black blood and sweat, eyes wide.

"Well, that sucked."

Four sets of eyes turned to land on Tadhg, who was pulling a chunk of something black and bloody from his hair. He looked up, seeing their incredulous gaze before shrugging. Wil let out a low chuckle before lowering onto a low cushion. Lithia's head began to swim as the pain started to creep in.

The room faded as she fell to the floor.

CALCAS

After Lithia collapsed, Cal offered to go out and clear the rest of the area and check on the horses. He didn't know what to do once they got her laid out and Wil and Narcos began looking over her injuries. Tadhg had raced upstairs to find their bags to heal and treat her wounds. She had looked fine in the moments after the fight, as exhausted as the rest, but fine. In a moment that had changed, she swayed on the spot and then went down.

They had rolled her over to find the vicious wounds left by the bottom feeder who had trapped them. He silently panicked. He had been angry with her since the moment Seren hadn't walked off that battlefield. He had spent years avoiding her, insulting her, hating her, and taking his hatred of her out on anyone in his path.

The moment the light left her eyes, though, the thread connecting him to that hate had fractured. He was still angry at her.

He still blamed her, at least a little. However much he needed to see her healed, he also couldn't bear to allow the others to witness that weakness in him.

He took a few deep gulps of fresh air, stepping out of the blood-tinged air of the inn. He was momentarily blinded by the sun after the darkness he had been in for days. Once his eyes adjusted, he took in the small village around him. What he didn't expect, however, was to exit the door of the inn only to find that there was no village whatsoever around them. Only the glittering trees of The Singing Wood and a door carved into the trunk of an enormous tree.

He let out a slow breath in a futile attempt to lower his heart rate and started walking to the right around the trunk. About 50 paces from the door, he came to a small stable cut directly into the side of the same tree. Despite their apparent plans to eat him and his party, the nassella had taken excellent care of their horses. He ran his hand down Redmaw's neck as he passed and continued around the tree.

Nearly half an hour later, he had circled what had to be the largest tree he had ever laid eyes on and found himself back at the door. He took a breath before letting himself back in. Four sets of eyes met his from the furthest end of the room near the small carved staircase. She was okay. The breath he let out was shakier than he expected it to be. Closing the door firmly behind him, he steeled his spine and made his way across the room.

Tadhg was sitting to the side with a small tabletop fire bowl cooking what seemed to be skewers of beef, looking drained. Lithia was leaning back on a cushion as Narcos and Wil attended to separate injuries. Her chest had been bandaged and Narcos was tying the wrapping on her arm. Wil was packing herbs around the puncture wounds on her leg to help speed their healing.

Tadhg looked up at Cal as he took a seat in front of him. "Did you find anyone else out in the village? I thought you would be out there longer."

Cal grabbed his waterskin and took a long drag, shaking his head as he swallowed.

"There is no village."

The others froze. Wil broke her reverie first, canting her head to one side as she spoke.

"Mmm. I was wondering if that would be the case. Nomira was more powerful than I thought. I expected they were using some ruins as a base for the glamour, but there was nothing at all but this building?"

Cal chuckled. "We aren't in a building. We're in a tree. And before you ask, the horses are all fed and accounted for."

All four sets of eyes blinked back at him incredulously.

"I know I lost a lot of blood, but did you say we're in a fucking tree?" Lithia asked, leaning up on her uninjured arm.

Cal shrugged. "That's exactly what I said. If it weren't for the door and the nook cut out for the stables, this part of the forest wouldn't look any different from the rest. It's the biggest tree I've ever seen."

A contemplative look fell over Narcos' face. "I wonder if it's a sister to the tree of beginnings in Fernholme."

"I've been to Fernholme many times and never seen a tree that big."

"You wouldn't have; it is in the castle's private garden. Only the Prime's family is allowed in as it is a holy place. Even as the Arcane Heir, you wouldn't have been permitted inside. It is believed that its roots touch all of Suviel. From the exterior of the castle, it appears to be a large grove of trees. However, it is only the tree of beginnings."

Cal tilted his head to the side in thought. He had seen that grove, or what he had assumed to be a grove, from outside the castle walls. Imagining it as one tree, he could easily picture it to be the same size. His eyes unfocused slowly as he thought.

"If we aren't in a ruin then Nomira was much stronger than I anticipated. We are lucky to have gotten away at all," Wil said quietly.

"Wil," Lithia started slowly, "can you tell us what the hell just happened? I thought the nassella were a myth, a story nursemaids tell younglings to keep them from wandering."

Wil heaved a sigh, tying off the final knot on the bandage she was holding and sitting back. Cal watched the contemplative gaze in Wil's eyes crack into a bone-deep exhaustion.

"You'll find that many things you believe to be legends are very real, simply well hidden."

"Explain," Lithia said with a hiss of pain as she adjusted on her cushion.

"When Mab united the courts, there were many fae who didn't conform. That is, they didn't want to be beholden to a court, as many found them to be lesser fae or creatures."

Lithia nodded, well aware of the treaty formation as it was their main form of contention with the voxis, even now. Wil reached out a hand, gesturing for a waterskin. Cal tossed it in her direction and she caught it, taking a long gulp before continuing.

"Mab formed the treaty, as you know, allowing any group not beholden to a court left to self-govern. They were given autonomy on the condition that they not be a danger to the fae under the protection of the courts. The treaty was bound in blood and still holds. The groups were mainly small family units at the time. Most are hidden in plain sight, others are in far remote regions in the sea or hidden in the mountains. There are many that have fallen under the guise of myth because of it."

"How ... how do you know all this?" Tadhg asked, eyes blown wide in shock.

"I know many things," Wil said with a pained smile.

Lithia's eyes landed on Wil, narrowing, but Cal had no idea if it was suspicion or confusion dancing across her features.

"Well, that's disconcerting, and I still have no idea what just happened or really what nassella are," said Tadhg, turning the meat over the fire.

Wil chuckled, throwing the waterskin at Tadhg, knocking him from his crouch onto his backside.

"Nassella are born from a voxis and a fae mating pair. It happens rarely if at all anymore, but they have extremely powerful glamour magic. Not full shifters like the voxis, but also without as much casual magic as the fae. They are highly predatory, using their glamours to trap and toy with their prey. It's why we saw a village where there was none."

"But she said it had been three days—how?"

"Ahh, that is where it gets interesting. Their glamour only extends so far, but what they enjoy most is lulling their prey into safety. There is a plant, felbore, that when watered with the blood of these halflings, amplifies their glamour. It essentially creates a drug that takes over the mind of the unwitting prey who consume it. In this case, us. It was likely laced in all of the food, and the incense as well."

Tadhg's eyes bulged. "So, they could have kept us trapped indefinitely? I mean, I did find a chest of not rotten food behind the counter, so I assume they weren't planning to starve us to death."

"I wouldn't be surprised if some of these fae," Wil replied, gesturing to the bodies on the floor, "had been trapped in their thrall for years, if not decades. It likely started the moment we entered the range of the smoke from the chimney. Otherwise, the name of the inn would have tipped their hand."

"How did you realize what was happening?"

Wil's stare turned distant for a moment and she shifted uncomfortably. "Had that fae not pulled me from the room, I don't know that I would have. I'm not sure what caused the ripple in the glamour, but once I saw it, I couldn't unsee it."

Wil cleared her throat and took a long drag from the waterskin.

"About that," Tadhg said, rubbing his palm over the back of his neck. "There isn't actually an upstairs. When I went to grab our things, it was just a large landing with our things piled in a corner. If she pulled you out of the room, where did she take you?"

Cal knew Wil was something of a mystery to all of them, but he also knew that being a spymaster likely meant that was necessary. He opened his mouth to defend her secrets but before the words formed on his tongue, Lithia sat up, groaning quietly, eyes narrowed once again on Wil.

"Willow."

Wil let out a low breath. "It is my job to notice things, Lia."

"Your noticing is very convenient lately," Lithia said, lying back and wincing.

"I know," Wil said quietly.

Cal stared at her, not wanting to push, but the feeling that she wasn't being entirely forthcoming nagged at his senses. Narcos cut into his thoughts with his quiet rumble.

"We can stay here for the night since the nassella are gone. There is no sense in moving on until the morning."

Cal grunted in acknowledgment before he stalked over to some moth-eaten cushions on the far wall and fell onto them, throwing his arm over his eyes and letting the exhaustion of the day finally settle. He listened to the low murmur of conversation as the others ate and slowly broke off to their corners to sleep.

LITHIA

Lithia woke with a low groan. Tadhg's healing combined with Wil's salve had healed the deepest parts of her wounds. Her head, however, had begun to ache, like a hot dagger was being dragged along her scalp. In the moments after the fight, the wounds had felt minor, but as the adrenaline wore off, the pain had rushed in at once, crumpling her.

She sat up, slowly disentangling herself from Narcos's limbs, and looked around the shadowed room. It looked like it was currently Tadhg's turn on watch. He was sitting on a cushion by the door with his head leaned back on the wooden wall, humming a low song.

She picked her way across the room gingerly, trying not to wake the others. She grabbed some of the leftover bread from the previous evening and a waterskin as she went. She slid down the wall beside him and offered him the water when he rolled his head in her direction.

"I can take your watch if you need more rest. I'm too sore to sleep well, anyway."

He chuckled, taking the proffered water and drinking deeply.

"What kind of Queen's Guard would I be if I slept while my queen kept watch? I can feel Cian's glare from here. Lean forward, let me heal you a little more."

She smiled gratefully, adjusting so he could lay his warm hands on her back. She rested her arms on her bent knees and turned her head to watch his face as he worked.

"What made you agree to become my guard, then?"

"You did." His face grew somber. "I was on that battlefield, as you obviously know. I saw you charging into battle like you were as expendable as the rest of us and I knew I would protect you with my dying breath."

Lithia blinked quickly, her eyes lined with silver. "That wasn't quite the joke I was expecting, Tadgh."

He rolled his eyes dramatically. "Fine, I joined because I figured guarding a battle-hardened warrior would be easy work because you're far too scary for anyone to attack."

They laughed, Litha nudging him with her foot.

"I guess you're a decent guard. You are at least fun to beat up in training."

"Please," he scoffed, "Finn won 50 gold off me the last time I lost to you. Goddess knows why anyone bet I would win."

"Hmm, I'm sure Cian would say something about gambling being unbecoming of a Queen's Guard. I say next time let me know so I can get in on that bet."

Tadhg leaned back and chucked the piece of bread he picked up at her head. They sat there laughing for a few minutes before a quiet settled over them both.

"Do you think the temple will have the information we need?"

"I don't," she replied, picking at a thread on her bandage. "To be quite honest, I am more than a little afraid this is a wild hunt, just chasing ghosts."

"Then why did you decide to do it?"

"There weren't any other options. I couldn't leave the stone unturned, and despite my frustration at her cryptic answers, I trust Wil with my life and she thinks this is the right path."

Tadhg smiled as they fell into a companionable silence. The room gradually lightened as dawn approached to the soft sounds of the forest waking, like a sigh of relief that it too had survived the night. The others rose with the sun, and they found themselves once again gathered around the low table. Mugs of hot tea and some fruits from their bags sat around Tadhg's map spread across the table's surface.

"If we are still relatively on track, we should only be a day's ride from the boundaries of The Singing Wood, and we should be able to camp outside the forest this evening," Tadhg said, pointing to their location in the forest.

Lithia squinted down at the map. "And how far from the temple?"

"It's hard to have an exact number given the temple's proclivity to hide. We are about three days from the Valley of Atropin. It will take about half a day to cross the Pass of Souls and after that, it is up to the gods."

"So, four-ish days until we intentionally get lost in the Tipping Peaks. Lovely, let's get a move on then," Cal said, slapping his thighs as he stood up and made for the door.

Narcos narrowed his eyes at his departure and Wil huffed a laugh as they gathered their things, following Cal out the door.

"Tadhg, have you seen the temple before?"

Tadhg stood, shifting his weight before answering.

"I got conscripted to the legion because I was the fourth child. I was young and afraid, but sixteen of us set out from our village deep in the mountains for the training camp in the pass. We got lost. We had run out of food a few days prior and could only thank the snow for water. One girl had already died of starvation. She was hungry before we ever left. Anyway, on the third day after the food ran out, suddenly it was there."

Lithia found herself leaning in.

"Two acolytes in long robes came rushing out into the snow with lanterns and ushered us all inside the temple. It was beautiful and warm, and I might have cried a little when I got the feeling back in my toes." He chuckled at the memory before continuing. "We stayed for nearly a week. When it was time to go, they gave us the choice to continue to the camp or stay as acolytes. The thought of not having to travel further was tempting, but in the end, only two stayed. We made it to the pass the next day, even though we should have been far from it."

He shook his head as if releasing the memories, and smiled at her. "It will find us, Mo Bhanrighit, don't worry."

He scooped up his bag and slipped out the door, stepping into the forest, leaving Lithia alone in the room. Gathering the last of her things and checking that her weapons were secure, she opened the door into the cool mist of the morning. As the door closed behind her, she saw the enormous tree for the first time. She hadn't thought Cal was lying, but seeing it was something wholly different.

The tree was magnificent. Massive and gnarled, with bark a rich copper streaked with silver. She moved forward and placed her palm on the bark. As soon as she touched it, a ripple of magic jolted through her. She could see everything. She could follow the roots of the tree to a tiny frog on the other side of the wood. She was sharing eyes with a tree.

The tree let out a sigh of relief at her magic. Faintly she heard her name being called, but she didn't want to move, or maybe she couldn't move, she wasn't sure. She stood, letting the warm pulses of magic ripple through her body until they slowed and the bark released her hand. As she opened her eyes, her senses flooded back, and she turned and found the others staring, not at her but past her, at the tree. She took a step back blinking hard a few times before she saw why. The door was gone. All signs that the nassella had ever scarred this tree had vanished like they never existed.

Narcos turned to her in awe. "You healed it."

He reached out to her, pulling her face to his.

"You are the most beautiful magic," he whispered before claiming her lips in a soul-shattering kiss.

A cough behind her had her step back to find a bemused Wil.

"I could see through the roots of the tree. Is that how it is at the Tree of Beginnings?"

"Yes, it is quite similar, though it is more like feeling through the tree."

"I'm going to touch it again and see what it was trying to show me."

"We will finish packing the horses." Narcos placed a small kiss on the tip of her nose before they turned back towards their horses.

Lithia walked in the opposite direction a few paces before finding a patch of soft moss nestled between a few of the tree roots. She sat facing the tree and took a slow breath as she gently placed her hand back on the tree's trunk. That same warm current flowed up her arm as her eyes shuttered closed.

The tree shuddered, and she gasped.

CALCAS

"Should we poke her or something?"

Cal chuckled quietly, looking over his shoulder just in time to see Narcos slap Tadhg on the back of the head.

"Ow! I was kidding ... mostly," Tadhg said, rubbing at his head.

Calcas turned back to Lithia, a furrow forming between his brows. It had been nearly an hour since Lithia sat on the tree's roots, her black eyes wide open, staring into the distance. The horses shifted uneasily. Wil reached over to stroke Daylis's muzzle, making a soft shushing sound. Redmaw nudged Cal's shoulder as he danced in place and let out a soft snort, just as a gasp sounded from the direction of the tree.

Lithia was swaying on the spot, blinking the moisture back into her eyes. She stood slowly, turning back to stare at the tree in awe. A heartbeat later, she whipped her head to their gathered party.

"We should move on."

She made for her horse, slipping into the saddle still seeming dazed. Calcas watched her for a moment, a little concerned she would slide off again, but shrugged and hauled himself onto Redmaw.

"The tree showed me a small group of voxis headed this way. They don't seem to be a threat, but I would rather not sit here and wait to greet them," she said, turning towards the road.

"Lead on," Cal said, falling into place behind her.

She dug her heels into Daylis and set off west at a brisk pace. The others followed suit, the vibrant metallics and greens of the forest blurring around them. Cal's ears filled with the rhythmic sound of hoofbeats and steady huffing breaths as Redmaw followed close behind Daylis.

Several hours passed before sunlight broke through the trees in front of him. The trees thinned and fell away as they reached the outskirts of The Singing Wood. Cal pulled up short in front of a narrow bridge, waiting for the others to arrive. Tadhg arrived at the rear of their party, bowing as he stopped alongside Lia.

"No one behind us on the path, Mo Bhanrighit. We should be safe to camp for tonight. Tomorrow we should reach Mt. Haven and sleep in a bed that isn't trying to eat us."

Cal let out a chuckle at how the guard could be so humorous at the worst times. There was no way that wasn't magic all its own.

He shook his head, turning toward the small bridge to cross into the valley.

The worn wood of the bridge looked like it had been lovely once. Intricate vines and thorns running along its railings had been worn smooth with time. Rich, dark wood had been bleached in the sun and an obvious path had been worn with time. For a fleeting moment, he wondered if the bridge was stable, but he stepped off the other side with no issues.

"So where are we camping?" came Tadhg's all too chipper voice as he stepped off the bridge.

Cal grunted, nudging Redmaw forward along the stream bank.

"We'll stick to the bank but move about a mile south towards the valley road. Had we not ended up off track with the nassella, we would have already been close to the road. As it is, we have to backtrack some."

He started forward, pulling a chunk of bread and an apple from his pack, taking a bite of the apple before feeding the rest to Redmaw and tearing into the bread. He stayed just ahead of the others, desperate for space he was sorely lacking.

They continued for only an hour or so before finding a flat area to make their camp for the night. He sat on a rolled sleeping mat near the fire, finishing the portion of rabbit they had roasted for dinner and staring off into the flames, when Lithia started speaking.

"So, the tree," she started, watching as all eyes turned to her and conversation died out. "It showed me a lot and I'm not sure quite how to explain. It showed me Mab. It was there, on its roots, where Mab got her magic."

"It showed you that far into the past?" Wil said in an awed whisper.

Lithia let out an unqueenly snort.

"It showed me creation. The goddess rested on that sapling, feeding it her magic until its roots reached all corners of Suviel. The first wars, Mab's near death, the creation of the queendom we know. It showed me the nassella and the pockets of blindness where its vision is being blocked. It showed me the pain it feels from the void. It showed me that group of voxis. Shit, it showed me a tree frog near Hearth."

"Did it show you the heart or anything about the curse?" Wil asked.

Lithia's shoulders slumped. "No, I think it tried, but there are these barriers in its memory, like the magic is blocking it. I'm also not sure it would have known exactly how to show me raw magic like that. It seemed to be showing me things as they were created."

"So you spoke to a tree for an hour and got a bedtime story? Helpful." Cal asked incredulously before he went back to his dinner.

Lithia picked up a rock and chucked it at him. It bounced off his shoulder and he threw her a glare, but he kept further insults to himself for now.

"It's not just that. I think that it showed me some of what I should have gotten from the stillness had the magic not been frayed. The priestess said that in the past the High Queens have spoken to their predecessors and to Aduna herself, but my connection was broken."

Wil leaned in, placing a hand on Lithia's knee. Cal stood, grabbing his bedroll and moving towards the outer edge of the firelight. It was a bedtime story from a fucking tree, not divine intervention. He rolled over, falling asleep to the low whispers of conversation.

He had just finished removing his armor when she barged into his tent. His heart faltered at the blinding smile on her face before she jumped into his arms. He buried his face in her neck, breathing in her lemon and thyme scent. He peppered small kisses up her neck, the salt of her sweat clinging to his lips.

Seren arched into him, clawing at his tunic with the same haste he pulled at her riding leathers. They undressed each other quickly as they fell back onto the bedroll in the corner, the furs soft on his back as she settled over him, her knees on either side of his hips. Nipping at her throat, he moved his feverish kisses to her pouty lips, his hands palming her breasts, her hard nipples scraping along his palms. She arched her back, and he took her peaked nipple into his hot mouth, biting down on the sensitive flesh.

Nails dug into his shoulder blades as Seren ground her soaking core down on his hard cock, coating his length in her arousal.

"Please," she whispered into his hair.

He reached between them, his fingers finding her dripping. He swirled his fingers around her clit, a feral noise tearing from his throat. He laid back, pulling on her hips until her knees settled by his ears.

"Sit. Now."

She looked down, eyes hooded with lust as he ran his tongue up her center. She reached up, pinching and rolling her nipples, head rolling to the side, eyes closed. He lapped and sucked at her clit, her arousal running down his chin. Her breaths turned to panting and a string of unintelligible keening flowed from her mouth. Grabbing her hips, he rolled them so she was under him before crawling up her body and letting her taste herself on his tongue.

Shadows rolled down his arms, snaking up and securing her hands above her head. He stared into her honey eyes and she squirmed beneath him.

"Don't worry, you're going to come, but it's been months and I need the first one to be on my cock."

She whimpered as he thrust into her, fully seating himself in her pussy, and a shiver ran through them both, magic sparking through the tent like an electric current. He started a steady rhythm, his *shadows rolling around her body as she reached a hand between them, deft fingers stroking her clit in perfect time.*

"Fuuuuck, Cal."

He felt the muscles of her body lock as her pussy convulsed around his cock, her orgasm dragging his out. He filled her with his own release, leaning down to pepper soft kisses on her chest and neck, his shadows releasing her hands. As soon as she was free, she pulled him to her mouth in a consuming kiss.

"I love you."

He looked down at her, a smile dimpling his cheek. Sliding his cock from her, he moved down, laying his head on her thigh and pushing his come back into her pussy, earning him another gasping moan.

"I love you too," he said, biting her thigh before hopping up and grabbing the washbasin from the table and settling it beside the bedroll. Her skin pebbled at the cool water as he ran the cloth over her, cleaning travel and sex from her body. She watched him, a pensive expression on her face. After several minutes of silence, she sighed.

"Cal, she loves you, too. She isn't trying to hurt either of us."

His shoulders fell. "I can't shake the feeling that she's wrong this time, Ser."

"I trust her."

LITHIA

Lithia stared at Calcas as he stalked away with his bedroll, the flashes of him in the fighting ring floating to the surface of her mind. It was her fault. His rage, his pain, was all her fault, but there was something else, and something in her chest ached at the thought.

"So, how do you feel about all of it, then?" Narcos asked, handing the rest of his bread to Lithia.

She accepted with a smile, "I think what I learned is important. I'm just not sure how yet. So the best path is the one we are already on. If anything, I think coming across a connection to Mab when mine is frayed means I'm where I should be, if we are putting any hope in fate."

They fell into silence. Wil stood to follow Calcas, laying out on her bedroll and blinking up at the stars. Tadhg leaned close to Narcos, talking about the best route through the mountains. Lithia rose and quietly made her way downstream, desperate to rinse some of the grime of travel from her skin. She moved until she was well out of sight of the campfire to begin slowly removing her riding leathers. After pulling off her leggings, she strapped her dagger back to her thigh, not wanting to be left entirely unarmed.

She knelt down and carefully rinsed her sweat-salted skin, careful to avoid her bandages and wishing she had thought to bring replacements with her. Soft, sure footfalls grew closer as she rinsed her face. Turning, she saw Narcos approaching, a small bag in his hands. She stood from her crouch, water rolling down her bare chest.

When he got close enough, he cleared his throat. "I thought I would help you change your bandages."

Her shoulders relaxed. "Thank you, Nars," she said with a soft, pained smile.

He tended to anticipate what she needed far more accurately than she did, and it was one of the things she liked most about him. He was so kind and so thoughtful and so ... what was wrong with her?

He gestured for her to sit on the small towel he pulled from the bag, and knelt in front of her. Silently, methodically, he cleaned her wounds and replaced her bandages. He finished tying off the bandage on her leg and stayed kneeling in front of her, his warm hand tracing light circles on her thigh.

"For a moment, when you crumpled to the floor in the cursed inn, I thought you were gone and all I could think was that you were going to die thinking I resented you. I'm sorry I allowed my jealousy to cloud the love I have for you, Mo Lunath."

"I should have told you where I was going that night, Nars, I was selfish."

"No. You have a right to keep your secrets. I was being petulant."

Lia huffed a laugh. "You? Never!"

Narcos grinned up at her, those tiny circles moving further up her thigh. He leaned down, placing a soft kiss on the inside of Lithia's knee.

"Really, Lia, all I want to do is pull you closer and instead I pushed you away."

Narcos continued with those infuriating circles on the tender inside of her thigh before looking up. The heated look in his vibrant green eyes sent lust pooling low in her core.

"Rest your leg on my shoulder. I wouldn't want you to strain that injury."

Lia fell back onto her elbows, eyes hooded. Narcos pulled her leg up onto his shoulder as he slowly kissed the tender flesh towards the apex of her thighs. Her eyes slid closed at the sensation.

"Look at me," he growled, biting down on her thigh.

She peeled her eyes open just in time to make eye contact with Narcos as he dragged his tongue up the length of her pussy, circling her clit. Groaning, she fought to keep herself from slamming her eyes closed again. The feral gleam in Narcos's eyes was enough to keep the eye contact.

He sucked hard on her clit at the same moment he plunged two strong fingers into her aching pussy. Litha gasped, throwing her head back as her orgasm built. Narcos's tongue danced around her clit in perfect time with the pace of his fingers pumping and curling inside her. Her fingers dug into the soft grass as she rolled her hips, grinding down on his face.

"Fuck, Nars, yes."

Stars burst behind Lithia's eyelids and she was sure her arms were going to give out any moment as her orgasm barreled into her. Waves of pleasure rolled through her body, and her pussy convulsed around his fingers as he worked her through the bliss. He slipped his fingers out, licking her over-sensitive clit gently, before leaning back to watch her breathing calm. All the while, he peppered her stomach and chest with small kisses on his way up to her mouth.

His lips finally landed on hers and he sucked her recovered breath from her as he kissed her greedily, making her taste herself on his tongue. Lithia leaned up into the kiss, clawing at the waistband of Narcos's leathers, desperate to have the taste of him on her tongue as well.

He chuckled into her mouth, laying a hand on hers.

"Not tonight. That was an apology. We need to get back to camp because we might scar Tadhg for life if they send him looking for us."

Lia barked a laugh, her breaths still uneven. Narcos reached down, gathered her clothes, and helped her dress before they started back towards the fire.

On their way back, Narcos slid an arm around her waist, pulling her into him and kissing her sweetly on the head.

"I love you, Lia, and I am honored I was chosen to be your king."

Lithia leaned into him with a gentle smile.

"I am honored to have you as my king, Nars."

One day, she would say the words. One day, she would love him the way he loved her, but Seren still took up too much space.

CALCAS

Tadhg managed to get both Lithia and Wil to sing bawdy drinking songs. Two of the deadliest women on the continent were singing about bedding barmaids and pissing in public. By the time their antics had settled back into silence, he could make out the shape of Mt. Haven in the distance. Curls of smoke coming from stone chimneys nestled among a tapestry of thatched roofs. They passed through the outlying homes. Farmers pulled in their herds and children for the day, as the sun dipped below the horizon. Several fae made their way toward town in search of their beds or a meal. Cal dipped his chin to a few as they passed.

Closer to town, the houses clotted together, forming small clusters. Large pastures and fields were replaced by small personal gardens. A few young females giggled, batting their lashes at him as he passed. Finally, the houses slowly turned into shop fronts, the dirt road becoming a nicely cobbled road.

Tadhg pulled up beside him.

"The Cork and Dagger is going to be our best chance at finding beds."

Cal nodded, turning left down a side road that would lead them to the town's square. He knew the inn. He had been many times before. They passed small shops, the smells of sugar and warm bread wafting from the open door of a bright blue storefront. It was syrupy, sweet, and utterly tempting. The large paned windows displayed rows of pastries, drizzled with sugar and honey, cakes dotted with candied flowers, and row upon row of fresh, warm bread.

The next few shops looked to be closed for the evening, a tailor and cobbler sat with dark windows across from a florist who looked to be pulling the large buckets of fresh stems inside as he closed for the evening. Thick ivy surrounded the warm golden light spilled from his shop window and into the street.

They neared the square, where the quiet closing shops turned into a bright street dotted with taverns and inns that were just waking up for the evening. There was something quieter about the square than he remembered. Rather than loud cheerful conversations and frenetic energy, it was a calmer sort of energy. The surrounding fae still seemed to hold cheerful conversations, but they were all restrained.

He pulled Redmaw to the right as they entered the square, towards a large three-story stone building. The Cork and Dagger was the largest building in the square. Several tables framing the walkway were already full of merchants, sentinels, and other travelers who had wandered in for the evening. To the left of the building was a rather large stable, where he led their group.

He dismounted quickly and began pulling his packs from the saddle, slinging them over his shoulder.

"I'm going to go see about rooms," he grumbled, moving past the others and toward the front door. He had wanted to be as far from Lia as possible after his dream last night, but in a small party it was impossible to do.

The tavern on the ground level of the Cork and Dagger was always busy. The high ceilings and long oak bar could almost convince you the room was open and airy rather than stiflingly crowded at all hours of the day. Calcas stepped through the door, his gaze sweeping over the round tables sticky with spilled drinks. All manner of people crowded around the table tops, tossing money into the pile for a card game, or eating what smelled like a spiced stew. A few were laughing heartily at a small male gesticulating wildly as he told some exaggerated story.

Cal turned towards the bar, scanning the nondescript door to the left of the bar before slipping his eyes across the bar top right into the enraged gaze of the portly looking female behind the bar. Her eyes burned directly into his, her knuckles white on the rag in her hand. Had she been holding a glass, it would have likely turned back to sand by now. He flashed her a grin.

He took a deep breath of the warm, sticky air and began pushing his way toward her. She looked much the same as the last time he saw her. Soft round cheeks that always held a red flush, a curly mop of grey-brown hair tied in a loose bun atop her head, and bright silver eyes that could cut down any man. RoseLynn was usually jovial and warm. She had owned the Cork and Dagger for centuries and had made an art of making everyone feel like they were coming home.

He jostled through the crowd of patrons, RoseLynn's eyes narrowing on him as he got closer. A rather round male drunkenly fell into Cal's path, stumbling and twisting as he fell. Cal caught the lush by the collar of his tunic inches before his nose hit the floor, pulling him up and standing him back on unsteady feet. The drunk fae blinked owlishly at him before stumbling back towards his table.

He got to the bar and slipped into the stool in front of Rose-Lynn, noticing as he did the scorch marks she was leaving on her rag.

"You'll end up with no way to wash up if you torch that rag, Rosie."

Her skin flushed a deeper shade of red as smoke began pouring from her nose in great puffs.

"Yeh think yeh can just stroll back in here, yeh great bloody brute?"

Cal winced. Her volume was no more than a whisper, but that was enough to cause a hush at the nearby tables.

"Yeh left here nigh on two years ago like Thahaos was nipping yer arse, not a word of when yeh would return, and yeh dare to come in here grinnin' at me?" She looked around and lowered her voice further. "Jofin was spittin' mad too, sai yeh'd end up costin' him gold by not fightin' all yer matches."

He chuckled. "I missed you too, Rosie."

He leaned over the counter to kiss her on the cheek while she swatted at him with her still smoldering rag, rolling her eyes.

"Now tell me why yer back. Yeh, look better than the last time."

"I don't know that I'm better, but I'm at least not alone."

She broke into a radiant smile.

"No alone? Is it a she that's finally caught yeh?"

"Not this time," he said with a laugh. "We are going to need five beds, if you have them to spare."

"I can'nah do five. I only have the big room in the attic open. It has two, but I'll have Hollia pull a few mattresses up there for yeh."

"That's perfect, Rosie. Can you get a booth cleared out for us too? We are a little too recognizable to be in the thick of it tonight."

"Now, jus how pretty are yeh assumin' yeh are? I'll not clear out my patrons for the likes of—oh."

Cal looked over his shoulder to see that the rest of his party had finally made it through the doors. A hush rolled through the patrons as they nudged each other's attention. Lithia stood a step ahead of the others, looking every bit the warrior queen despite the dust and injuries of their ride.

She smiled at patrons as they greeted her, clearing a path in front of her as they all made their way toward Cal. The others may not have been as recognizable but commanded the same amount of awe. In Wil's case, it was likely a little fear as well because she cut a terrifying figure in all her weaponry.

The rag snapped across the back of Cal's head and he turned, finding those angry eyes once again.

"Yeh could have started with tellin' me yeh were traveling wi' the queen, yeh oaf."

She tossed her rag at him as she turned, bustling off to tell her girls to get their rooms ready and likely to clear out a booth near the back for them. He chuckled, watching her scurry about even though she had met Lithia many times before.

The others finally reached him and he turned to see an amused look on all their faces.

"Rosie looks like she got herself all worked up." Wil chuckled.

"She got so flustered seeing the queen come in, I don't even think she saw you, Wil. I imagine we'll hear the squeal—"

"AAHHHHH MY SHE! Come here and let me look at yeh!"

"—when she sees you," he finished with a laugh.

RoseLynn had raced around the bar and scooped Wil into a bone-crushing hug. She now held the much taller female's face between her strong hands, turning it this way and that as if she could read the passage of time in Wil's milky white eyes. He left the two females to catch up, Rosie talking animatedly while Wil's stoic features faded into familiar warmth.

"She's getting the attic ready for us," he said, leaning towards the others. "Might not have five beds but we'll make do. It's better than the ground."

Lithia nodded just as Rosie rounded on her.

"Oh, I have'nah seen yeh in ages. I 'spose it's Mo Bhanrighit now, not General. Yeh look a lot happier than the last time, though. It's been nigh on six years since yeh marched through here?"

Lithia's smile dimmed slightly, but she recovered in the same heartbeat.

"I don't know if I'll ever heal entirely, but I am not alone."

The echo of the words Cal had spoken moments ago replayed in his mind. The two females shifted into a warm embrace, clinging to each other as Rosie whispered something into Lia's hair that made her eyes shine with silver.

He cleared his throat. "Let's go put our things in the room and wash up before supper."

They murmured an agreement and began up the stairs. Rosie caught him by the elbow before he moved.

"Be kind to tha one, she's still broken."

He nodded curtly before moving towards the stairs.

"OH," she called behind him, "and the booth at the back will be empty for yeh when yeh come back down," she finished with a wink.

Cal turned towards the stairs, his thoughts tripping to keep up with the pulsing tug in his chest.

LITHIA

Lithia pulled her body up the stairs towards the attic room. The strain in her muscles from riding and sleeping on the ground finally set in as the idea of a warm bed and a hot meal commandeered her thoughts.

After they ate, Lithia thought her stomach might burst. The stew was hearty, with tender chunks of beef and earthy vegetables in a fragrant broth. And Rosie kept refilling their bowls and rushing over with loaves of the buttery brown bread. When she first brought it out, she dramatically stage-whispered to Lia that she "knows it's Cal's favorite," which pulled a fond eye roll from the broody male. The way he ate nearly an entire loaf on his own, however, proved that to be an accurate assessment.

They had all finally had to tell her they were likely to keel over if they ate another bite when she tried to fill their bowls a third time, except for Tadhg, who was on his fourth, his stomach clearly a bottomless pit.

They sat in relative silence, watching the room bustle and move around them like a stone parting a stream. Guilt settled in the pit of Lia's stomach. She should be doing more not sitting here happily eating.

Wil leaned into her. "We'll find it."

Lithia turned a pained smile to her friend. "But will it be enough when we do?"

Wil shrugged, refilling her cup. "We won't know until we try."

Lithia smiled, clinking her cup to Wil's, as the door by the bar flew open and the largest male she had ever seen filled the threshold. He was tall and broad, wearing a leather vest that had nearly as many scars as his large, muscled arms. His oily hair was a deep blue, pulled back at the base of his skull. The look on his face was nothing short of feral as he scanned the bar with his sharp, ice-blue eyes. No, not eyes, eye. Where his left eye should have been was a gnarled, raised scar that cut through his eyebrow to the hollow of his cheek.

"Shit," Cal whispered, downing the rest of the ale from his cup.

Before she had time to register more, the male's gaze landed on their table, his lip curling into a snarl as he started in their direction, the crowd parting around him, desperate to avoid his warpath. Her hand went immediately to the hilt on her thigh, all but Cal doing the same.

"For the love of the goddess, do not draw your weapons. He's coming for me," Cal breathed, straightening in his seat and raising his chin.

"Calcas, you piece of rotting amphiptere dung, you owe me a fight."

Cal let out a slow breath. "Lovely as always to see you too, Jofin, but you'll find I don't owe you a fight, seeing as you got to keep all of my winnings."

The larger male, Jofin, it seemed, loomed over their table.

"You cost me several customers who decided I was no longer reliable when you didn't show up to your last fight." His scummy gaze scanned the table holding on Lithia's for a beat before cutting back to Cal. "You're up in an hour."

He turned on his heel, not acknowledging the rest of them. They watched as he stalked back to the door, swiping a large ale off the end of the counter on his way past. When the door closed behind him, four pairs of eyes landed on Cal. A muscle in his jaw ticked as he breathed heavily through his nose, his shadows writhing around his arm.

"Who the hell was that?" Narcos asked, narrowing accusing eyes at Calcas.

"Jofin," Calcas said with a sigh, "runs the fighting ring that operates below the Cork and Dagger, as well as several similar spots throughout Suviel."

"I've never heard of a fighting ring here."

"Well, you wouldn't have, given it isn't typically somewhere you would find the son of a Prime whose tunic costs as much as half the fighters make in a year."

A red flush crept up Narcos's neck.

"You are just as pampered as I am, Cal, despite your determination to pretend otherwise. If the gilded slipper fits, wear it," Narcos bit out.

Cal's eyes narrowed on Narcos, fingers twitching as he inhaled through his teeth.

Wil's hand came down hard on the table. "That's more than enough," she hissed, eyes flitting between them.

She narrowed her eyes knowingly at Cal, a conversation passing between them in silence. Lithia made a note to pry information out of Wil later if Cal didn't cough it up.

"I used to fight in his rings regularly. When I left, it was rather unexpected and I missed a couple of already scheduled fights. It sounds like he lost a few wealthier customers because of it, so he's making me fight tonight to make up for it. Should be fun."

Cal refilled his drink and swallowed it in one.

"Why did you leave?" Lithia asked, a sinking feeling in her gut.

He paused, looking over her before grimacing into his drink. "I was unceremoniously dragged back into polite society for a new queen."

Wil's knee made contact with Lia's, signaling for her to stop her line of questioning as Cal stood from the table and stalked up the stairs, cutting her off. She tracked his progress until he disappeared around the corner of the landing.

"Well, I guess we're watching a fight." Tadgh said, leaning back in his chair.

The fighting ring had the metallic scent of blood mixed with the noxious body odor of the greasy-looking fae around its perimeter. The ring was more of a cage. High iron bars set into the sandy floor. They were all standing on a battered wooden deck, looking down on the fighters. A small girl swept the gouges and footprints from the floor of the ring to ready it for the next fight.

Looking over the gathered fae, Lithia watched as money changed hands and females clung to the wealthiest patrons. There was a clear distinction between the assembled fae. Wealthy patrons in finely tailored tunics, many of their faces concealed in hoods or masks standing next to dirty-looking fae who appeared to have just been in a fight themselves.

Glancing around, she found Jofin standing near the open door to the ring, three of the wealthier looking males in front of him talking animatedly as they handed over heavy purses of coin. He bowed to each of the males before stepping into the ring and sending them up the steps to join the spectators.

The crowd ebbed and churned as the gathered fae found their places around the ring. As Lithia scanned the crowd, she felt a small nudge, drawing her eyes down to a terrified youngling beside her. She glanced quickly back at the fighting ring before turning and kneeling down beside the small girl.

"What in the goddess's name are you doing in a place like this."

Tears lined the girl's eyes as she stared wide-eyed at Lithia.

"Can you speak? Do you understand me?"

The small girl nodded slowly and eked out a small "yes."

Lithia placed a hand on the girl's shoulder and noticed her trembling. The sound of the fight ringing behind her.

"Come, stand with me and do *not* watch the fight. You shouldn't be here, it isn't safe."

She stood and tucked the youngling into her side, shielding her face from the fight. When she looked up, she found Wil watching her, worry etched into her features as she glanced between the youngling and the greasy male in the center of the ring.

"Good evening, my lovely guests," his voice, magically amplified, boomed through the pit. The magic containing it to this room must be extremely strong, given how it rattled Lithia's teeth.

Jofin's sour smile landed on her as he continued, malice flickering in his eyes.

"I have the most delicious of treats for you tonight. One of your favorites has returned" —he flourished his arm dramatically towards the entrance door— "the Shadow of the South!"

The roar was near deafening as Cal strode out into the sandy pit. He had changed into a pair of leather leggings, all weapons removed except for the sword held tightly in his hand. His chest was bare, showing his tanned skin and corded muscle marred with small scars. His swirling black tattoos were on full display.

"The rules, as always, are simple. To the death. Magic is allowed, especially given his opponent.

Judging by the set of Cal's jaw, something was coming, and it wasn't what he planned for.

"His challenger for the evening is one of the most fearsome creatures to crawl this plane." Jofin paused for an excruciatingly long moment as he backed toward the door to the ring, his grin turning feral. "The hema!"

Lithia's stomach threatened to revolt as a door opened in the sandy bottom of the pit and the first of the hema's eight legs emerged.

LITHIA

As the monstrous spider pulled itself onto the sand, Lithia pulled the youngling further into her, determined to shield her. How the fuck did Jofin even have access to a hema? They were notoriously territorial and rarely left their nests in the mountains. Its body was enormous, nearly as tall as Calcas, though it was likely small for its kind, and covered in iridescent hairs that reflected the light as it moved across the sand. Each of its eight legs was adorned with black spurs that glinted in the light.

Most lethal, however, were the fangs, long and curved, oozing with venom. Ordinarily, these massive creatures would be frightening because of a small gland on their back that they could use to secrete a powerful hallucinogen into the air. These hallucinations created visions of extreme rage, often causing their attackers to turn on each other before they ever reached the nest. This creature, judging by the large scar on its back, has been divested of that defense mechanism.

Lithia watched, chewing on the inside of her cheek, the taste of metal coating her tongue as Cal circled the ring. Eight glistening legs moved with unsettling grace across from him as beady eyes sized him up. Cal adjusted his grip on his sword, shifting his circle to bring him closer to the hema. As soon as the creature sensed the altered course, it reared up on its hind legs, its massive fangs clicking ominously.

"Come on then," Cal roared.

The hema lunged, its legs skittering across the sand in a blur of motion. Calcas swung out as a leg came spearing towards him and he twisted, barely dodging the strike. On his next turn, Cal's blade found a home in one of the hema's leg joints, making its legs flail wildly as it screeched in pain.

Lithia dug her nails into her palms as she watched Cal struggle to keep track of all eight legs. Sweat dripped from his face, his breath coming in ragged gasps. He feinted left, his shadows unfurling and cutting off the legs on the hema's right. As its body tilted, Cal drove his sword into its underbelly. The hema shrieked, its remaining legs twitching erratically.

One of its legs came up, catching Cal in the chest, a barb finding a home in his side and tearing a ribbon of flesh from his body. Cal screamed as he pulled his blade up through the hema's body, rending it in two, thick black blood oozing onto the sand.

The ring went silent as Cal's breaths sawed in and out for another moment before the sound erupted again.

Wil moved closer to Lithia as the crowd jostled them to get a closer look at the carnage.

"Why did that feel so ... easy?" Lithia asked, yelling to be heard.

"I doubt Cal would call it easy, but did you see the blood at the end? Not to mention it was already injured. They removed its toxin gland. Given it's a magical being, I would think it's like removing a limb."

"No doubt it's more profitable for Jofin if the hema dies," Lithia added, disgust lacing her tone.

Lithia stroked the hair of the youngling still clinging to her leg. "Now, what to do with you?"

Tadhg and Narcos filtered over from their places elsewhere in the ring, and the swirl of patrons quickly slipped through the few doors and into the night. As the room began to clear, Lithia knelt in front of the small fae.

"Out with it, what are you doing in a place like this?"

An abashed smile crept across the girl's face.

"We come here to pick up the loose coins."

"We?" Lithia said at the same time Tadhg barked a laugh and said, "*loose coins*?"

The girl looked down at her ratty slippers.

"My brother and I."

"And just what do you really mean by pickup loose coins?"

Cal stumbled up to the group with a small boy, slightly taller than the girl at her side, with a wide grin on his face and a small pouch in his hands. The girl's eyes went wide as dinner plates.

"Elias!" she hissed, "Someone is going to come looking for that much."

Lithia chuckled. "Ah so these loose coins, they wouldn't happen to reside in people's pockets, would they?"

The girl looked down again, a red flush creeping up her neck. Elias blushed deeply as well.

"I didn't steal this one though, Ayla! He gave it to me!"

The group all turned their gaze to Cal.

His wheezing breaths turned to a laugh, "I did give it to him, but after I caught him trying to steal from Jofin." He turned to the boy. "You can have it on the promise you won't come back here to steal or to fight."

Elias bounced eagerly on his toes.

Lithia stood looking down at the boy, a crease forming between her brows.

"Why are you stealing, anyway? Where are your parents?"

Both children shrank further into themselves.

Elias straightened, sniffling, "Our parents died when we were little, our brother raises us, but he's—"

He looked to his sister.

"He was working with the blacksmith; he has an affinity for metals. A few months ago, his magic—"

"HIS MAGIC IS GONE AND NO ONE WILL EMPLOY HIM," Elias blurted, his face going an ashen grey after.

Lithia froze in shock. She blinked rapidly, turning to Wil.

Wil nodded. "I'll get a message to Neda." She turned and slipped up the stairs.

"Okay, take this money home tonight and ask your brother to come meet us here in the morning. We want to talk to him about his magic, it's important."

They agreed excitedly, Ayla jumping to hug Cal, who groaned in pain.

She jumped back, apologizing, before coming back to hug Lia.

"What's your name?" the girl asked, wide eyed.

Lia smiled, squatting down to bring herself to eye level with the girl.

"My name is Lithia Caileanach."

Ayla's eyes went wide and she squealed, hugging Lia before turning to drag her equally wide-eyed brother out a small door to the left of the arena.

"Do you think it was smart to give her your name?" Cal asked, as Tadhg slid in to help support his weight.

Lithia's gaze turned cold.

"It is mine to give."

Calcas

T he ache had settled fully into Cal's body by the time he reached the attic room, leaning heavily on Tadhg's shoulder. The hema got in several good shots but that barb to the side may have done more damage than he thought, now that he could feel every breath like a bolt of lightning. Once in the room, he dropped hard onto one of the mattresses on the floor, groaning in pain as his sore limbs jostled.

"Let me get my healing supplies. Do you want a drink?"

Cal groaned. "A strong one, please."

Tadhg chuckled as he pulled the bandages and tinctures from his bag, along with a copper flask. He flopped down on the floor beside the mattress and handed the flask to Cal as he sorted through the supplies. Cal drank deeply from the flask, the floral notes of the gin burning a path down his throat. Tadhg watched him for a moment before holding his hand out to take the flask. Cal took another drag before handing it over.

"They mostly look superficial, so I'll let you deal with them, but that one," he said, gesturing to the still bleeding gash near his ribs, "needs to be healed. Do you need something to bite on?"

Cal shook his head and laid back. Tadhg poured gin on the wound without warning and Cal let out a string of curses. Then, carefully, he cleaned the wound, concentration etched into his features. Pain licked at his nerves as if he was flaying the skin from Cal's body as he began to sweat. Tadhg grimaced, shaking his head to himself, sifting through the bag again.

"What?" Cal grunted through clenched teeth.

"Something is wrong. You shouldn't be bleeding so heavily. Do you mind if I—"

He held his hand up.

Cal gave him a curt nod, his jaw flexing. Why was it so goddess-damned hot?

The same warm golden glow as before filled the space between his body and Tadhg's hand, and oddly warm sensation flowing through his body and pulling like a tide.

"Shit, I'll be back."

"What are you—" Cal started, but Tadgh was out the door in a blur of motion.

He laid back, staring at the old wood of the ceiling, his breathing loud in his ears, sweat rolling down his temples. The door opened and multiple pairs of feet moved towards him. Rolling his head, he found Tadhg and Wil with matching looks of concern on their faces speaking quickly. After a few moments, Tadhg took his spot beside Cal and Wil kneeled by his head.

"Cal, part of the barb broke off and is lodged by your lung. We are going to have to get it out. I'm going to hold you down."

Wil's voice was soft, which scared him more than her words. He nodded, or at least he was pretty sure he nodded. Wil laid warm hands on his shoulder and her magic fizzled through him, locking his limbs in place. Pain like white-hot lighting shot through his body, searing every nerve ending.

Everything was pain and he was nothing.

He cracked his eyes open. The pain had settled to a dull ache. The room was dark and silent, with no indicator of the time. Shifting his weight, he rolled. Tadhg's hands appeared at his sides to help maneuver him into a sitting position and to slide a pillow behind him where he leaned on the wall. He nodded his thanks. Tadhg plopped back down in the small nest of blankets he had made by the mattress, offering Cal some of the food on the large platter between them. He grabbed a large piece of herb bread and took slow bites.

Tadhg looked exhausted, his shirt still stained with Cal's blood and dark circles beneath his violet eyes. His curly silver hair looked like he had run his hands through it several times. He took in small silver tattoos on the male's ears, curling up to the point, standing out starkly on his warm brown skin. A thought itched at the back of his mind and he stared at the other fae taking in his features as if a puzzle had plopped itself in his lap.

Suddenly something clicked into place. The elegant features reminded him starkly of Halos.

"Tadhg?"

He turned his weary eyes towards Cal and smiled.

"You can ask. I can practically hear your brain working."

Cal huffed but relented easily, his curiosity nudging him.

"Are you related to the Celestial Prime? You look strikingly like Halos."

His warm smile turned strained.

"Halos is my half brother. We share a father, though I don't think I've spoken to either since I left for the legion. I always tell the story that my being conscripted was because of my birth order, but in truth, I was a bastard that they wanted to hide."

Cal grimaced, at the guilt that he had scratched an old wound.

"Well, since we are sharing, can I ask about the fighting? Is that where you disappeared to after the battle in the Valley of Atropin?"

Cal took a long drink from the water jug by the bed and leaned his head back on the wall.

"When I left that command tent after it was over, the last of me broke. My mate was gone, the only person I trusted no longer trusted me, and I had been relieved of my command. I stumbled back to Dragos, the rage building with every step. I was standing in the street looking at the lights of my childhood home and I wanted to burn it all to the ground. So I stumbled into a tavern and drank until I was dumb enough to get into a fight. Jofin found me there."

Tadgh opened his mouth to reply, his brow creased. A voice from the door answered before he could.

"*Mate*?" Lithia's eyes were wide and lined in silver, her chest heaving.

Cal's head whipped to the door, his breath halting. She turned and left without waiting for a response.

"Fuck," he said, slamming his head back to the wall.

"Well, that'll make for a fun evening I'm sure," Tadhg said with a frown. "Well, I should probably stop sitting here covered in blood. I healed a good portion of that wound since the blade did damage on its way out. You'll be weak for a few hours because it pulls from your magic and mine. I'll do another round in the morning after I finish with Lia's."

He stood up and moved towards the wash basin, un-tucking his tunic and pulling it over his head. Cal let out an involuntary hiss. On his back were two nearly identical vertical scars. Gnarled and raised, they ran from each shoulder blade to the middle of his back. Tadhg silently washed the blood from his arms before returning to his blanket nest.

"I take it you hadn't considered that I was a Celestial Fae and should have wings."

"You don't have to tell me, Tadhg."

He shrugged.

"Bastards don't deserve wings. Especially a bastard with no air magic."

Cal's head tilted, brows furrowed.

Shrugging, Tadhg continued, "I suspect had they known I was a healer, it would have gone differently. Lucky for me, I had been in the legion for five years before my abilities appeared."

He glanced at Cal's still confused and righteously angry face.

"I was treated better by the legion than I ever would as the bastard son of the Prime held as their court healer. My wings were taken as a youngling; I don't remember much." A smile slid across his face when he added, "Lithia told me about those shadow wings she made. That means you have to be the one to teach her to fly."

Cal broke into laughter. Tadhg clearly didn't need his pity, so he wouldn't give it to him.

"Fine, leave me with the baby dragon."

They ate the remainder of the food in silence before sleep won out.

LITHIA

Her feet pounded on the stairs. That word echoed in her ears and clanging through her brain. The thread in Lia's chest pulsed.

Mate.

Mate.

Mate.

It was like losing her all over again. Seren left a void in Lia's chest. She knew, of course, that Cal and Seren loved each other. There were no secrets, no whispers of unfaithfulness, because they had all known. Mates, though, that was different altogether. She always assumed that when the time came, Seren would be her mate. Fated mates were a rarity, the goddess of love keeping that blessing sacred. Bound mates, however, were much more common. The unions were blessed by the temple, their soul threads

223

wound together by the priestesses. Bound was what she would be to Nars, assuming they didn't die first.

Had they been soul bound? How could they do that without telling her? She always felt the tug in her chest and knew that Seren was her fated; she thought Seren knew too. Her breath came in heaving pants as she reached the bottom of the stairs. Her gaze swept around the room, finding Narcos and Wil in deep conversation. She skirted around the other side of the room, making for the door.

Slipping into the cool night air, she finally took a full breath. Her eyes scanned the square, warm lights floating in the air and the murmur of drunken conversation filling her senses. Her heart slammed in her chest and turning, she made her way towards a quieter street. She wandered down the cobbled street, looking at all the businesses that had long since closed for the evening.

She was dizzy, as though the world had been knocked off course. She looked around at the quiet street and realized that maybe it wasn't the world that was off course. Perhaps she had simply had her center of gravity struck by the betrayal and she needed to find it again. She needed something comforting.

Peering into one large diamond-paned window, she took in the rows and rows of books. A window seat surrounded by leafy plants cradled a rather large cat curled on its cushion. Oh, to be a cat in a bookseller's window. A few shops down, light spilled from the window of a small bakery. She stepped inside and found a male with a kind round face cleaning the inside of his display case. He looked up and flashed her a warm smile.

"I'm cleaning up for the evening, but I still have a few pastries left if you want one."

Lithia pushed a smile onto her face.

"Yes please, do you have any moonberry?"

He smiled warmly. "I do believe I have some moonberry tart left."

She took a seat on one of the high stools as he shuffled around the counter. He rustled around for a few minutes before returning with a small square tart on a plate and slid it onto the counter in front of her. She took a bite and nearly moaned. The tart berry flavor bursting on her tongue while the buttery crust melted in her mouth.

The baker laughed. "Those were always my daughter's favorites too."

He slid her a cup of tea and went back to his nightly cleaning, leaving her to her thoughts and the pastry in front of her. She finished the pastry in a few bites, her head still swimming with confusion. The older male flipped his closed sign, and she stood, reaching in her pockets for her coin bag. Seeing her motion, the older fae smiled and shook his head.

"It was an honor to serve you, High Queen."

He reached behind the counter and pulled out a paper bag.

"For your companions."

Then he walked her to the door, bowing as she left.

Standing on the street, she blinked hard a few times at the bag in her hand before laughing and making her way back towards the Cork & Dagger. A scuffle sound in the alley to her left drew her attention, and she paused, moving to the wall of the shop to listen.

"You know she told us to stay out of the towns. We draw attention," a low voice hissed.

"I know, but I swear, the kid said that the queen was here. If we were the ones to find her—"

"That is not our job, you're going to get us both killed. We need to get back to camp before anyone notices your stupidity and she kills us both."

The scraping footsteps began to fade as they moved towards the far end of the alley. Lithia peeked around the corner, seeing the shape of two armed voxis before they turned the corner. Shit. She took off towards the inn, trying to calm her pounding heart as she reentered the Cork & Dagger. A glance around the room told her Narcos and Wil were likely upstairs. She huffed a sigh as she snaked her way toward the stairs and a room full of people likely pissed at her for leaving.

She took the stairs two at a time, nearly running into Cal's chest as she passed the shared washroom on their floor. He hissed in pain, stumbling back into the wall, and she reached out a hand that he quickly pushed aside. He sidestepped her, and she stood there another moment before continuing toward their rooms. When she got to the door, she could hear a low argument beyond and winced as she opened the door, three heads whipping in her direction.

"I brought pastries," she said, holding the bag up.

Wil looked back to Narcos with a raised brow, gesturing at Lia before plopping onto the bed. Tadhg swiped the bag from her hand, moving to sit beside Wil. She rolled her eyes with a laugh before looking back to Narcos, who was glaring at her.

"Where in the hell did you go? Why would you go out alone at all?"

She made her way to the other bed, unstrapping her baldric as she went and tossing it on the bed. Looking back at Narcos, his face had softened some but the tension around his eyes remained.

"It wasn't a great idea but I'm fine, I just—" She sighed. "I needed some air."

"I told you she would be fine, Narcos. She's scarier than most of us, anyway," Wil said with a wink to Lia as she bit into a sticky-looking bun.

"Holy shit, I'm not even mad, these are delicious. Feel free to sneak away for sweets whenever you like," Tadhg said, his cheeks full.

Cal scoffed, stepping into the room and leaning on the door frame. "Didn't you just eat?"

Tadhg shrugged, taking another large bite.

"I apologize if I worried you but I did overhear something concerning." She leaned forward, resting her elbows on her knees. "There were a couple voxis in the alley near the bakery who seemed to be looking for me. They said that *the kid* said the queen was here."

Cal shifted from leaning on the door frame to standing straight, his brows pulling further down. "So, I was right that you shouldn't have told that little thief your name."

"Oh fuck off, Calcas."

She waited a beat, staring at him. His silence echoing in the room.

"I think they likely just overheard her. It's not like I have been hiding who I am."

She turned back to the others, ignoring the glare she could feel leveled on the side of her face.

"Anyway, they also said that *she* told them to stay out of the towns, and *she* would kill them if they didn't get back to camp."

The room was silent.

Wil cleared her throat. "So, we were right to be concerned that they were organizing again. It's happening again."

Lithia nodded. "We can rotate a watch; we need to rest. To-morrow, while Cal and I, talk to the tiny thieves, the rest of you can quietly ask around and see if anyone knows where this camp is."

Cal sat back down on the mattress with a grunt. "I'll take watch. I just woke up anyway."

They all mumbled their agreement. Wil slipped down into her bed as Tadgh made his way to the other mattress on the floor. Lithia pulled off her boots and shuffled off her leggings, folding them before setting them on the floor by her boots. In her loose tunic and undershorts, she slid into the bed, Narcos at her back, and fell asleep as her head hit the pillow.

Calcas

He sat against the wall, watching the clouds roll across the sky as dawn crept into the sky. He watched the others slowly wake with the sun, pulling themselves from their beds and quietly getting ready for the day. Once the last of them woke and began dressing, he slipped out of the room to the tavern below. He could feel Lithia's eyes on him and he knew she was going to corner him before the younglings got here and he needed an out.

Rosie had the same table as the previous evening set with breakfast for them. He sat, piling a plate with bacon and hash and peppery fried eggs. After downing several pieces of bacon and his second cup of tea, the others joined him, quietly digging into the best breakfast they would likely have for a while.

"I think we should do what we can to leave Mt. Haven by noon," Lithia said, setting her teacup down with a clink. "Tadhg,

Nars, gather supplies for the next leg. We'll stop at the fort in the pass to drop the horses, but they won't have many provisions to restock us, so get extra and make your inquiries as you go." Both males nodded and moved to leave the table.

"I already have plans to seek out my contacts," Wil said, sliding off the bench behind the others.

Cal sat, watching the wheels turn in Lithia's midnight eyes. She picked up her cup and leaned back on her bench, watching him over the rim as she took a sip.

He broke her gaze and sat back, watching the other patrons mosey down the stairs following the smell of bacon.

"Cal."

The muscles in his shoulders tightened as his eyes slid back to Lithia. She tracked his movement, a smug smirk barely kept itself from her face, her mouth tipping at the corner. He hardened his heart. His only defense to having this conversation was going to have to be pissing her off.

"What did you mean by mate?"

He scoffed, "You are my queen, but I do not owe you my secrets."

"You're right, you owe me no secrets."

He moved to take another sip of his tea but stopped just short of his mouth at her voice.

"You do, however, owe me your life."

She waited. Her glare, hot on his skin.

He sighed, hanging his head. "This conversation is too important to have right now, Lia."

"Then when are we supposed to have it? Why were the last ten years not good enough?"

"I'm–"

He took a deep breath turning towards her in time to see the hurt well in her eyes. At the same moment, the door opened and the two small fae from the night before stepped over the threshold.

"I'm just not ready," he finished lamely.

"Is it fair of you to get to be the only one who decides that?"

Lia shifted in her seat with a smile and waved over the younglings. The hurt in her eyes had been replaced with a false joy, her shoulders relaxed and the smile on her face had settled into a softness he had rarely seen from her.

"Elias, Ayla, thank you for coming back to talk to me. Where is your brother?"

Ayla scooted in close to Lia and threw her arms around her middle. She tensed before placing an arm around the small girl as she beamed up at her.

"He's on his way. He stopped to talk to Miss. Rosie."

"He'll never make it then," Cal said, winking at Elias, who was shoving bacon into his mouth.

They sat quietly watching the two shovel an enormous amount of food into their mouths. Ayla wriggled in her seat, chattering an endless stream of nonsense to Lia, crumbs flying from her mouth. Lia sat calmly listening along, though he was sure she couldn't understand a word she said.

"Kieran! Over here!"

Cal turned and watched as a tall male with broad shoulders and muscled arms made his way across the room, greeting a few others before settling on the bench beside Elias and ruffling his hair. The three siblings looked so similar, with deep brown hair streaked, emerald eyes framed with thick lashes and freckles dotted across fair skin.

Kieran bowed to Lia. "Mo Bhanrighit, it is an honor that you wanted to speak to me." Then to Cal, he offered a more contained nod. "Heir Calcas."

Cal's eyebrows rose impressed. "I'm impressed that you recognize me."

Kieran's ears flushed pink. "I actually met you once, when I was a youngling. I was traveling with the blacksmith to Dragos to visit the goldsmith. You let me try to hold your morning star and it nearly pulled my shoulder from its socket."

Cal laughed. "You look like you could wield it properly now."

Kieran's flush deepened, but he sat up a bit straighter in his chair.

Lia's quiet voice cut into their introduction, "I'm sorry to jump to the point, but would you mind telling us about your magic?"

His shoulders fell once more as he looked down at his rough hands, peppered with small burns and scars, before looking back to Lia, his brows knit together.

"Are you going to fix it?"

Lia's smile fell a fraction.

"We are going to try. We are hoping your story can give us a little insight as to how it happens."

He nodded in silence for a few moments before taking a shaky breath.

"We are all Hearth fae. Their higher magics haven't developed yet, but mine had. I have—" He sighed. "*had* an affinity for metals. I started to apprentice with the smith when I was thirteen and I worked with him for nearly twenty years. I was especially good with blades, daggers being my favorite."

He pulled a small dagger from his belt and handed it to Cal. The blade was light and perfectly balanced. The double-edged blade was wickedly sharp with a mesmerizing pattern subtly etched into the steel that caught the light in loops and swirls. The hilt was a rich ebony wood inlaid with steel detailing. Intricate floral and vine patterns snaked their way around the grip. In the crossguard, he could make out a set of runes that matched the ones running down Lia's arms.

He moved to pass it back to Kieran, but he smiled and shook his head.

"It's for her," he said, nodding to Lithia.

She took it, eyes wide, like she had never been given a gift before. Cal watched as he passed her an equally intricate iron scabbard. When he turned back to Kieran, he found a proffered blade similar to the one he had given Lia. He took the gift, heat prickling the back of his throat. Looking down, he found that this hilt had been inlaid to make it resemble the scales of the amphipter that roamed the skies of his home court.

"Thank you. I'm honored."

Kieran looked down as the tips of his ears turned pink once again.

"Anyway, it was about six months ago. I was working and nothing was coming out properly. I thought maybe I had just been working too much, but we needed the coin, so I pushed through. It just got worse until three months ago when it was gone. I couldn't pull on my magic at all. There wasn't any way for me to continue working for the smith, which is how these two ended up in the arena last night." He threw a glare at his siblings. "Even though they know better."

The small fae looked to have been thoroughly chastised about the issue before they arrived.

"That's all of it? Did you notice anything that may have triggered it, like an odd interaction, weather patterns, an injury?" Lia asked, leaning forward in her seat.

"Not that I can think of. All sorts come to a forge, so plenty of interactions were odd and injuries as well."

"Could you feel anything else, or was it just there then gone?"

"I felt it like the strength leaving me; I got sickly and tired. More so as time went by. Even now I don't have but half the strength I used to have. I feel like I heal slower as well."

Lithia sat back, chewing on her lip.

Cal leaned into the table, turning his back on the room at large to cover his words as much as he could.

"Do you know if you have interacted with any voxis recently?"

His eyes grew wide, and his breathing altered.

"It's okay, you aren't in trouble."

He darted a look around the room.

"Before I started losing my magic, one of them came in and asked if we could fill a large weapons order. Arrows, broadswords, and spears, mostly. The smith told him to get lost, but I wasn't sure why they thought to come to us in the first place because we haven't ever been in the business of arming the voxis."

"Thank you so much for speaking to us. Please, stay and eat. I'll be back."

"Wait," Kieran said, chewing his lip. "Am I ... am I going to go missing?"

Lia shot Cal a concerned look. "Why would you think that?"

"It's just the other fae that have lost their magic have gone missing a little while later."

Cal leaned forward. "All of them? Do you know of any that have gone missing with their magic intact?"

"As far as I know, all of the ones from here that are missing lost their magic first."

Kieran looked between them, confused, before Lithia stood, dropping a kiss on Ayla's head.

"Thank you, Kieran."

She slipped from the table and made quickly for the door. Kieran pulled a plate of pastries towards himself and grinned at Cal.

"Did she just leave you with babysitting duty?"

Cal rolled his eyes and swiped the apple tart from Kieran's hand. "She can't help herself."

He popped the whole tart in his mouth as Ayla started her never ending stream of mindless chatter again.

An hour later, Ayla had fallen asleep with her head on Kieran's lap, and Elias had roped them into a game of cards that seemed to be entirely made up and rigged for Elias to win. Just as Elias was winning the fifth round in a row, Wil and Lia stepped up to the side of the table with a man Cal didn't recognize.

Wil bowed in greeting. "My name is Willow. I sent word to Neda that the three of you will be taking up residence in the citadel."

Kieran straightened so fast Cal was surprised his spine didn't audibly snap.

"Neda? The Legion High General? *THE CITADEL*?"

He looked to Lia for some sort of assurance.

She smiled that warm smile.

"Yes, please allow me to shelter you in my home. The blacksmith there will take you on as an apprentice so you can learn to work again without the aid of your magic, as several of my best armors do."

"One of my contacts is going to escort you to the capital. Neda and the Arcane Prime will be there to greet you. Be safe."

Kieran shot up from his seat, Cal barely catching Ayla before she hit her head, and ran around the table, throwing his arms around Lithia.

"Thank you," he whispered into her shoulder.

She hugged him back, something in her eyes more hollow than happy.

LITHIA

Kieran followed Wil from the tavern, talking quietly about what all they had room to bring. The two younger fae happily bounced out after them, likely entirely unsure what just happened. Lia watched as Ayla skipped up and grabbed Wil's hand and began her endless chatter. She wasn't sure how one small fae could have so much to say.

She turned back to the table to find Cal gone and just caught a glimpse of the heel of his boot as he rounded the stairs, disappearing from sight, running from her again. Rolling her eyes, she turned to follow him, but two steps in, Rosie stepped into her path.

"I know yer plannin' on leavin' before lunch, so I made yeh somethin' yeh can eat on yer way."

She took the linen bag from Rosie and looked inside, finding enough meat hand pies to feed a group twice their size. She opened a smaller paper sack and found a single moonberry tart. She turned back to Rosie's cheerful face and grinned, leaning in to kiss the older fae on the cheek.

"Bah. Anything for ye lot. Mr. Honeycourt, the baker, told me to sneak yeh that tart, so don' let that hungry one get to it."

She winked, squeezing Lia's hand before bustling away to fuss at one of her girls. The door swung open and Tadhg, the hungry one in question, came striding in, Narcos a few steps behind him. He sniffed the air as he got close to her, a smile spreading on his face.

"Do I smell food?"

Lia slapped his hand as it started for the bag.

"Yes, but it's not for you to eat now, it's lunch."

He opened his mouth to respond just as one of Rosie's girls popped up beside them, blushing furiously.

"Ma'am said to bring this to yeh, sir."

She held a plate out to Tadhg, who took it with a thank you. His eyes lit as he picked up the hand pie on it and took a large bite before hustling across the room to kiss Rosie full on the mouth. They laughed as she swatted him with her tea towel, blushing furiously and shooed him away.

"Everything is ready to go once Wil gets back," said Narcos, who then turned to Tadhg. "Will you run up and let Calcas know we are ready to leave?"

Tadhg bounded up the stairs, still happily munching his pastry.

Narcos reached out, pulling Lithia closer to him, arms slung low on her waist, and nuzzled her neck.

"That was a sweet thing you did for those younglings, Mo Lunath."

She closed her eyes leaning into his warmth. "I couldn't leave them here to starve."

"No." He pulled back and kissed her on her nose. "You could have, but you didn't."

Then he walked out the door leaving her feeling unsteady once again.

Lia nudged Daylis forward and slowly made her way down the side street she had wandered down the night before, bowing to the baker as she passed. The narrow, cobbled streets were a bustle of activity this morning. People flitted from shop to shop, groups gathered talking, a florist was braiding pixie's breath blooms into the hair of a gaggle of younglings while they talked animatedly.

She forced herself to smile at people as she passed, a pit growing in her gut as they drew closer to the reaches of Mt. Haven. The buildings shrank and grew sparse. Cobbled roads lined with shops flattened to a wide dirt road flanked by farmland. An hour after the city faded behind them, she reached into her bag and tossed them all lunch, quietly eating her moonberry tart as she rode.

By the time they pulled to the side of the road to camp, the sun was setting, quickly slipping beneath the horizon. They made a small fire in a pit on the open plane, sitting quietly around it and eating the last of the hand pies from Rosie. The chill of the evening had begun to settle when Wil returned from setting up wards. The wards likely weren't even necessary, as they could see someone coming easily in the flat landscape.

When Wil had settled in her seat and finished eating, Lithia nudged her.

"Did you find anything out about the voxis camp in town today?"

Wil tilted her head to the side.

"Yes and no. Many of the people I spoke to have had more interactions than usual with the voxis as of late. However, they seem to be attempting to blend in when they come into town and none of them have started any trouble."

The others quieted their low conversation as Wil spoke.

"Has anyone seen where they are coming from or going to?"

"Not that I can tell. Most didn't even recognize them as voxis until they had been interacting with them for a while. Apparently, they are coming in disguised when they can."

Lithia nodded, brow knit in thought.

"Did you get an idea of what they were in town for?" came Narcos's low voice.

"It seemed they were seeking out supplies, rations, cloth, weapons, medicine. They are certainly gathering in large numbers somewhere."

"That is deeply concerning. Do you think the ones near Mab's tree in The Singing Wood were near the camp?" Narcos asked, his face pinched.

"It's possible. I think it's also likely that they have spread themselves out more than we realize. If they are that close to Mt. Haven, who knows what other cities they are close to."

Lia's face twisted in thought. "Send crows in the morning to Neda and the Primes. Have them look for evidence of voxis gathering supplies elsewhere. When we spoke to the younglings today, he told us a voxis had come to buy weapons but the smith turned them away. Try to get any information on what kind of supplies they have gathered as well."

"He also told us that all of the missing fae had lost their magic before going missing." Cal looked up from the dagger in his hand, his eyes locking with Wil's. "This isn't something we connected before. We thought the numbers were separate or that any overlap was coincidental. Have them check on the voided fae and compare the records we have to look for the pattern."

"We should have someone keep an eye on Jofin as well," said Narcos. "That hema wasn't a random find, and it bled black like the voxis in the woods. He could be trading with them."

Cal nodded. "Even if he's not, he may lead you to a place where the voiding is infecting other creatures."

"Either way, I'll have one of my crows keep an eye on him. He seems the kind to want to talk," Wil agreed with a nod.

Lia spoke, her eyes fixed far beyond their group. "Everyone get some rest. I want to leave at sunrise so we make it to the valley by nightfall. I can take first watch."

They mumbled good nights and dispersed into their own spaces before slipping into their own dreams. As their breathing turned deep and even, Lia stared into the sky, watching as the stars popped into existence, the night sighing deeply around her.

CALCAS

They rode hard through the day, watching as the Tipping Peaks grew larger. The flatness of the plain gave them no respite from the sun, and it beat down on his neck. Around midday, he had pulled a thin piece of fabric from his bag and draped it around his head and shoulders to give himself the smallest relief.

The plain started to narrow, the rushing sound of the river growing louder as they approached the mouth of the valley. The Idris River originated high in the mountains, forming Lake Clotho in the western bowl of the valley before snaking its way towards the southern coast. As the road began to bend north, the Idris came into sight, crashing and tumbling over rocks as it roared past.

Slowly the road came level with the river as it widened and smoothed, a blue-grey ribbon cutting through the land. The mountains loomed over them as they slowed, a patrol blocking the road into the valley. Cal pulled back, allowing Lithia to approach first. She dismounted Daylis quickly and passed the reins to Narcos, walking the last stretch to the waiting patrol.

As Lithia approached, the gathered patrol of sentinels snapped to attention and bowed.

"I apologize, Mo Bhanrighit, but we can't let anyone into the valley after dark," said the young sentinel in the middle.

"Thank you. The road is closed at nightfall? Why is that?" Lithia said, motioning for them to straighten.

They tentatively looked around before deferring to the older fae.

"In recent weeks we have noticed the lachis, the spirits in the valley, have grown more agitated. Before they behaved as you would expect from a shade, wandering aimlessly, not interacting. A few weeks ago, however, they began attacking patrols and travelers. We decided limiting access to the road after sunset was the safest option for now."

"It takes longer than a day to reach The Pass of Souls."

"Yes, Mo Bhanrighit. We have a waypoint set up in one of the old manors. Captain Marshhold is a Hearth fae and fortified the lower walls. It's not exactly comfortable, but it's safe for the night."

"Thank you. We will camp nearby for the night."

Lithia turned back to their group, a wrinkle forming between her brows as she reached back and twirled the end of her braid. She mounted Daylis in one swift motion and gestured back the way they came.

"Let's set up camp out of the way."

Out of the way most certainly meant out of earshot. They backtracked until the border station was just within sight before pulling into the soft grass opposite the river. So close to the valley the river was broad and slow. If you weren't paying attention it looked nearly still. The sun fully fell below the horizon by the time they sat down to eat. Narcos was the first to break the uneasy silence.

"Why weren't we warned about the lachis? Have they not let Neda know?"

Lia tilted her head to the side. "I know that she had reports about some incidents in the valley, but we both assumed them to be voxis attacks."

Wil leaned forward, placing her empty skewer at her feet.

"The lachis have never been violent before, they are simply misplaced spirits, doomed to wander until they find their way to Thahaos. There are many in the valley after the last battle, but they shouldn't be able to interact with the physical plane."

There were several minutes of silence before Cal spoke.

"This curse is upending eons of nature. The nassella were entirely too powerful for halflings, the voxis are solitary but gathering in large numbers, and now the lachis are able to cross the veil? The magic at work here is old."

Wil nodded, staring towards the mountains.

"I hope Thahaos's priestesses have some answers for us. I fear it is going to get far worse before it gets better."

The next morning, a pit settled in Cal's stomach as they passed the sentinels from the night before and entered the valley. There wasn't anything different about the road on the other side of the border, but a creeping dread hung in the air. A chill, like a sharp nail running down his spine, told him to leave this place where so much death clung to the air.

He noticed the others seemed to be shifting uncomfortably in their saddles as well, while Wil sat unnaturally still on her mount. The Valley of Atropin would be picturesque without the stench of death. The mountains curved around the valley like a crown while the Idris pooled into Lake Clotho, which reflected the sky like a mirror. On the far banks of Clotho, you could just make out the shapes of crumbling manor homes.

The valley had once been popular among the wealthy fae in the spring and summer months. The crystal clear water and lush valley were the perfect backdrop. After the final battle destroyed the majority of the homes and the dark aura settled, no one had come back to rebuild, so the once opulent manors continued to deteriorate as nature reclaimed them.

"The sentinel from last night said it likely won't take the whole day to reach the waypoint, but it isn't possible to make it the entire distance in a day," Lithia said pulling up beside him.

"It will give the horses a chance to rest some after the stretch yesterday."

Lithia nodded and moved forward until she was riding level with Narcos.

The morning passed quickly, the serene appearance of the valley at odds with the stifling energy. They stopped on the lake shore at midday and Tadhg tossed them all some dried rabbit and bread from the night before, and Lia pulled out a small bag of fruit for them to pick at.

While the surface of Lake Clotho reflected the bright blue sky from a distance, up close, you could almost be fooled into believing there was no water in front of you at all. The water from the mountain flowed so clear, you could count the individual pebbles on the lake bottom. Calcas always found the lake to be more eerie than beautiful, its clear water lulling you into its deceptively deep waters. Like most fae, he preferred the small lagoons and hot springs that could be found closer to the mountains, where the manors are situated.

"We are only a few more hours from the waypoint," Lithia said, refocusing his attention. "They have it set up in one of the larger manors. Hopefully that means we are able to get good rest, but with the lachis, I have a feeling that isn't going to happen."

"I hope the hot springs are close, because I could really use a bath," Tadhg said, sniffing at his shirt and grimacing.

"Trust me, I know." Wil chuckled, tightening the strap on the saddle bag.

Lithia stood staring out over the water, leaning into Narcos and whispering. Cal turned, nudging Tadhg towards the horses to give them a moment.

They made it to the first manor about two hours past midday. A large boulder sat nestled in what used to be its upper floors. The creeping vines had all but covered most of the intact façade, while small birds flitted in and out of its bones. The next few were much the same. One looked nearly whole, but scorch marks indicated the inside had been entirely consumed in fire.

Lia pulled them to a stop outside the most complete-looking home. It had an obvious hole on one end of the upper floors, but otherwise looked unscathed by battle. The lower floor had been blocked entirely with a thick stone wall. Just as Cal was going to ask how they were supposed to get in, a large section of wall lowered, exposing the front door. A tall fae that looked startlingly like Narcos stepped out.

As he got closer, it was clear he was likely several centuries older than Narcos, but the white blond hair and angular features were all there.

"Nephew, I got a letter from your sister a few days ago saying you would be coming this way!"

Cal looked to Narcos, who had a grimace plastered on his face that tugged at his scar and his knuckles were white around the reins.

"Uncle Calum. I didn't realize you were stationed in the pass. What did you do to deserve that honor?"

The older fae scoffed, "There's that self-importance you got from your father; I was sure it was in there somewhere."

Narcos pushed his chest out as he took a breath to respond, or more likely to berate his uncle, when Lia interrupted him.

"Do you not find it appropriate to address your High Queen before antagonizing her riding party?" Lithia raised her chin. "We are stopping at this waypoint out of necessity, Captain Marshhold. I will not have you disrespecting my companions, as they are all your superiors. Now, show us where to stable our horses and direct us to the nearest springs."

Calum blustered before bowing and mumbling out a greeting. Cal held back a chuckle, flashing a look at Tadhg and Wil and finding them doing the same. Calum barked a few commands over his shoulder before turning to show them into the small compound.

LITHIA

The lagoon was the softest milky blue color. Situated in a cavern below the manor like an underground bath, it was warm and inviting after riding for so long. Lithia sat on the edge submerged up to her collarbone with her head resting back on the stone lip. Above her, the cave wall glittered with condensation and streaks of bioluminescent algae, creating constellations throughout the space.

Narcos was to her left under the low waterfall that fed the lagoon, while Tadhg floated out in the middle. Cal was laid out on the far side, much like she was, though he seemed to have fallen asleep. Beside her, Wil sat running her fingers through the water, sending glittering ripples across the surface.

Lia smiled and looked back towards the cavern ceiling.

"Have you been to Thahaos's temple before?"

Wil didn't answer, so Lia looked back to find her staring at the swirling constellations on the ceiling as well. Thinking she was lost in thought and finished talking, Lia lay back and traced the swirling patterns as well.

"Many times," Wil responded in a low voice. "But not in a very long time."

Narcos moved toward them and Wil smiled a small smile and moved toward Cal. Settling in the spot Wil had just vacated, Narcos moved in close to Lia and laid his head back beside hers.

"My always hospitable uncle said he would prefer we were back in the main house by sundown."

Lia scoffed, "He's certainly full of himself. Why did he greet you like that?"

Narcos let out a small sigh. "He and my father grew up constantly pitted against each other. Twins and the oldest children, either had the right to be heir, and my Grandsire loved to dangle the position in front of them both. When he was fading, he named my father heir. Calum was always too hotheaded, too irrational. He is an excellent sentinel, but he never had the head for politics. I think had Grandsire made it clear when they were younger that they were better suited for different roles, he wouldn't have become so bitter, but it's far too late for that now."

Lia couldn't really imagine the dynamics of having so many siblings. The destiny of her family had been set: one daughter. Only one; there was never a spare, so family politics never really rooted in her brain because there was no need. She had gotten a crash course in sibling behavior when she first joined the legion, but even that seemed different from the dynamics at play in a family as large as Narcos's.

She turned her head, admiring the angular planes of his face glistening with the water of the lagoon. The ends of his hair that touched that water fanned out around him like a halo of white in the chalky blue pool. She reached up and traced the blunted tip of his ear, following the scar down to his mouth.

"I don't think I'll ever be able to tell you how sorry I am for this."

He smiled, his eyes closed as he grabbed her hand and kissed each of her fingertips.

"I'll tell you until I run out of breath that I don't need an apology. I would take that blade for you every time, in this life and the next, Mo Lunath."

She leaned over, kissing him softly. He ran his tongue along the seam of her lips, coaxing them apart as he deepened the kiss, pulling her against his side. A wave of water crashed over them and they pulled apart quickly, finding Tadhg with a self-satisfied grin staring back at them, slowly swimming away.

"This is a public lagoon, can't have anything upsetting my delicate sensibilities."

Narcos chuckled, resting his forehead on hers.

"I love you, Lia. I know you aren't ready to say it, but I love you enough for the both of us. I am, however, going to have to leave you while I drown Tadhg."

She laughed as he launched himself towards the guard, who turned and swam quickly away from Narcos's reaching hands. Cal frowned and Wil looked to Lia with a crooked smile on her face. Just as Lia turned back to the chaos that was Narcos attempting to catch Tadhg, an ear-splitting shriek ripped through the cavern.

High pitched and wailing, it echoed off the cavern walls. Everyone froze.

"What is—" Tadhg started but was cut off by another shrill scream, this one followed by a low thundering sound.

"It sounds like … a necsite, a water demon, but why would it be this far upriver?" Wil said in a panicked whisper. "Get out of the water. GET OUT NOW!" she screamed, pulling herself out of the water as a second scream pierced the air.

Cal and Lia followed quickly, Tadhg and Narcos swimming as hard as they could manage. They had ended up much further out than she realized.

"We have to do something."

"They can make—"

Another shriek, like nails gouging her ears. They clamped their hands over their ears as the necsite's head broke the surface. Seeming to be made of the water itself, the form of a massive warhorse rose from the surface, its eyes glowing red. It paused and tilted its head, watching the two fae swimming for the edge. It shook out its mane, its body rippling until it resembled the shape of a fae but stretched, with long limbs and a narrow face still set with those red eyes. It cracked a horrifying smile, its mouth full of jagged teeth like shards of sea glass.

They were so close. Lia knelt, holding a hand out, Cal and Wil mirroring the action beside her.

She screamed for the necsite to leave them be.

Screamed as the necsite lunged forward, latching onto two legs, its razor-sharp claws digging into flesh.

Screamed as hands disappeared into the swirling water just before she could reach them.

Screamed as two heads disappeared below the surface.

Lithia tried to jump into the water. Wil's powerful arms wrapped around her, her magic sinking into Lia's skin, bringing her to her knees. A blur of motion flew past her as Calcas dove into the water. She would not allow anyone to take that risk in her place. She inhaled deeply, pushing Wil's arms from her, and jumped.

The warm water closed over her head as the lagoon embraced her once again. Through the frothing water, she could just make out the churning motion of the two males deep below her, Cal moving quickly ahead of her. With every powerful stroke, she pulled herself deeper, each moment pressing down on her with enormous weight.

Cal got to them first, reaching for the closest limbs to him. As he pulled at Tadhg, the necsite whipped around, its red eyes narrowing on the two of them. The large creature sent a wall of warm water towards Lithia, sending her spinning. Her senses dulled in the water, she could hear nothing but her frantic heartbeat in her ears. She turned in a circle, trying to find her bearings, and found a wall of darkness in front of her.

Cal dragged Narcos and Tadhg with him through the water. Lithia swam forward, a low vibration rippling through the water, and took Narcos's weight from Cal as both of them kicked for the surface. The mixture of shadow and water pulsed behind her, obscuring the water behind them as they moved.

If Cal's shadows could blind the necsite for long enough for them to get out of the water they might stand a chance. She was struggling to remember much about their magic at the moment, too focused on swimming. One more stroke and her head broke the surface. She gulped lungfuls of the heavy, humid air of the cavern as she hoisted Narcos up and began swimming towards shore.

It wasn't fast enough.

The necsite broke the surface with a shriek. Lithia's magic throbbed in her core. She dug at the water, trying to get to shore. She prodded at her magic; there in the lagoon she found it, the boiling rage of the necsite's magic. She stopped trying to swim away, took a breath, and pulled at its magic. The priestess had said something about being careful not to drain someone, but maybe she could drain something on purpose, too.

She heard a scrape as Wil helped Cal and Tadgh climb from the water.

The lagoon churned as the necsite's screeches became a wail of agony. Narcos groaned in her arms she hefted him again afraid of losing her focus. She pulled at the threads of magic bringing them into her magical core. It smelled like salty sea spray but also acrid like brimstone. As she pulled a final time she smelled a thread of earthy moss and soil before two threads snapped.

The walls of the cavern shuddered around them as the necsite dissolved into a wave that pushed her under. As the lagoon claimed her for the third time, she lost hold of Narcos, tumbling into a rapid of her own making. Strong arms came around her and as she spotted the surface, she wondered for a moment how much she even wanted to breach it.

As she swallowed down air in the cavern once again, she watched as Willow pulled Narcos onto the shore. If she stayed in the water, she could pretend he was just unconscious. If she stayed in the water, he was fine. Nothing was real until she got out of the water.

She crawled through the shallows and up the shore until she was kneeling next to Narcos. He was still breathing, but only barely. She moved to where she was right beside his face and brushed a lock of wet hair behind his mangled ear.

His eyes finally focused on her. "You ... had ... to ..."

"No, Nars, I didn't," she choked on a sob and squeezed her eyes shut.

"Don't ... blame ... *love* ..."

She opened her eyes to find Narcos's vibrant green eyes staring dully beyond her.

"Lia." Wil's warm, honeyed voice came from behind her as she wrapped her arms around her. "He's gone. You don't need to see him like this."

She screamed.

Not a sob, or a shrill shriek, but a guttural, soul-rending wail of agony. The warm arms holding her were replaced with larger powerful arms that held her tightly as she folded in on herself. She wailed into his chest. The sounds of boots on stairs fading in the background. Cal's strong arms shifted, lifting her from the cavern floor.

"I CAN'T LEAVE HIM HERE."

She thrashed, the arms banding tighter around her.

"*Shhhhh*, Lia, we aren't leaving him here. He is coming with us."

Her wailing turned into sobs as he carried her from the second death to take a piece of her soul.

CALCAS

He stood on a balcony watching as the sun set for the second night after the attack in the lagoon. Lia hadn't moved from the window by the chair in nearly that long. The necsite had shredded one of Tadhg's legs. He told Cal earlier that he should be healed enough to travel tomorrow, but it was unlikely to ever heal entirely, adding to the map of gruesome scars already on the guard's body.

Wil came up beside him, placed her hands on the railing, and looked out over the lake.

"I let Calum know that the wagon will be here tomorrow for me to return Tadhg and Narcos to Arachin, although Tadhg is fairly adamant that he can ride."

Cal huffed a small laugh. He couldn't stand, let alone ride.

"I sent a crow to Neda." She paused. "Your mother responded. Our favorite general hasn't left the training pits in two days. She is going to go down tonight and force her to get some sleep." She stopped and stared out at the valley again. "We have to leave tomorrow," Wil said quietly.

"Have you spoken to Lia yet?" Cal asked.

She sighed. "I've spoken at her, but I don't know that she's listening."

"You're about to ask me to talk to her, aren't you?"

Wil laughed, and he turned, leaning against the railing to look her in the eye.

"Why would she listen to me? She just lost her fiancé. I don't think big-brute-who-yells-a lot is who she is going to react to," Cal said, needing someone to say they would do it for him.

A small smile slipped onto Wil's face as she stared out at the lake.

He huffed. "Fine, but you have to deal with her when I piss her off."

He had been sitting in the chair beside her for nearly twenty minutes and he wasn't even sure she knew he was there, so he decided to just talk.

"Wil and Tadhg are leaving in the morning to take Narcos back to Arachin. Back to Neda and Nylian. We, you and I, need to continue towards the temple. We still need answers."

He waited. Nothing.

"Lithia. *Lithia*, look at me."

Nothing.

He sighed, leaning forward in his chair.

"You don't have to talk, but what if I told you about how poorly I handled Seren's death? It's not a good example of healthy grieving, but it's ... well it's better than the silence right now."

She blinked rapidly down at his face as if just recognizing he was in the room.

He took a deep breath.

Her head tilted to the side as she watched him pull up his courage.

"When she died, I blamed you; but in truth, I blamed everyone. Every sentinel who could have taken that final blow, every voxis that led us to this valley. I blamed myself because I thought I should have been there to save her. I shouldn't have let her die alone."

He took another breath, this one shaky and broken.

"In the years after the last battle, you know that I took to fighting in the rings for Jofin, but it was so much worse than that. I lost control of my shadows entirely. They fed on my rage and hatred. I killed twelve females. I would find them after a fight, bed them, then my shadows would rip their soul from their body.

The last time it happened was the same night Wil found me and dragged me back."

Lithia's eyes held the shock he expected, and tears rolled down her cheeks.

"I know it's terrifying. To be honest, I'm afraid of myself. It's why you don't see me use my shadows as casually as I used to. It's why, regardless of anything else, I never would have taken your offer to be your Queen's Guard. I have done horrible things and the worst of it is that I'm not even sure why. I think had I dealt with my grief rather than fighting it, literally, it may not have happened, but now, I just don't know."

Cal slipped out of his chair and knelt in front of her, taking her hands. Lithia flinched slightly. A hot dagger of pain radiated through his heart and he saw the moment she registered her reaction, an apology flashed in her eyes. He nodded and continued.

"I don't want to be that person. I don't want my grief to be uncontrollable, Lia. I don't want to be a shadow of myself. More than that, I can't stand to watch you become a shadow of the person I know you are. Do not bow to this grief, as I should not have bowed to mine."

Lia blinked hard at him as if he said something he shouldn't have.

"I shouldn't have left you to that pain alone, just like I shouldn't have held myself in that pain alone. I can't allow you to become a shell right now. We need you. We have to leave for the temple in the morning. I know you feel like you are abandoning him, but you aren't. I know this isn't enough time to mourn, but we have so many other lives depending on us. I know you love him—"

She scoffed, and Cal froze as her eyes fully cleared.

Her voice cracked as she spoke for the first time in two days.

"You think this is because I love him?" A tear rolled hot down her cheek. "This is because no matter how much he loved me, I could never love him back, and he died knowing I didn't love him."

Cal stared at her, the words dying before they ever reached his tongue. He sat back on his feet as she looked down at their clasped hands, her thumb tracing the crescent-shaped scar on his thumb. He waited quietly for her to continue or retreat into herself.

"You know, I always believed Seren was my fated."

He looked up sharply.

Shrugging, she continued, "Maybe she wasn't, but I felt the tug. I know it snapped that day. You should also know that she didn't die alone in the end. I held her as her soul left this plane."

Cal nodded, realizing the only reason Lithia hadn't realized that they were mates was because she thought she was mated to someone else. Someone he loved. Someone whose eyes floated in his dreams and his nightmares. He shook the visions of Seren's honey-colored eyes from his mind and looked back at Lia. She was still tracing the small scar on his hand. Fate was a bitch.

"I still feel the tug, like a phantom limb scratching on my soul."

They sat there in silence for a while. It could have been minutes or hours when she finally spoke again.

"I killed them both. I watched them both die, in an arena of my own making, and I did nothing to save them. The fates of this valley want my soul, Cal."

Cal opened his mouth, entirely unsure what he was going to say when she spoke again.

"You were always right, Cal, the blood always comes from my hands." Her hands trembled before she let go of him and stood sharply. "We should leave at first light. I would like to say goodbye to Narcos."

She turned and strode out the door, leaving Cal kneeling on the floor, his mind spinning.

LITHIA

Lithia spent hours the previous night sitting beside Narcos's shrouded body, entirely unsure of what to say. She wanted to say goodbye, but once she was in his presence, she couldn't find the words. They all stuck on her tongue. So she just sat, holding his hand until she eventually fell asleep, waking to the gentle nudging of Wil as they readied to leave.

She kissed him quietly on the nose before slipping from the room.

"Rest where no shadows fall."

Lithia and Cal made it to the Pass of Souls quickly, stopping at the fort only to restock and stable the horses before they began the trek through the pass and into the mountains. The pass was safe enough for the horses, but they would never make it through the more treacherous mountain paths. With no idea how long they would find themselves trudging through the mountains, it was also easier to not have to account for extra supplies, so the horses stayed.

The pass itself was a stunning sight. Wide enough that four or five could walk side by side comfortably, it carved its way between two peaks. The path sloped in such a way that it seemed to end abruptly in the sky, like the next step would be into nothingness. The grey rock rose around the pass streaked with iridescent veins of glowing opaline. The first fae believed that when your soul returned to Aduna, it crystallized to form opaline. Lithia wasn't sure that was true, but believing that the magic of all those she had lost pulsed around her was the only comfort she had.

She ran her fingers over the stone as they climbed wordlessly through the pass, the only sound the scraping of boots on stone. head of her, Cal moved slower than his usual brutal pace, keeping to the worn heart of the path.

Lithia could feel a deep thrum of magic coursing through her fingers where they brushed the opaline fissures in the wall. She paused a moment, staring at the lacework of stone veins in the wall. Cal turned, likely hearing her paused footfalls, and took the few steps back to meet her.

"Good point to stop for lunch," Cal said with a nod, his eyes flashing to where she studied the wall.

Nearly twenty minutes later, Lia was sitting with her back against the mountain and had just finished the chicken and bread they pulled out for lunch when Cal finally spoke.

"Do you believe their souls rest here?"

She shifted and settled her arms on her knees not looking toward him.

Cal continued in her silence, "I believe that my desire for them to be here is all that's going to get me up this mountain. I believe that this would be the most peaceful place for a soul to land. Most of all, I believe that if the world dies, they are the only ones safe from the void."

Lithia sighed, staring at the opaline fissures running through the walls of the pass.

"I've been through this pass many times and it was just a pretty rock hallway, but now when I walk through it feels like the souls are reaching for me." Lithia turned to see Cal's face as she continued, a crease forming between her brows. "Wil always said she could feel them brush against her here, and I always said she was being intentionally mysterious because I never felt the souls like she did." Lithia smiled softly. "She liked to remind me often that just because something doesn't reach out and grab you, doesn't mean it's not there."

Lia expected Cal to huff or scoff, but instead, he cleared his throat.

"We should get moving. We should make it to the mouth of the pass by nightfall and we can camp for the night. I think" —he shifted uncomfortably— "I think maybe we should talk to them as we move through, leave our guilt here with the souls. They might be the only ones who can take it."

Lithia blinked at him, shocked, but nodded, feeling the thread in her heart warm.

As the afternoon burned overhead, Lia spoke. To her parents, she poured out years of stories and apologies. She gave them her shame and her fear and she told them about The Void and their hopes of finding answers. The words she whispered to Seren were carried away in the wind. She gave Narcos all the regret she carried for not making room in her heart for him fast enough. She apologized to one for loving them too much, and to the other for not loving them enough. The tears rolled hot down her cheeks before the wind swept them away, leaving only the echoes of her voice.

The sky mirrored their pain as rain poured from an iron sky, soaking through to her skin, the cold seeping into her bones. For four days, they had walked. While not entirely aimless—Tadhg had told them to keep moving towards the center of the range—it still felt to Lia like hopeless wandering. Her patience was grinding thinner by the day. She had left so much shame and sorrow in the pass, and now found that rage was all that remained.

She waited for a moment under a small overhang while Cal scouted the paths ahead in search of someplace dry to stop, with the rain not seeming to let up. Cal jogged up after a few minutes to tell her he found a cave they could dry out in for the night. She took a bracing breath before stepping back into the icy downpour, hoping the cave was close. Ten minutes later, they were standing in the mouth of a small cave listening to the rain echo off the rock outside.

It wasn't a large cave, but it seemed to be deep, the hazy light from the opening not reaching far enough for her to get a decent look. They began peeling off their soaked leathers and laying out the things from the pack that had gotten wet as Cal built a small fire to warm them up.

An hour later she was sitting close to the fire, finally warm, mostly dry, and fed. Cal was wandering around the small space restless. Lia had closed her eyes and let the rhythmic sound of the rain slow her breathing and drown out the thoughts racing through her mind on a loop.

Lia started to sing quietly, an old lullaby from her mother.
Where the green of the hills meets the sky's velvet blue,
Where pixies dance lightly on gold morning dew,
Hear a lullaby sung on the whispering breeze,
As it touches the leaves of the old knowing trees.
In the still breath of night, where shadows all sleep,
May your dreams be calm as the black of the deep.
Hear the lilt of the wind or the call of the sea
as your soul finds rest safe here with me
So sleep well, my love, while the night fills your scars,
The world softly humming under the blanket of stars.

A soft kiss to your brow and this song in your ear,

Sleep now in peace knowing love's always near.

Lia let the tear roll from the corner of her eye.

Her quiet moment was interrupted when Cal shouted a curse. She opened her eyes just in time to see a cauldron of bats swoop from the back of the cave and out into the night. They both stared after them, shocked for a moment.

"I guess this cave is a little more occupied than we thought." She chuckled, sniffling as Cal moved back into the firelight.

Cal nodded, grabbing a lantern from his back, lighting it from the fire, and shouldering his morning star before slowly moving out of their circle of light. She stood, hefting her sword and stepping around the fire to follow him. He shook his head, opening his mouth to insist he clear it before she followed him.

"It's cute that you think I would just wait here," Lia said, rolling her eyes and gesturing for him to lead the way.

CALCAS

Cal barely contained his answering eye roll as Lia armed herself and lit another lantern. He just wanted to make sure the cave didn't turn out to be something's den that they hadn't noticed in the blackness. This was more than likely a short walk to a small alcove, but those bats had come from somewhere. But sure, why not be dramatic about it? Finally, Lia gestured broadly into the cave.

"Lead the way."

He turned towards the darkness outside their firelight and began slowly walking forward, scanning the floor for any pitfalls or holes. The cave went back further than he expected, but not far. They could still clearly see their camp from where they stood.

"I guess I just spooked them when I was poking around," he said, turning to her.

Lia looked mildly disappointed that their little quest had only been about 100 steps, but she looked over his shoulder and got a strange look on her face. He watched as she moved around him toward the wall and held her lantern up to its surface. She took two steps to the left, turned to him, and grinned before she took another step and disappeared into the stone.

Cal blinked a few times at the spot she just vacated for a few seconds before she reappeared, smiling broadly before disappearing again. He moved toward the wall and held his lantern up. Once he was close to the stone, he realized there was a gap in the stone large enough for someone much larger than him to slip through, but the way the stone overlapped, it looked to be one solid wall from a distance.

He slipped through the opening and found himself in a cavernous room. The floor was inlaid with small white tiles of some sort forming a spiral around a small raised dais where Lia currently stood, her head thrown back, staring in awe at the ceiling. He raised his eyes slowly, taking in the smooth black walls glittering with veins of opaline, large braziers filling the room with flickering light. When his eyes finally found the ceiling, his breath stuck in his throat.

On the ceiling was another mosaic like the one under the temple in Arachin. Laid out in intricate tiles, the looping swirls of glass accented with flashes of gemstones filled the entire expanse of the domed ceiling. A tall figure cloaked in black stood in the center, arms outstretched wide. From his head grew two horns, thick and curved like a ram. His face was half in shadow, the bottom half appearing as if made from bone. Cal's eyes traced down the cloaked figure, taking in the swirls of shadow that formed his cloak.

The figure's right hand was a rich brown, with long fingers held out while a line of fae climbed each other to reach his open palm, where a fae male lay curled in sleep. His left hand, made of bone, held a fae made entirely from opaline. From his hand flowed a line of opaline fae. They stretched across a field of blood-red poppies that glittered in the firelight. At the figure's feet, his cloak swirled, like Cal's own writhing shadows, and a city of black formed in its depths.

Cal stared up at the ceiling in awe, his eyes watering at the angle. He looked down to find Lia staring at him, equally slack-jawed.

"Thahaos," Lia said, her voice smaller than he had heard before.

He looked over to find her standing with her head bowed.

"Is this the temple?" he asked.

"No, I don't think so," came Lia's hushed response. "This is definitely a temple, but I don't think it's the one we seek. I've never seen anything like this."

"It matches the one in Arachin, though?"

"The mosaic does, yes, obviously with a different image but the workmanship has to be the same. The rest though," she said, eyes sweeping the immaculate chamber, "is vastly different. I don't see any exits in here. We should go back; I feel like we shouldn't be here."

As they turned towards the door, a small gasp left Lithia as she stepped from the dais and she froze, her eyes glued to the floor. She looked up, face ashen.

"It's bone. I think this is a tomb"

He looked down at the swirling stone floor to find that what he had assumed to be stone was a precisely inlaid pattern made from bone. Fae bone, by the look of the partial skull Cal could pick out by his foot.

"I think we should go with that plan to get the fuck out of here."

They moved quickly towards the gap in the rock they had come from. Cal scanned the room one last time and noticed, on the far wall, a large circle of runes. He couldn't quite make out the pattern, but he also had no intention of standing on a pile of the dead for longer than he needed to. So he moved quickly out of the chamber a few steps behind Lia.

A few hours later, they were sitting around the fire in a tense silence when Lia spoke.

"I'll take the first watch; it's my turn. We should both get some sleep. We are of no use otherwise."

His smile was thin, but he nodded and went back to staring into the flames.

***

Cal woke to a scuffing noise and cracked his eyes open slowly. A lantern was disappearing through the stone at the back of the cave, and he sighed deeply. He lay still for a moment, debating letting her doom herself before a little nudge in his chest reminded him that they needed her. Grudgingly, he stood and slipped to the rear of the cave, feeling along the wall for the opening before disappearing inside. He found Lia seated on the dais, her legs crossed and eyes fixed on the mosaic. Instead of saying anything, he made his way to the center of the room and sat beside her, looking up at Thahaos, and waited.

"Do you think they have the answers we need, Cal?"

He chuckled. "Oh, I am absolutely positive they have the answers. Getting to the answers is a different beast entirely. However, if Thahaos has effectively abandoned his creation like Aduna has hers, it may be harder to get to the truth."

Lithia stared up at the hooded face. They remained like that in silence for several more minutes, before prickles of unease crept up his spine.

"We should go back; this place was not built for us," Cal said, his eyes sweeping the massive room.

Lia took his hand and allowed him to help pull her to standing before following him silently from the chamber.

Cal took up a post by the cave mouth, watching the mist settle over the mountains as the clouds finally cleared. Leaning his head back on the rough stone, he sighed and sent a silent prayer to whatever god would take it that they would find answers soon.

An hour before dawn, a crow landed on his knee and extended its leg, offering him the attached letter bearing his name in a tidy scrawl.

Calcas,

The priestesses have received Narcos and he is being taken back to his court to rest with our ancestors. I know you have no interest in orders from me even though I am your general, but keep her safe. I know she intends to shoulder the guilt like she did with Seren. I need you to tell her none of us blame her.

Be safe and stop scowling at this message.

Neda

Legion High General

He read the message several times. He very much doubted Lithia thought anyone blamed her more than she blamed herself. He heard her speaking to Narcos in the pass. Heard her explaining how she hadn't sensed the intertwined magic until it was far too late, how she would never know how to trust her magic again. She had felt the pain when her magic took his life, entirely out of her control. Blame was only the first mountain.

LITHIA

Two fucking weeks.

It had been two weeks since they entered the pass. Lia sat watching the sun peek over the mountains while Cal milled around, slowly repacking camp. They vaguely knew where in the range they were, but the last two days they hadn't been in any rush to move. Cal and Lia both grew more unbearably frustrated with every step they took, their tempers likely to clash at any moment.

She held back a well of angry tears. They didn't have time to play some fickle god's game of hide and seek. The lives of everyone in Suviel were set on this ever-unbalanced scale, and no matter what she did, it would continue to tip out of reach. Cal sat down beside her and offered her what she was pretty sure was the last of the tea. She took it with a tilt of her head.

"The sun coming over the peaks is about the only thing reminding me this isn't hopeless," Cal said, his eyes closed and face tipped towards the sun.

Lia looked out and really took in the mountains before her. The mountain faces still clung to the inky blue of the night as the sun spilled its soft golden light over the edges. The highest peaks glistened like molten gold at first light. A wisp of mist swirled through the dips and valleys, sprinkling the morning with dew as the texture of the mountains was thrown into a dramatic contrast.

"It just reminds me that if we fail, the sun will rise on the ashes we leave behind," Lia said, looking down into her tea.

Cal looked at her, a crease forming between his brows.

"I've never heard you sound so defeated."

"I've never been so defeated. Whatever this curse is. I won't survive it."

"What makes you think that?"

Lithia sat quietly for a moment, staring at the brightening pinks and yellows of the sky, and took a deep breath.

"I don't think the voiding just started. When the tree showed me ... well, everything, I saw that in the year or so after the battle, its sight started to dim around the edges. I don't know what this is, but I think it's a lot further along than we feared, and I don't know that we can stop it."

"Why didn't you tell us?"

"Would it have mattered?"

"Trust always matters, Lia."

Lia silently stood, holding a hand down to Cal, who took it and pulled himself up beside her.

"Then let's trust that the end of this journey holds answers."

They walked slowly, their pace unimportant since they were chasing a temple that seemed in no rush to reveal itself to them. They walked for most of the day, stopping under one of the lone trees to eat during the hottest part of the day before turning up a path that inched higher into the range. This path was narrow and winding, the blind curves setting her teeth on edge.

A couple hours before sunset, something in the air shifted. They paused and waited, Cal scanning their surroundings for whatever was coming. A ground-rumbling roar set the stones around them skittering. Lithia looked up to the clouds as a massive amphiptere circled above them. Its massive serpent-like body undulated through the clouds, armor-like scales glistening in the setting sun. Each beat of its massive wings sent a pulse of wind toward them. It circled for a moment above them before letting out another bellow and flying parallel to the path they were on.

Breaking her awed stare, she found Cal grinning broadly. Cal had an almost youngling-like energy buzzing about him at their unexpected visitor. She rolled her eyes and kicked a small rock at his feet, causing him to stumble slightly given his fixation on the sky. It seemed even her sour mood couldn't dull his excitement at the moment because he was right back to marveling at the creature a beat later.

"I think he wants us to follow him. We must be close," Cal said in an awed whisper.

She snapped her head towards him as he nodded toward the form that had paused further up the path and begun circling, like it was waiting for them. Cal began moving up the path, leaving her briefly confused and mildly horror-struck on the path behind him before she followed.

As they walked, she took in the amphiptere above her. Its scales were vibrant shades of reds and purples that reminded her of the sunrise with the way they faded into each other. Each wing was covered in soft iridescent feathers on the top, but the inside looked like a soft membrane, like a bat. The membrane was the same fiery colors as its scales. This was the first male she had ever seen so close. In the past, the amphiptere she'd interacted with had been the ones the Arcane riders bonded to. Since only the females bond to riders, instead of the brightly colored scales like this one, they were all a glistening black.

She was so focused on the swirling flash of color above her that she nearly missed her first glimpse of the temple. At the end of the path, carved into black stone peak of the mountain, was an enormous structure. Easily seven stories high with open air balconies at each level and three tall spires, the temple loomed over the entire mountain range. Set at the bottom was an intricately inlaid circular door surrounded by runes.

Their escort circled one of the spires before landing softly on one of the balconies and disappearing from sight. They slowly approached the door, casting each other concerned glances. As they drew nearer, she got the same heavy feeling in her gut as when she stepped off the dais in that cave. The door was inlaid with glistening white bone. She shuddered as she took in the gently curving slopes of the filigree tree the bones made on the door. She looked around, unsure of how to proceed, and turned to Cal.

"Do we knock?"

Before Cal had even opened his mouth to respond, the door began to shift.

The great round door began to rotate and as the macabre tree became entirely inverted, the door split down and slid open. Warm orange light spilled onto the grey stone, washing over them in a breath of warmth. A tall figure stood in the gap of the door, backlit so she couldn't make out their features, and began moving down the gentle slope toward them.

Once they passed the doors, their features came into view. A statuesque female dressed in a sweeping black dress with opaline detailing on the corset glided their way. Her skin was a deep brown, her hair a halo of silver white curls that faded to a light purple at the ends, and a woven band of onyx rested on her brow. She had high cheekbones and full lips painted a deep glittering purple. It was her eyes, though, that arrested Lia's breath in her lungs. They were an extremely light shade of purple, nearly white, with thin black pupils. She glanced at Cal and found a deep wrinkle between his brows.

As she grew closer, Lia could make out glittering tattoos covering her skin in intricate patterns. They reminded her of the tattoos that most Celestial Fae had peppering their skin, but where theirs tended toward single stars and dainty constellations, she seemed to have entire galaxies swirling across every inch of exposed skin. It was hypnotic.

There was a swirl of silence as the statuesque woman turned, looking as if she expected their party to be larger. A flash of disappointment crossed her features at the absence of their companions.

"Welcome, Mo Bhanrighit, Calcas, it is an honor to have you here. I am Miana, The Consort and High Priestess."

Calcas

"Consort?"

Lia's face had shifted from awe at Miana's appearance to a furrowed brow he knew matched his own. Whose consort would she be?

"Ah, yes. Well, even after this long, I guess it's to be expected that there is much you do not know," she said, a haunted tinge to her voice.

She turned, gesturing for them to follow.

"We have a suite ready for you. We will allow you to rest for the evening; all your questions can wait until morning. It is quite late." She paused and looked over her shoulder as Calcas moved up beside her.

"Our matters are quite urgent," Cal said before they passed through the doors.

"I am aware, but alas, it will need to wait one more night."

He tamped down the urge to demand they be heard immediately, knowing he was walking into a domain not his own and acting ... like himself ... wouldn't be helpful.

They stayed on her heels as she moved quickly through the doors, which closed silently behind them. Inside, they found themselves in a large open chamber. It mirrored the sanctuary in Arachin with a massive pool dominating the room, this one crafted from onyx rather than gold, and more stunning, it was filled with dancing golden flame.

Coming around the side of the pool of flame, he found the back wall entirely made of glass. He longed to see the world stretching out under the mountain, but that could wait. There were two small fae washing the stone, who stood and bowed to their group as they passed. He bowed to each as they passed through a carved archway leading to a wide set of stairs.

The entire building looked to be hewn from the black stone of the mountain, the stairs looking more like a natural feature than cut stone. The stairs curled steadily upwards, archways cut every so often leading to whatever mysteries lay in a temple. After climbing a seemingly endless number of stairs, Miana stepped through a simple archway.

On the other side, he found they were in a wide hallway with doors lining each side. She stopped halfway down the hall before a door on the right. The door was made from a deep-colored wood with a detailed crown carved into it resembling the Crown of Suviel and dripping with glittering rubies.

"The guest chambers are on this floor near the acolytes; the priestesses are upstairs on the top floor. If you need anything, there is a bell pull right inside the door and one of the acolytes will be here quickly. There are five bedchambers each with washrooms connected to a small living area. Someone will bring dinner up to you in the next hour. I will come for you in the morning. Sleep well."

She opened the door and moved to the side to let them in before pulling it shut behind them.

Turning, he scanned the cozy room. It was much simpler than he expected: a soft seating area surrounded a large fireplace, with a dining table large enough for six set by the windows.

Lithia had moved toward the doors along the back wall and stood motionless, staring at them. Moving to stand beside her, he waited for a moment, not sure why she had frozen, until her voice, small and quiet, broke the silence.

"There are five rooms."

He nodded

"They knew." She looked at him. "They knew we were coming and expected us. They prepared a room for us. The five of us."

Cal shrugged. "I have a feeling they know a lot."

He stepped forward, pushing through the third door.

He wasn't quite sure what he expected, but a massive bed wasn't it.

The bed was large enough to fit three of him comfortably, with plush blankets and a small warming pan poking from beneath the sheets. There was a small table beside the bed and a wooden bench set at the end. Scanning the room, he also found a small writing desk, a chair, and a chest of drawers. There was nothing frivolous in the room, but the few things that were there were of extremely high quality. He set his pack down on the bench before he moved towards the chest of drawers and placed all his weapons on its surface and kicking off his boots.

Slowly he moved to the bathing room and sighed in relief at the sight of the upright shower, meaning he wouldn't have to worry with a bath, though his muscles could use a soak. He pulled off his sweat-and-dust-streaked clothes before calling a stream of hot water to the spout. The rhythmic pounding of the water soothed the muscles in his back and shoulders.

He washed quickly and exited the steam-filled room to find a stack of clean clothes on the bed that someone had clearly dropped in while he showered. He picked up the tunic, running the soft cotton between his fingers. He pulled on the lightweight tunic and pants before slipping back out into the common area.

He flopped down into the chair across from Lithia and pulled the jug of wine towards him, filling his glass and emptying it before looking up. Lia was wearing a similar soft grey tunic to his and was consuming her wine at a much more appropriate pace.

He removed the covers to all three platters on the table and set them to the side. Underneath, they found roasted lamb, potatoes, some buttery vegetables, and small chocolate cakes. It was simple but smelled heavenly after two weeks of rations and the occasional meat if they found something. They ate in silence before Lithia finally spoke.

"Do we need a plan for tomorrow?"

Cal leaned forward, staring into the dregs of his wine. "Probably, but to be honest, I think we need to just ask. We don't have more time to waste. We've been wandering these fucking mountains for weeks."

Lithia nodded. "We should likely at least explain why we are looking for it."

He scoffed. "I can't imagine they have no idea what's happening, if they knew enough to know how many of us were coming at some point."

Lithia's eyes glazed as she stared off into the fire. He sat there a few minutes longer before making his way to his room and crawling into the warmed sheets.

LITHIA

They were seated in a richly decorated sitting room on one of the lower floors of the temple. Deep purples and reds draped the walls and supple leather couches surrounded a low table with a shallow brazier of flickering flames. A kind-looking acolyte with emerald-green hair brought them all a warm melted chocolate drink that made Lia immediately feel like she wanted to take a nap.

They had been waiting a few hours for Miana to finish with something important and join them. Cal had been staring at the door, a muscle flexing in his jaw for the last hour, and it was beginning to make Lithia anxious.

"Do you think staring is going to make her appear faster?"

He shot her a rude hand gesture, and she chuckled, going back to reading the reports they had gotten on their journey along with a stack of reports Miana had shared with her. The voiding had spread further inland and the number of fae with draining magic was growing. She was worried they were too many steps behind and wouldn't be able to catch up in time.

She was reading through a letter from Astris for the fourth time when Miana finally swept into the room. She bowed to them both and motioned for the few others lounging in the room to leave before settling on the couch opposite Lia.

"I hope you got some rest."

"Yes, thank you, our rooms are lovely. If you don't mind my asking, how did you know we were coming?" Lia said, setting the stack of reports on the couch beside her.

"Oathis has been tracking you since you exited the pass, though the crows told me to watch for you weeks ago when you left Arachin."

"Oathis?"

"The amphiptere," she said with a soft smile. "Tell me, High Queen, what knowledge you have sought us out for?"

"Do you know of The Voiding already?"

Miana nodded, urging her to continue.

"The priestesses in Arachin fear that a curse has been set on the heart of Suviel. We believe it is some form of withering curse; the Hearth Prime is looking into this magic for us. However, we have an issue of not knowing the location of the heart. We were hoping you would hold this knowledge."

She sat silently for several minutes, allowing room for the tension in the air to grow taut. Lia's knuckles were bleached white, her heart racing. Miana sat back on the couch, sipping at her drink before answering.

"Thahaos was the first of the gods to ever take a consort. I had been a wraith for hundreds of years before we crossed paths the first time, but soon after that first meeting, I saw him everywhere. At first, I assumed that it was coincidental, but quickly realized he had been shifting his days to collide with mine."

Cal and Lia exchanged a wary glance.

"We courted for nearly 300 years before he decided to make me consort. It had never been done, raising a mortal being to an immortal life span. The other gods were furious that he believed he deserved any happiness after they cast him into The Beneath. After we were mated, the others, in their fury, bound me to this mountain. I have been here since before Mab was a spark in her mother's womb and I will remain here until the sky cracks into the sea."

She paused for so long, Lia wasn't sure she was going to continue. She opened her mouth, to say what, she didn't know. In the end, it didn't matter because, after a long breath, Miana did continue.

"I tell you all this so you believe me when I say I have been here for lifetimes and I have seen of much of history as it unfolded. As it happens, I do have knowledge as to the fate of the heart." She leaned forward, rubbing her temple. "There is not one heart."

Lithia sat up quickly trading a panicked look with Calcas.

"What do you mean? The High Priestess specifically said that Suviel has a heart; it's written in their texts."

"They are not inaccurate, but the texts they are using obviously stop tracing the heart at the moment it was taken by Thahaos as he fell into The Beneath. There is no longer one heart, there are five."

"Five?" Lia rasped.

"Why are there five?" Cal asked, leaning forward on his elbows.

"As Thahaos fell, his intention was of course to take the heart into The Beneath with him. To be honest with you, I am unsure what his goal was. What I do know is that when the magic struck the veil between Suviel and The Beneath, it shattered. Aduna's magic retreated to its origins to protect itself. So there are five: one for each court."

"There are only four courts, though," replied Cal, a furrow between his brows.

"There are four elemental courts; the final heart belongs to the wild magic. The magic outside the courts, creatures, the wild fae, and Mab's line."

She gave Lithia a weighted look.

"How are we supposed to know which heart is affected? Where are they all?"

"If it is as you say, then I would assume that they are all affected. While there are five, they are all pieces of the whole. If one is dying, then they all are. From what I understand, you are seeing the effects across all the courts?" Lithia nodded. "And you and the creatures are feeling the void as well?" Another nod. "Then most certainly all five pieces are in peril."

"Well, in that vein, though, if they are pieces of a whole, would curing one fix all of them?"

Miana gave her a sad smile. "I'm sorry, but that kind of knowledge is beyond me as well."

"Do you have any idea how to find them?"

"I fear I have far fewer answers than you hoped for, Mo Bhanrighit, but I believe I can find out more if you'll give me a day."

"Of course, your information so far has been invaluable. We need to begin forming a plan, since this has become far more complicated than we had hoped. Thank you, Miana."

"Of course. I will send word to Thahaos that his knowledge is required."

"Thahaos?"

"Who better to ask?"

Lia felt all the blood drain from her face before her heart began to pound. She was going to have to ask a god. Miana rose and glided from the room, leaving them both in stunned silence.

CALCAS

An acolyte had taken Cal to collect several books and maps from the library on his way back to their rooms. When he stepped back in, it looked to him like a storm had blown through the room. Notes, scrolls, books, and maps covered every flat surface. She had only been up here for a couple of hours but had somehow made the room look like a war tent mid-battle.

She looked up when he opened the door, and the relief on her face was palpable. Cal strode over to where Lia was worrying over a map and placed a hand on her shoulder.

"Tell me what you need."

"I know we don't have a ton of information yet, but I would like to start forming the shape of a plan so we can fill it in quickly after getting the information we need."

"Okay, maybe let's start with organizing the information we do have, because its going to be impossible to find anything in here."

Lithia looked around the room for a moment, the fog in her eyes clearing.

"Ah, I do seem to have made a mess."

Cal barked a laugh, setting down the stack of books the temple had lent him before starting to gather the spread pages. Lia narrowed her eyes at him before she smiled and helped him gather and sort the strewn paperwork.

Several hours later, all of the information was sorted into neat piles on a long table brought in by several acolytes and they were seated at the small dinner table, a map of Suviel spread before them. They had been attempting to plot out a course of action but realized that without the needed information on how to combat the magic, there wasn't much they could plan.

What they settled on was lodging guesses as to where the hearts were stored. They started with the most obvious answer, that they were all held in the capital temples, but Cal had a feeling they wouldn't be so lucky. She suggested they also include the physical center of the territories, but they ran into the issue of having no idea where that would be in the Tidal Court.

Lithia was growing progressively frustrated as the day waned. They had come here for a very specific reason, and while they had gotten that answer, it didn't lead them to any functional plans.

He could see her mind spinning and he wished he could give her something to grab a hold of.

After several hours, they had more than a dozen markers on the map of possible locations. It was less of a start and more of a game of places they could name in groups of five. They had essentially wasted the day waiting on Thahaos. Without his input, they were aimless. Cal settled in to the plush chair by the fire and tossed his knife in the air, catching it with his shadows.

Twenty minutes later, the door to their room opened unexpectedly, and they were both on their feet in the next breath. Cal's mind slowly caught up with what was happening. He and Lia both had daggers drawn, aimed at the door. Cal followed the line of his shadows to the door, where the jeweled dagger he had been tossing was pressed into Miana's throat.

To her credit, the ancient wraith stood there calmly with a small smile on her face. Neither of them moved quickly to disarm themselves, though Cal slowly removed his blade from her throat, pulling his shadows back until the dagger slid into his palm.

"Consort?"

"I came to let you all know we will be having dinner upstairs in the private dining room this evening. The acolytes are on their way with clothing for you all."

"Thank you," Lithia said with a bow of her head. "We would be honored to join you."

Miana bowed to Lithia and turned to leave, inclining her head again to Cal as she turned.

Cal stood in his room and admired the clothing the acolyte gave him as he laid out the pieces on the bed. A black tunic with delicate gold embroidery looping and whirling over the soft cotton contrasted the rich black leather leggings. The leather was supple and perfectly worn where he'd expected it would be stiff and uncomfortable. He dressed quickly, fidgeting with the full-length sleeves, as he preferred his arms to be bare. He considered tearing them off but decided potentially disrespecting a god and his consort wasn't the best move.

He slipped on his own boots and slid several daggers into them, strapping the jeweled dagger from Kieran to his belt. He wet his hands in the basin and ran them through his hair in a half-hearted attempt to make it look decent. With a sigh, he left his room, plopped on the couch, and poured a glass of wine while he waited for Lithia to be ready.

Lia stepped out twenty minutes later in a sleek black dress that flowed like water down her curves, gold snakes writhing around the bodice that plunged between her breasts nearly to her navel. Her skirt was slit up to her hip, her jeweled dagger strapped to her exposed thigh. A gold and onyx crown was braided into her curls before they were pulled into an elaborate style at her nape, displaying her runes along the broad line of her shoulders.

Lithia squared her shoulders and moved quickly past him to the door. Taking that as the sign to move, Cal fell into step behind her. They walked quietly down the hall and up the steps to a hall similar to the one on the floor below but shorter, with a massive set of double doors at the end.

The doors were inlaid with gold that depicted the night sky, and as they got closer, he saw that they were moving and swirling, a glittering river of stars. As Lithia reached the doors, she tensed, her spine snapping straight.

"What is it?" he asked in a low tone, his hand falling to his dagger.

She shook her head. He took a small step back, realizing that she was putting on her facade. She was a queen and that is exactly how she wanted to look when those doors opened. He stepped to the side so she would be the only image filling the doorway.

LITHIA

Though she was mentally preparing herself to come face to face with the God of Death, there was a small part of her that still held it as an impossibility. While she knew that Aduna did things like speak to her line, she didn't walk in their world any longer. Thahaos, however, was banished to The Beneath. This temple was in between those worlds, so it made sense that he could come here to the place where his consort was bound.

The door swung open on silent hinges to reveal Miana dressed in a draping grey dress that faded to a deep wine color at the bottom. Her purple and white curls were accented with the same woven onyx band set on her brow. She smiled warmly at them, stepping to the side and gesturing them inside.

She stepped through, spine straight, Calcas at her back. She entered into a cavernous room, to the left deep leather couches with plush throws surrounded a fireplace that she could have easily walked into without ducking her head. On the left was a table large enough to seat 12 comfortably.

Directly in front of her was a wall of books, floor to ceiling, with two rolling ladders and a pair of worn armchairs. Standing behind one of the armchairs was a tall male with the same deep brown skin as Miana. Braided white hair sat under a crown of flickering black flames. His eyes were deep and knowing and they were tracking her entry, his mouth set in a firm line.

His gaze flashed to Calcas before settling back on Lithia and softening the slightest bit. He swirled a small glass of amber liquid in his hand before bowing to Lithia. She straightened her shoulders before bowing low in return. She heard the rustle of fabric as Cal followed her movements. Thahaos's expression cracked, and he smiled broadly at them all. The unexpected expression sent a shiver down Lia's spine.

"Come, dine with us."

His voice was deep and layered, rattling with something ancient that settled heavily around her shoulders. They moved past the long dining table and through a doorway set into the far corner of the room. Stepping through, she found herself in a much more intimate dining area where a smaller round table was set for four.

Thahaos moved to the far side of the table facing the door and pulled out the seat to the right of his for Miana, before turning and pulling out the seat to the left and holding his hand out to Lia. As she watched the God of Death's movements, she noticed that his skin seemed to shift. The rich brown flickered to skeletal in flashes. She took his hand and slid onto the cushioned leather chair, tipping her head in thanks. She watched Cal hold his arm out to Miana before sliding himself into the one beside Lia.

"Thank you, King Thahaos, for honoring us with your presence."

The King of The Beneath smiled warmly at her.

"Thank you, Mo Bhanrighit, for sacrificing so much to seek help from me. I am honored to be of service to the queen who has earned the respect of so many who have entered my gates, even the wraiths."

"Thank you, King Thahaos, and please call me Lia. We will be here all night if you have to say Mo Bhanrighit every time."

"Then I insist you call me Ahbba. It is only fitting that you, all of you," he said, his gaze sweeping the others, "refer to me as my family does."

Lia bowed her head, smiling as the others bowed their heads in thanks as well.

"If you don't mind, what does Ahbba mean?"

"Ah, it means *father*," he said, smiling warmly. "Now, let's eat. We can save the more serious conversation for after."

Miana gestured towards the covered dishes on the table and stood, moving the covers to a low table set against the wall. The room filled with the aroma of warm herbs and earthy vegetables. There was a rich red soup, set beside a large platter of roasted meat that smelled to Lia to be pork with a deep green herb sauce. There was a large bowl of small roasted potatoes beside a bowl of mixed vegetables, and a plate piled with warm brown bread.

Lia waited for Thahaos and Miana to fill their plates before reaching out and filling her bowl, she saw Cal begin serving himself from the corner of her eye but when she looked back to her plate, she realized he had filled her plate instead, tasting the food as he did. Thahaos watched him with a bemused smile before giving him a nod of respect. Lia stared at him, utterly bewildered.

He leaned into her whispering quietly.

"He may be a god, but I would be a piss poor sentinel if I allowed my queen to eat untested food."

"I eat plenty of untested food, Calcas."

"No. You don't."

She looked over to find him filling his own plate, a smug smile on his face. They ate in relative quiet. As the meal passed, her shoulders slowly loosened, and she relaxed into her seat. Every few minutes, though, something would remind her that she was in the presence of a god and a shiver of tension would ripple through her.

The table had been cleared and decanters of wine set on its polished surface after the meal was through. Thahaos sat back in his chair, puffing on a long pipe carved from what looked to be bone. The smoke wafting from it smelled sweet and floral, and filled the room with a low haze.

"Can I ask? I have heard the term a few times, but I find my knowledge lacking. What exactly is a wraith? I have only the most basic understanding," Lithia asked as the four of them settled in to talk.

"A good question. It is unlikely that a living fae would know much unless they have spent time here in the temple really, and not many do. The wraiths were made by me when I first formed The Beneath. Originally, they were my attempt at something resembling fae, but I did not have the patience to fill a kingdom. Now they serve as reapers. There are only a small number of wraiths, hand-selected by me when they die. They join The Hunt and reap souls that have remained on the mortal plane too long."

"Do your original wraiths still exist?"

"Oh yes, but none are a part of The Hunt, fresher souls are needed for that. They all serve in The Beneath, similar to the Primes in Suviel. Miana is one of my original wraiths," he added with a warm smile before continuing. "Now, tell me, Lia, what can I do to help you?"

Lia leaned forward, clasping her hands on the table, inhaling deeply.

"Miana has already explained to us how the heart shattered when you tried to pull it through the veil."

Thahaos nodded silently.

"So with that new information, we laid out as many guesses as we could as to where these hearts exist, but we have essentially no information and we are hoping you have some knowledge as to where the pieces of the heart are."

She stared down at her hands, the realization that they were flying entirely blind into all of this tightened like a vise around her throat. She swallowed hard before lifting her chin to meet the deep red eyes of the God of Death.

Thahaos took another long drag off his pipe before leaning forward and matching Lia's posture.

"Unfortunately, all I have for you is speculation."

Lia twisted her fingers in her lap. "Anything is more than we have now, Ahbba."

"I don't know where the shards landed. They stayed on your side of the veil and I have been banished to this side since then. I believe there is one in the mountains, though I can't be sure, but I can feel it when I am in the temple."

"Do you know what form they take?" Cal asked, leaning in.

"That I have a better answer for. The original magic was housed in what is now Arachin, in a cavern under the island where the temple sits now. When I found it, it was formless, a nexus of power pulsing with light and energy. It wasn't possible for me to transport it that way, so I took the magic into myself, planning to use myself as a vessel for it until I could place it in The Beneath. It was ripped from me when I entered the veil. I flew into the veil and the magic flew five directions out of the veil."

"So it is likely they are formless once more?" Lithia clarified.

"That is what I believe, though I do not know the exact locations of these nexuses."

He took another drag of his pipe, breathing out slowly.

Miana cleared her throat. "Given the amount of magic they put off, it's likely they are drawing some sort of unconscious magical attention. Temples or shrines may be a good starting place."

Lithia's spine snapped straight, her head whipping around to Cal.

"I think we know where at least one is," Cal said, his eyes wide. "We came across an ornate chamber hidden in a cave several days from the pass of souls, and Ahbba, you said you could feel one here in the mountains?" The god tilted his head thoughtfully. "It's worth looking, we have to pass it on our way out, anyway."

Lia was shaking her head. "But there was nothing in there, just a pretty empty room."

"Beauty hides many wicked things, Mo Bhanrighit," said Thahaos, a cloud of smoke rolling from his lips.

LITHIA

She sat on the window seat in their shared sitting room, a map spread on her lap, staring out into the rain. While they were sure stopping in the cave was the best option, they had replayed the guessing game again. This was all good information, but with just the two of them, she wasn't sure it was enough. Hopefully, if they were right about the cave, it would put them on the right track.

Cal had a working theory that the Arcane nexus was somewhere on Darke Mountain. It was an excellent theory, but it led to hours of arguing not only the vastness of the mountain but the dangers. Not only was the mountain an active volcano, but it remained the only nesting ground of the amphiptere.

They had marked several places within the Hearth boundaries that could be of significance, including the tree Nars had told them about hidden within the walls of the capital. The Tidal Court was one massive mystery. The majority of the islands were uncharted, and searching the sea would be a laughable undertaking.

"Should we focus on the nexus we have located to see what it's going to take to heal it?" Cal asked, running his hands through his hair.

Lia rolled her head towards him. "We should just focus on making sure we have actually located one."

"I guess that's fair."

Lithia groaned and hopped down from the window seat, plopping into a chair at the table.

"Do you think I can just draw the curse out of the heart?"

"Pretending that isn't a terrible self-sacrificing idea, where is that magic supposed to go once you pull it out?" Cal asked, leaning forward on the table.

"Into me, I'm assuming."

They sat in a tense silence for a few minutes before Cal shook his head.

"We would have to find somewhere for you to direct that magic. You can't hold it in your body, Lia, and we don't even know that you could syphon it out and into something else effectively."

"As of right now, we aren't even sure that's what is going to happen, so I'm not worrying about it. The more imminent issue is we need a plan and we have nothing." Lia clenched her jaw, pulled out a new map, and rolled it out onto the table. "We know one of five is here," she started, circling the relative location of the cave on the map. Darke Mountain is a good assessment of where the Arcane shard is located."

She circled the mountain and sat back.

"I like the idea of The Tree of Beginnings being a good place to start in Hearth. We should talk to Neda or Nylian, though, they may have a better idea. Along that same vein, we should call on Aegaea as well because I would assume the shard here in the cave to be the Celestial shard, given how central the cave is in The Tipping Peaks."

"That just leaves Mab's heart, right?"

Lia nodded silently for several seconds.

"I think it's in Arachin."

She looked up, locking eyes with Cal and saw the moment he made the connection.

"The sea cave."

Lia made a noise of agreement before continuing. "It makes sense, the mosaic is so similar to the one of Thahaos, and it's directly under the citadel."

"So what's the plan?"

Cal's eyes landed heavily on Lia. Her gift had always been strategy, but there in that moment, she felt like the world was crumbling to ash in her hands. If she twitched her pinky, the mountains would crumble into the sea and the trees would wither to their roots.

"Send messages to Neda and Aegaea. We should have them meet us in the valley. Then send word to Calum to refortify one of the other manors for us to use as a base. We will have Miana send all our information ahead of us so they can begin while we head for the cave."

They spent the next few hours making sure Wil and Neda would have the most comprehensive possible information to begin with, so they could begin the search on two fronts. After a while, her back began to ache, and she stood from the table without another word and slipped into her bedroom. Quietly, she closed the door behind her before sliding down the polished wood to the floor, burying her face in her hands.

Hot rain landed on her face as she stared out at the carnage around her. Scanning the body-littered valley, something in her chest cracked open, a hot tongue of flame licking out and searing it all into her memory.

A flash of red caught her eye, and she looked down to find a perfectly circular drop of blood on her hand. As she stared, more followed. She looked up and, to her horror, found the rain was sheets of blood falling from the sky. It bathed her memory until nothing but red remained.

She screamed.

She woke with a start, the scream still raw in her throat. Hot tears stung her cheeks as she rapidly blinked, trying to clear the lingering red from her vision. As the room came into focus Calcas rushed through the door, his terror-stricken face stopping at the end of her bed and running his hands through his sleep mussed hair. His breathing matched her own ragged gasps, his chest rising and falling rapidly.

"Dream," she whispered.

He scrubbed his hand over his face before answering groggily. "Tea."

He turned and walked out the door, rubbing at his eyes. She stared after him, utterly bewildered by him being there, but more so at his sudden exit. Cold sweat stuck her clothes to her body as she began to shiver. She pulled her blankets up and cuddled back into the soft pillows.

A few minutes later, Cal returned, two cups of tea in his hands. The warm scent of honey and chamomile floated around her as he sat, leaning on the headboard beside her. He offered her one of the cups and they sipped in silence for several minutes.

"I get them too. I'm not sure if anyone who walked out of that valley is free of them."

Lithia sighed and dropped her head back with a thunk as it hit the headboard.

"I am responsible for every life lost that day. On both sides."

Cal didn't respond, just took the teacup from her hand and set it on the table.

"Go back to sleep, Lia. You need rest."

She slid down into the warmth of the blankets and she felt the bed shift beside her. Reaching out, her hand landed on his arm as he moved to leave.

"Stay. Please?"

He tensed before he slowly released a breath and shifted, laying down on top of the blankets.

"Thank you."

She closed her eyes, slipping quickly back into sleep.

Calcas

Just before midday, Calcas waited in the atrium. Lia entered, Miana walking close to her as they exchanged goodbyes. As they drew closer, their conversation tapered off until they stood before him.

"Calcas," Miana said, bowing her head. "It was lovely to meet you, even given the dire circumstances."

She reached out, pulling him into a hug. She took a step back and smiled softly at them both, placing her fist against her heart and bowing.

"Be swift and be vigilant, Mo Bhanrighit."

"We should make it to the cave in a week's time."

"Actually," Miana started, tilting her head. "The temple may let you out closer to your destination than you expect."

Lia's brow furrowed, the question dancing in her eyes as Miana smiled and moved towards the large circular door.

"The temple is not in the mountains, it is in the veil. The door is the judge, it takes you where you need to be, which is why the temple is not plotted on any map or set on any definable course. The door comes to you just as it will put you where you need to be when you leave."

Cal stared up at the massive doors, the tree of bone mirrored on its interior.

"It's a portal?"

"In a manner of speaking."

Fire flashed behind Lia's eyes. "So could it take us to the other hearts as well?"

Cal's eyes cut to Miana, and he watched her shoulders droop.

"While I'm sure in theory it could, it does not work that way, it—"

"It's duty is to judge the souls that pass through it. It is less a means of travel and more of a link between The Beneath and the surface; it is tethered," came Thahaos's layered voice from behind Miana's shoulder, as he materialized.

Cal shuddered, knowing nothing would ever be so simple.

"Good luck, Mo Bhanrighit," the god said, lowering his head in a bow.

They both bowed low as Miana turned, placing her palm on the door near the base of the tree. Cal felt a warm shiver of magic run down his spine as the door shifted and split opening back to

The Tipping Peaks. On the other side was a stone ledge, entirely different from where they entered the temple. He stepped out the door ahead of Lia, turning to get his bearings.

He quickly noted they had come out much further south, towards The Pass of Souls, than where he expected. Pulling the map from his bag, he noted they were likely only a day, maybe less from the cave. Lia stepped up beside him, a deep crease between her brows, her mouth turned down at the corners.

"We aren't far from the cave, less than a day."

"That's good. That will make up for the time it took to find the temple."

He turned and started off towards the main path. He turned back toward the door one last time to find nothing but rough stone.

"Well, that's unsettling," Lia said, looking at the place the door was just moments before.

"Agreed."

As he turned, he caught a flash of color disappearing into the clouds.

They moved quickly, making camp under a small overhang for the evening and waking covered in dew. They moved on quickly the following morning as the sun rose. It was nearing mid-morning when the landscape began to look familiar. He heard Lia sigh beside him as the gently curved path revealed a small opening in the rock face.

Lia plopped onto a smooth boulder outside the cave mouth and pulled out her waterskin, taking several long sips. Cal sat down beside her, pulling out dried fruit and offering her the bag. She accepted it with a nod.

"Do we have a plan?"

She shook her head.

"Honestly … no. Until we find the heart and figure out what it is, there isn't really a way to plan."

"When we were in there last time, I saw a large circle on the wall that looked like runes. I'm wondering if it's like the door of the temple."

"Like the cave is just the gateway to somewhere else?"

"No, I think it's a door tethered to the heart. Hopefully, that means it will let us through, though I can't say I have much hope for it being simple."

"Who hides ancient life-sustaining magic where it's easy to find?" Lia said, her mouth ticking up at the corner.

Cal raised his eyebrows, taking a sip of his own water.

"So, are you stalling for a reason or are we going in?"

Lia huffed.

"Let's go."

She stood, shifting her bag and shifting the jeweled dagger from her thigh sheath to her palm. Taking a deep breath, she stood frozen for a moment before slipping a small torch from her pack and holding it out for Cal to light.

Much like last time, they found the outer cave quiet and undisturbed, a slight scorch mark from their first fire remaining on the ground. She moved quietly in front of him, her small flame lighting their way. Making it to the back wall, Lia searched for a moment before finding the small opening and spilling through, leaving Cal in darkness for only a moment before he followed.

As he entered, he found the chamber just as breathtaking as the first time. The mosaic ceiling was even more chilling after meeting the God of Death in the flesh. He looked back down, finding Lia placing her bag by the door and checking that all her weapons were accounted for. He followed, hefting his morning star from his back, taking comfort in its weight in his palm.

They began a slow circle the chamber, poking and prodding, looking for any concealed doors or alcoves. They circled the entire chamber, finding nothing but the runes. Turning, Cal moved back to the circle of runes running his fingers along the etchings. He turned to find Lia staring at the ground, circling the dais.

A sickly-sweet smell rolled through the room like too many flowers. He scratched his nose, suddenly irritated by the emptiness of the room. Why the fuck were they staring at blank walls?

"What are you looking at?" he asked, annoyance seeping into his tone.

Her shoulders tensed, her nose wrinkling.

"I am simply being thorough, Calcas."

"Which is why I asked what you were looking at."

Something flared in her eyes. The calm demeanor of the last few days had vanished entirely.

"I understand you don't trust me, I do, but could you pretend for just a moment that you do?" she bit.

Cal had no idea where her sudden hostility was coming from, but his own anger reared up in response.

"What about me risking my fucking life to traipse after you in the goddess forsaken mountains makes you think I don't trust you?"

She crossed her arms. "Oh, I don't know, maybe the decade of you hating me? Or you telling me that you don't trust me? Oh, or how about the constant questioning of my choices?"

"What the fuck are you talking about?" he asked, throwing his arms up.

"I'm talking about how you continue to hold Seren's death over my neck like an axe ready to fall, Cal."

"Well, you did make the decisions that led to her death."

Lia stalked across the room toward him, her knuckles white on her dagger.

"It's not just that. You hated me for decades before that because I took pieces of her attention away from you. You couldn't stand that she loved me, that she let me touch her, that she belonged to anyone but you."

Cal could hear his pulse pounding in his ears, his vision dimming at the edges. Something was wrong. The rage wasn't his. He pushed at it. Fought it. The rage won.

"I was mad that my mate—"

"Mate," Lia spit the word at him coated in venom. "Your precious fucking *mate* found *me* on the battlefield. She kissed *me* before she died. *My* name was the last name on her lips."

The dam in Cal's chest cracked and the flood of rage pulled him under. He knew no matter how hard he swam against it, he would pull her with him.

"YOU ARE MY GODDESS-DAMNED MATE, LITHIA."

She stared at him, eyes wide as saucers, lips parted. The rage slipped from his body in a grinding, unnatural way. Like a veil lifted, his consciousness snapped back into his body. Lithia looked as confused as he was, but before he could say anything, he saw movement in the corner of his eye. Shit.

"Hema."

LITHIA

The fog of rage slipped slowly from her mind as she stared at Cal in shock. She blinked hard before a shiver of awareness crept up her spine.

"Hema."

Fear filled Cal's eyes as the word fell from his lips. Lia turned, finding a low shimmering red haze seeping from the room. The anger was the hema's hallucinogenic—they had been poisoned. How long had someone known they were here? Around the perimeter of the room, a dozen voxis moved, surrounding them. Their eyes glinted in the firelight as they shifted and twitched, baring their teeth and stalking them like prey.

On some silent command, they moved, letting out a layered cacophony of snarls. Lia tossed her dagger to her left hand and slid the Sword of Mab from its sheath. The sight of the sword caused the voxis charging her to stumble a few ste, but he recovered quickly, lunging at her and slashing down with his sharpened claws. Catching the claws with a shrill scrape on the blade of her sword, she slashed out. A hot well of black blood spilled from the gaping wound in its throat.

As the first fell to the floor, another was upon her, clawing at her scraping her bare arms with its talons. With a grunt, she buried the dagger in its gut, pushing it back and bringing the sword down with all her power, rending its head from its body. Chest heaving, she pivoted just in time for two voxis to be upon her, talons ripping through her leathers and drawing blood from her leg as she pushed back another.

There were too many.

More seemed to be coming.

Cal moved like a shadow, melting into the dark before bringing his morning star down, black blood arcing in its wake. She danced backward, avoiding a well-aimed talon searching for anything to give them the high ground.

"You should be able to channel power into the blade as you wield it if you syphon it from me first," Cal called above the chaos.

Slashing quickly at an oncoming voxis, she shook her head, "No, I could hurt you, Like Nars. I can't."

"Do it, Lithia."

"No."

"DO IT NOW."

Without thinking, she plunged the blade into the heart of the voxis charging her direction, and in another breath, she called to Cal's fire. For less than a heartbeat, nothing happened. Then, like an avenging fury, roiling black flames licked up her blade, turning the voxis to ash before her.

The room froze for a moment before the voxis began closing in on them. Her blade flashed, severing limbs and heads, scorching any who got near it. Just as she thought they were making headway, more spilled into the room.

Her eyes frantically scanned the room for Cal, finding him near the dais on his back, a voxis looming over him, jaws snapping. Before she could make a move toward him, he was throwing the voxis off, his shadows retreating back to his arms. With a mighty roar, he pulled the great sword from his back and split the oncoming voxis in two. He moved quickly, scooping his morning star from the floor and whirling to find her, his eyes widening in awe at the flame-dipped sword.

Several more voxis closed in on her, turning to ash at the end of her blade. The minutes stretched, feeling like hours as the barrage continued, the floor becoming slick. Then, as suddenly as they appeared, on some silent signal they disappeared.

"Cal, are you hurt? Did I take too much?" she rushed out in a panicked croak.

"No, it's fine, I hardly felt it, to be honest."

She didn't believe him after the way it seemed to pain Narcos to share magic, but he had continued fighting like nothing was wrong.

Lia and Cal stood in the carnage, chests heaving blood, both black and red painting their faces. She looked at Cal, her face crinkling in confusion as the adrenaline wore off.

"What the fuck just happened?"

"I don't know but we need to finish what we came here for and quickly before it happens again."

Lia nodded her agreement, staring down at the sword. She moved towards their bags to find their belongings scattered across the floor. With a roll of her eyes, she gathered what was salvageable of their belongings. Repacking her bag, she grabbed a tunic and waterskin and scrubbed at her face. The soft grey tunic came back covered in thick black blood. She assessed her injuries, finding none of them concerning.

"Cal?"

"Hmm?"

"Did any of the voxis have weapons?"

Cal froze, his waterskin nearly to his lips, his mouth turning down at the corner. He turned, stalking back across the room, Lithia close on his heals. Inspecting each of the fallen voxis, rolling them with his foot, and searching the ground all around them, they found no fallen weapons.

"I don't understand, the voxis have access to weapons, they use them often. Why would they not be armed? The way they attacked was nearly feral. I never saw the hema either. We felt its magic, obviously, but the beast itself wasn't in the fight."

Cal's gaze focused far behind her.

"They weren't all that difficult fight off, either."

"No, they fell rather quickly. We shouldn't be standing after an ambush like that."

"I don't know, that flaming sword was a good trick."

She rolled her eyes.

"Even still."

"Do you think it's the curse?"

"I think it's the only thing that makes sense. Black blood and nearly feral, it has to be that.

"I wonder if that's why they are gathering. It's not plotting, it's fear."

"Maybe. If they would speak to us rather than trying to eat our faces, maybe we could help."

"Let's get this over with. I need to bathe."

She chuckled, moving towards the large circle of runes inlaid into the wall. They looked different from any rune she had seen before, but that made sense given the ancient nature of the power they hid. Cal ran his finger along one of the runes, tracing it. Lia mirrored his movements on the other side of the circle.

As she did, she noticed a faint line carved by one of the runes. She placed her finger on it, tracing it from the outer circle towards the center. As she reached the middle of the spiral, she noticed the faintest impression just larger than her finger. As her finger settled in the hollow, there was a sharp pain. Stumbling back, she looked down at her finger; a trickle of blood ran over blackened flesh. Cal moved quickly to her side, cradling her hand, worry lines deepening on his forehead.

"The fuck was that?"

She opened her mouth to answer but was cut off by a low grinding of stone on stone. They looked up quickly to find the once empty circle filled with an intricate knot formed from pulsing light. As they watched, the light slowly slipped away from the wall before the circle of stone sank into the floor. Gathering their bags, they slowly moved through the doorway.

On the other side, they found a less ornate chamber, with a sleek black stone floor and ceiling cast in a warm glow by flickering torches. Inside the small chamber was a railing marking the top of a staircase that spiraled into darkness below. They exchanged a wary glance.

"I'm going first. Stay close."

Cal drew his sword and started slowly descending, Lia a step behind. As they sank lower into the mountain, the air grew cold and the smooth black walls constricted, like they were closing in. It took ages before they finally reached the bottom. Looking up, there was nothing but darkness, no flicker of light from the entrance they came through. Ahead, they found a hall lined on each side with plain wooden doors.

As they passed, they checked each but inside found only dust. The hall continued bending and sloping down, toward what she didn't know. Slowly the sound of moving water began to overtake the silence. Coming around a bend in the hall, Cal came to an abrupt halt. Stepping around his form, she found out why.

Instead of another elaborate chamber like the one above or the black stone of the stairs and hall, they found themselves in a lush garden unlike anything she had seen before. Large trees floated above the soil, their roots swaying in the air, oddly shaped fruit weighing down their branches. A row of flowers turned to watch them as they stepped onto the glimmering moonstone path.

As they walked, strange new plants came into view, the rich colors of night sliced through with the soft pastels of the dawn. Deep blue-black orchids framed by a pale pink leafy plant she had never seen before lined the path. Deeper in, the source of the water sounds became apparent: a large lagoon fed by a waterfall nestled in the floating trees. The rippling surface of the dark water reflected pinpoints of light, making it seem as though the heavens swirled within its depths. Maybe they did.

The path curled inward upon itself, sending them in yet another spiral towards the heart of the garden. As they came to the last bend, a large eight-sided courtyard spread out before them. The moonstone swirling with veins of silver made it glitter.

Lia gasped.

There in the courtyard, floating above the ground, was a swirling nebula pulsing with power. As she got near, she could see it was made of millions of stars swirling in an endless dance. Cal stood so close he brushed her shoulder.

"Definitely Celestial. Look just there."

He pointed to a spot just off the nebula's heart. It was black and dull, the stars parting around it like a rock in a stream. Lia reached out, but just before she made contact, Cal pulled her wrist back.

"What in the goddess's tits do you think you're doing?"

"I don't know! Syphoning?"

"You can't just touch it! It could kill you."

"Do you have a better plan, then?"

He stood there for several minutes, the scowl on his face deepening.

"That's what I thought."

She looked at him, seeing the conflict dance behind his eyes.

"I have to try. The priestess said that I wasn't holding the magic I was borrowing, so maybe we'll get lucky and I won't hold this either."

He gave her a skeptical look.

Reaching out, her hand made contact with the void, and for a moment, nothing happened. Then a few seconds later the void began to shrink. Licks of magic shot through her body and her fingertips began to turn black. As the void winked out of existence, she began pulling her hand back, watching the black swirl beneath her skin.

"That seemed too easy."

There was blinding pain and the world went black.

CALCAS

Lithia's body seized as she crumpled. He caught her, shifting so she landed on him, not the floor. Her body was wracked with tremors, though she was at least breathing on her own. He cradled her head on one arm, lifting her blackened hand up. The tips of her fingers had gone entirely black, fading to grey, like she had dipped her fingers in ash.

He looked back at the magic swirling above them and saw blackness seeping back in. It hadn't worked. He was stupid for letting her try. As her body continued to seize, he looked around desperately for anything to wake her but found nothing.

"Oh my, how disappointing."

The honeyed voice sent shockwaves through his body. Before he could turn towards its source, a white-hot lightning bolt of pain struck his temple and everything faded.

Throbbing filled his head as his senses slowly returned. Attempting to shift, his muscles screamed in protest on the hard surface beneath him. He groaned at the pain rippling through his body.

"Cal?" a voice to his left whispered.

He peeled his eyes open, the dim surroundings saving him the pain of adjusting to the light. Underneath him, he could feel the uneven texture of a rough-hewn floor, damp and spongy with what he hoped desperately was moss. He took several deep breaths, hoping the nausea would settle some before he moved.

"Cal, are you awake? Please be awake," came the voice again.

He turned his head, finding Lia on the other side of a set of iron bars. Adrenaline coursed through his body as his brain caught up to their situation and he sat up quickly, his head spinning and the nausea coming back in full force. He groaned again, bringing his knees to his chest and hanging his head.

"Shhhh. Don't move too quickly, you've been out for a while." she rasped, scooting closer to their shared wall of bars.

"Where ..." he started, barely lifting his head.

"I'm not sure. I woke up here a few hours ago. It seems to be some form of dungeon, but I'm not sure where we actually are."

"I gathered the dungeon part," he said, attempting a laugh but hissing in pain instead.

"Nice to know a blow to the head won't make you less of an ass," Lithia said.

He blinked heavily, noting a small copper band engraved with runes around his wrist. Holding it up to inspect, he heard a soft sigh from Lia.

"They dampened our magic."

Dragging himself along the floor to the bars, he sat beside her, leaning his head on the damp wall and taking in the cramped space. The cells were small, hardly large enough for him to lie down fully in either direction. Iron bars comprised three of the walls, with a mossy stone wall at the back. As far as he could see, there were eight, maybe more, cells in a line a thin strip of walkway in front. One torch illuminated the space set near the center of the block of cells a few over from theirs.

"Have you seen anyone since you woke?"

"No, but you can hear them moving and speaking in low voices further down the hall. Did you see anyone before they took us?"

"No. There was a female voice that sounded like—" he cleared his throat, shaking his head.

"What did she say?"

"'Oh my, how disappointing.' Then someone struck me, and I woke up here," he touched the spot on his temple, wincing when he felt dried blood where the skin had split.

"Did it work at least?" Lithia asked.

He looked at her, at the hope dancing in her eyes, knowing he was about to crush it. His eyes tracked down to her still-blackened fingers before meeting her eyes again and slowly shaking his head.

"Fuck." She leaned her head back on the stone, staring up at the beams of the ceiling.

"I think we were on the right track, because it was working; it just didn't hold. But we are missing something."

"I could feel it pooling in my hand, hot and sticky. Then it sank into my skin and I thought it was over but—" She held her fingers up, inspecting them.

"I felt it in my chest when you dropped. Like a hot knife."

She was silent for several minutes.

"Why didn't you just tell me I was your mate when you found out? Why did it take decades of anger boiling over and being forced out by magic?"

He let out a slow breath.

"In the beginning, when I first sensed the pull of the magic, I didn't know it was you. I loved Ser so much I would have been able to convince myself it was her no matter what, which you understand." Cal's smile was brittle.

Lia nodded slowly.

"I didn't figure it out until a few years before that battle, but I refused to believe it. So I went on existing as if it was her."

"But you told Tadhg your mate was gone."

"You were. I could see your brokenness written all over your face and still I blamed you for her death. I wanted nothing to do with you."

"You should have told me. You should have told me long before you hated me."

"That's true. I thought about it, and I knew we loved each other at one point, but I knew we would resent each other if we forced it. The only blessing of this bond is that it doesn't force you to choose and it can't make you love."

Lia scoffed, rubbing her chest. "It's heavily suggestive though."

Cal smiled, nodding.

"I wish you had come to me in the last ten years. You knew how much I loved her, and you had to have known how much I needed you."

"I should have, but I was too far gone. I did terrible things in the years after the war. I killed innocent women. I fought for profit. I lied and stole and did things I never thought I could be redeemed of. After a certain point, I didn't think coming back was an option."

Lia hummed in acknowledgment and Cal assumed the conversation was over until a quiet voice floated through the bars. He looked over to find her deep black eyes rimmed with tears.

"I missed you, Calcas."

He opened his mouth to respond but was cut off by a deep, rumbling voice.

"As touching as this little heart to heart is, we have other plans."

They both startled, finding a large fae standing in front of the cells. He had somehow come upon them in eerie silence. He was tall and broad and wearing armor Cal had never seen before. It was a gleaming silver inlaid with an opaline crest on the front, two crossed swords with a battle helm.

Something itched at the back of his mind as he stared at the crest, but his mind couldn't quite place it. The male moved to the door of Cal's cell and swung it open. Cal exchanged a look with Lia before pulling himself to his feet, swaying lightly, his vision pulsing at the change.

"Where are we going?" Cal asked, eyeing him warily, realizing he wasn't moving to pull Lia from her cell.

"Just do as you're told," the broad male scoffed.

The male sneered at him as he moved through the door and pushed him forward.

Turning towards Lia, Cal stopped. "Are we not both going?"

"I'm sorry that I wasn't clear enough. Do as you're told and do it silently. Move."

He pushed at Cal's shoulder again, herding him towards the low door at the end of the hall. He turned to look at Lia before he was out of her sight and found her clinging to the bars, fear painted across her face as another fae materialized in front of her cell in the same shining armor. The male in front of him chuckled, a deep unnerving sound.

"Don't worry, she's got her own party to attend."

Calcas

C al was led along a rough, winding corridor. The soft echo of footsteps reverberated off the damp stone walls as he followed the large male. The air was cool and stale, carrying the odor of mildew and decay. As they continued, the hall sloped upward and branched often into dark corridors filled with heavy wooden doors.

The longer they walked, the more disoriented he became until eventually he lost the path back to Lia entirely. The hallways seemed to stretch endlessly in an intricate maze before eventually, the floor sloped up sharply, leading to a short set of stairs, opening up into what looked to be a small throne room. Carved in on the far wall stood a large rough throne that looked like the same black rock as the mountain, with a smooth black wall rising above it.

A large chandelier of curved white stone hung from the ceiling, casting a warm glow on the room. Standing around the throne room were several more fae in the same armor as the one who came to gather him. He was led to the center of the room and pushed forcefully to his knees. Once down, he saw with horror that the floor, like the chamber in the cave, was inlaid with bone. Cold metal seared his skin as a collar was slipped around his throat.

As soon as the latch clicked into place, a shiver of magic ran down his body as chains slithered up from the floor and attached to the sides of the collar before slinking down to bind his wrists together by the magic-suppressing shackles already there. A large male leaned down, locking eyes with Cal, who barely contained the urge to spit in his face.

"Sorry, for this next part, wouldn't want her to think we went easy on you." The gleam of malice in his eyes said everything but sorry.

Cal barely had time to tense before the blow landed, snapping his head backward and rocking him on his knees. Steadying himself once again, he looked up at the brute of a fae scowling down at him and smiled.

The next stepped up, a feral smile on his face, and paused dramatically, making a show of planting his feet squarely before he landed a powerful hit directly in Cal's gut, knocking the wind out of him and doubling him over. Cal looked up just in time for the next to land several in rapid succession, his approach more aggressive than focused or flashy. It continued with them trading hits until Cal lost count.

Time passed marked by the rhythmic thud of fists on flesh. It could have been minutes or hours, he couldn't say. He could feel blood drying on his lips as they tightened and cracked, though all but the first male had avoided hitting his face. He supposed he needed to stay conscious for whatever came next; how lucky. Finally, the battery came to an end, and he spat blood out onto the floor before him, earning a snarl from the large female standing nearest to him as it splattered onto her plated boots.

A soft swish of a door followed by measured armored footfalls sounded behind him, and the surrounding fae snapped to attention. He waited, unable to turn his head, as a tall fae in the same pristine armor stepped in front of him. The armor was largely the same; the one glaring difference was the crowned helm they wore. A sparkling opaline crown rose from the top of an ornate full-faced helm blocking the wearer's features entirely.

They paused in front of him, leaning down to look into his face before moving toward the throne. As they turned to seat themselves, they lifted the helm from their head, and warm brown hair threaded with gold spilled down her back. A gentle flick of her wrist and the armor melted into a simmering opaline dress cut low in the back.

Cal's breath caught in his chest, a strangled sound escaping him as she turned, seating herself on the throne and arranging her dress. She leaned back, placing her hands on the armrests, a predatory smile curling on her face.

"Bring him to me," she purred in the same honeyed voice he'd heard earlier when Lithia had collapsed.

The chains dropped, slithering away as he was pulled harshly to his feet and shoved toward the throne. As he drew closer, he found himself staring at a horrifyingly familiar ring of honey gold. He fell to his knees in front of her watching as she adjusted the spiked rings on her fingers, the smell of lemon and thyme filling his senses making his stomach roil.

Before he could catch the words rattling around in his brain and push them out of his mouth, the wall behind her shifted. It cracked as a large red eye blinked back at him, what appeared to be a wall unfurling its lithe body to wrap a protective tail around the throne.

The glittering black amphiptere shook out its wings as it settled its serpentine body in a protective coil behind the throne, perching its large head to the right of the throne, facing Cal. The protectiveness of a dragon, poised to strike like a snake, added to the aura of terror unfurling before him.

On the throne, she made a small gesture with her hand before reaching out to stroke the beast's scales and he heard the sounds of the armored fae leaving the imitation throne room.

As the room fell back into silence, he looked back into the familiar golden gaze, all words lost to him. Fear and grief warred for dominance in his stomach, his emotions slowly slipping into numbness as he panicked. Her lips parted on a smile before she spoke.

"Hello, Cal."

He stood there for another moment expecting her to shift or disappear on the wind. When nothing changed, he croaked out the only word clanging around his head.

"Ser?"

LITHIA

L ia watched the large fae push Cal through the door. The first time in ten years that they had ended a conversation better than it started and he was taken from her immediately. She could feel the thread in her heart go taught, the ache settling in now that she understood what it meant. She turned to sit back on the grimy floor and found a large female in the same gleaming armor watching her from outside the cell, a cruel smile on her face.

"Don't worry, they'll take good care of your little mate. You get to come with me."

A ripple of unease ran through Lithia as the fae unlocked the cell door. She noticed a crest on the armor that she didn't know to belong to any of the houses in Suviel, and filed it away, hoping that at some point she would be out of here and it would be useful. She followed her captor through the same door Calcas had left through several minutes ago.

They walked through dank, gently sloping halls for what seemed like hours until, finally, they came to a set of spiral stairs. Her guard stepped to the side and gestured for her to go first, and they climbed. The stone steps were steep and narrow, worn smooth in the middle after likely centuries of use. She climbed until her legs burned, her breath coming in pants. Her captor, however, didn't seem to be struggling. She was so silent that Lithia wasn't sure she was breathing at all; she had to keep checking to be sure she was even there.

Finally, they reached the top of the stairs. On a small landing was only a single door. Lithia stopped on the landing and waited, not thinking this was the time or place for the initiative.

"For Thahaos's sake, open the fucking door. Where else would you be going?"

Lithia bit down on the inside of her cheek before reaching out and turning the door handle. What she found on the other side was not at all what she expected. A warm bed chamber draped in plush reds and golds. Set directly across from the large bed, along the wall, crackled a large fireplace. She stepped into the room, the clean spiced scent thick after the musty scent of the dungeon.

She moved towards the fire and saw to the side of the room sat a screen separating the room from small tub, filled with a steaming bath. She turned to the door to find the large female filling the door frame, her nose curling in disgust.

"Interesting way to treat a prisoner. You are to bathe and change into the clothes provided. Don't do anything stupid because I'm staying in the room."

Lithia pursed her lips to hold back the insults swelling on her tongue, scanning the room again, looking for anything that could be a weapon. Unfortunately, besides the bed and the drapery, everything seemed to have been removed. She stepped behind the screen and quickly removed her clothing before stepping into the hot water. She hissed as it touched her skin, but pushed through, wanting to dress quickly. The water burned her skin, leaving it raw as she scrubbed at the grime and voxis blood caked on her from the last few days, the small sliver of lemon soap finally chasing away the smell of death.

She stepped out of the tub and reached out for the towel to dry herself and caught sight of her blackened hand. Only it wasn't just a blackened hand any longer; it had reached her shoulder. The blackness was spreading. The void was spreading. Her breathing quickened as she dried herself off.

The clothing left for her was a long black dress with spiderwebs of lace over the length. She pulled it on, piling her hair on top of her head, and stepped out from behind the screen, setting her face into a mask of neutrality. Her guard was sitting in a chair with her feet kicked up on the table, tossing a coin into the air. She didn't react to Lithia's presence.

She cleared her throat, pushing her shoulders back. "I'm ready, though, I would like to be told where I am going."

With a sigh, the guard's boots slammed to the floor. "You're going to dinner, princess."

"High Queen."

"Alright," she scoffed, holding her hands up to Lia. "High Queen, you are going to dinner."

Lithia raised her chin. "With whom?"

The other fae moved across the room with predatory grace, stopping directly in front of Lia, who refused to cower.

"You might be the High Queen of the living, but I don't give a fuck who you are. Now stop asking questions before I bloody you up like they did your mate."

Lithia didn't move, but swallowed thickly. The guard turned on her heel and pushed open a door Lithia hadn't seen until now, gesturing with a flourish. She moved through the door quickly, the guard on her heels. It was small and cramped, like a servants' passage. After a few minutes of being directed through turns, Lithia pushed through a door and found herself in a large dining room.

"Sit."

"I am not an animal," she said, squaring her shoulders at her guard once again, before turning and taking the seat at the head of the long table.

Her guard laughed, a low chafing sound, before leaning against the wall by the main door. Lia sat in silence for nearly twenty minutes before she heard distant footsteps in the hall. She locked her spine in place and as she did, a pain like ice shot through her heart.

Looking down, she saw that the creeping tendrils of the void had reached down across her chest, finally approaching her heart. She looked up at her guard, panic in her eyes.

"Fuck is wrong with you?"

She stood, and the world tilted.

"LIA!"

"Cal?" she croaked as his face swam into view above her, purple bruises blooming across one cheek and blood caking his lip.

"Lia, what's wrong?"

"The void. It's moving?"

She could feel Cal touching her frantically and heard the light tap of quickly approaching heels before she heard nothing at all.

EPILOGUE

Wil was leaning over the stack of papers Lithia and Cal had sent ahead of them. She had just arrived with Neda and Tadhg a few hours ago and she had already read through most of Lithia's handwritten notes. Worry growing in the pit of her stomach, she wished they had come back first, or sent word and waited for help before going alone.

Neda threw the doors of what used to be a library wide, striding in with a wild look on her face. Wil looked up, rolling her eyes at the theatrics.

"Willow." Shit, Neda never used her full name. "Can you tell me why a fucking amphiptere just brought you a letter?"

Wil jumped, standing to her full height. "What? Where is it?"

"Outside, obviously."

"No, you—" she rubbed her eyes, "The letter, Neda."

Neda cocked her hip to the side. "It's outside, the damn thing won't give it to me."

Wil raced passed Neda, through the crumbing manor, to find Oathis out on the lawn ... with Tadhg scratching his belly. She moved quickly over to them, raising an eyebrow at Tadgh, who shrugged.

"We met when I spent time in the temple as a youngling," he said, holding her gaze.

She nodded and turned, reaching for the letter tied to his ankle, her name in elegant looping script on the front. She pulled it off, patting his snout once.

"Go home."

He chuffed, billowing steam at her before soaring into the sky as she tore it open.

Willow,
Lithia's soul has arrived in The Beneath, something is wrong, it is not her time.
Ahbba

ACKNOWLEDGEMENTS

I don't even know where to start these acknowledgments, to be honest. I feel like I am very much a village of support in a trench coat pretending to be a single author.

Thank you to Di and Carrie for reading the mess that was the first draft and still believing in me. To Jayme for giving me critical feedback while being my creative partner in magical crime. To Hillary for never being annoyed with my endless questions about how literally any of this author stuff works, you are my hero. To Whitney for fixing my mess of a blurb and always having the tea when I needed a break. To my discord server for being my safe place, we will build that commune one day. (Rileigh...I'm sorry about the spiders...)

Thank you to Chyanne for being my fierce solo beta reader and my forever biggest cheerleader. I would have quit 100 times without you.

Thank you so much to AJ for being quite possibly the most intelligent human I know and an absolutely incredible editor and teacher. I am so sorry I didn't get rid of Tadhg like you wanted but I love him. Thank you to Taylor for having a much better mastery of commas than I do, I'm sorry, I fear it's too late for me to ever learn where they go.

A massive thank you to Rachel for the absolutely stunning cover and to Kiley for bringing my girl to life. You are both incredibly talented and I can't wait to see what we do in the next book!

Thank you to my family for being excited for me even if they haven't read a book in years. Thank you to my mother, for excitedly telling people about my book so I have a heart attack when they follow me on Instagram. I love you all, please don't read my book.

Last but most importantly, to my husband and son for losing me to a keyboard every free hour and loving me anyway. I love you so very much. I would be absolutely nothing and nowhere without you both and I wouldn't want to be.

About the Author

Poppy Roberts has always been a passionate lover of stories and has finally decided it was time to tell one of her own.

As a child she always enjoyed playing pretend, inventing stories, and immersing herself in imaginary worlds. Now, as an adult, she still gets excited about fairy rings, magical creatures, and discovering entirely new worlds. Her mother encouraged her love of reading at a young age, and Poppy's search for that magical feeling has only grown stronger over time.